"I know if I _____ **have to go back to** _____ **id.**

"I just want someone to talk to. Women tend to look at things differently than men. I'll have some important decisions to make soon, and I want to make sure I'm doing the right thing."

"I wish I could help you make your decision—but you're right. If you succeed, I'll fail—"

"You won't fail."

"I'll fail at my reason for coming." And she would have to go back alone—which was the last thing she wanted. The boys deserved to be raised in a proper place, with good schools, and hospitals, and comfort— the frontier was far too dangerous a place to grow up.

"You've already accomplished a great deal since you've been here, and all of us are grateful," he said. "I'm hopeful about Little Falls, but I'm also realistic. I've been involved in several town prospects that have failed, even when they looked this hopeful."

He was trying to make her feel better, and for that she was thankful. But she must not allow her heart to soften toward him. There would be nothing but heartache and devastation if she did.

Gabrielle Meyer lives in central Minnesota on the banks of the Mississippi River with her husband and four young children. As an employee of the Minnesota Historical Society, she fell in love with the rich history of her state and enjoys writing fictional stories inspired by real people and events. Gabrielle can be found at www.gabriellemeyer.com, where she writes about her passion for history, Minnesota and her faith.

Books by Gabrielle Meyer

Love Inspired Historical

A Mother in the Making
A Family Arrangement

GABRIELLE MEYER

A Family Arrangement

H **HARLEQUIN**® LOVE INSPIRED® HISTORICAL

Recycling programs
for this product may
not exist in your area.

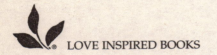 LOVE INSPIRED BOOKS

ISBN-13: 978-0-373-28388-0

A Family Arrangement

Printed in U.S.A.

Trust in the Lord, and do good; so shalt
thou dwell in the land, and verily thou shalt be fed.
—*Psalms* 37:3

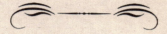

To my sister, Andrea.
You were the first person who had to put up with my vivid imagination and my unusual love for history. Thank you for always playing along.

Chapter One

Little Falls, Minnesota Territory
November 1, 1854

What had her sister been thinking when she followed Abram Cooper to the wilds of Minnesota Territory? Charlotte Lee shaded her eyes as she surveyed the sawmill, the two-story home and the barn on the banks of the Mississippi. The rough-lumber buildings were the only structures to mark the crude settlement.

This was the town Abram and Susanne had built out of the wilderness? Seeing it now, Charlotte realized Susanne had been exaggerating in her letters. This was not a town. It could hardly be called a farm.

The dust from the departing stagecoach settled around Charlotte as she let out a painful sigh. "Oh, Susanne." She whispered her sister's name, her breath puffing out into the cold evening air. If only Susanne had listened and stayed in Iowa City, where everything was safe and civilized, maybe she'd still be alive.

The pale November sky boasted a pink sunset, which did little to warm her shivering body. Charlotte strode down the single-wagon road toward the sawmill. The brown grass and bare branches of the oaks, elms and maples attested to the coming winter. Thankfully the snow had held off long enough for her to travel. Hopefully the clear sky would continue to hold for just a few days more until the stagecoach returned to take her back to Iowa.

Water rushed past the wing dam in the river, down a narrow sluice, and pushed the waterwheel into motion on the side of the sawmill. Charlotte balanced across a narrow plank and opened the door into a dimly lit room. Large cogs whirled to her right and a bulky rod pumped up and down, creating a loud grinding noise. Piles of rough-cut lumber littered the floor and cobwebs crisscrossed the rafters. Seeing no one on the main level, she lifted the hem of her gown and started up a set of stairs just ahead.

A tall man stood with his back toward her, a clipboard in his hand, while two shorter men stacked lumber in the corner of the large room. A thick log advanced through a sash saw, and with each up-and-down thrust of the blade, the log moved a fraction of an inch forward. One of the men stacking lumber noticed her and stopped his work, causing the tall man with the clipboard to turn.

His startled blue eyes looked crystal clear amid his shaggy brown hair and beard.

Was this Abram Cooper? The handsome young man Susanne had eloped with six years ago? It couldn't be. This man looked much older and much tougher around the edges.

Recognition slowly dawned in his eyes. "Charlotte?"

Yes, this was Abram Cooper. Charlotte recognized the determination and focus in the set of his shoulders.

"What are you doing here?" he asked.

She swallowed her nerves. "I've come to collect my nephews and take them back to Iowa."

Abram stared at her for a moment.

She stared back, trying not to falter under his intense gaze.

He glanced at the loud saw and then reached over and pushed a lever forward. The sash immediately stopped and silence filled the dusty room. Pale sunshine streamed through the large cracks in the plank walls and bathed him in bars of pink light. The two other men stopped working and watched in quiet fascination.

"What did you say?" Abram asked.

Charlotte stood taller than most women, but Abram was taller still. She was forced to look up into his face as she cleared her throat. "I'm here for the boys. The stage will return for us in three days."

Incredulity widened his eyes. "You're not taking my children."

"Susanne asked me to take them if—"

"She never said anything to me—"

"After Robert was born," Charlotte said quickly, "she told me if anything ever happened to her, she wanted me to take care of him."

Abram glanced over his shoulder at the two young men and then looked back at Charlotte, indicating the stairs. "Let's continue this conversation downstairs."

She almost sighed in relief. It was difficult enough to confront her brother-in-law, but to do so with an audience was far worse.

Charlotte descended the stairs and waited at the bottom.

Abram strode down, irritation—or was that fear—emanating from his countenance.

"Do you honestly think I would send my children four hundred miles away—with *you*?" he asked through clenched teeth. "After the way you treated me, I'm surprised you'd show your face here at all, Charlotte."

She blinked several times, her mouth parting. "The way I treated you?" The pain and loneliness she'd felt for the past six years seeped out in one breath. "You stole my sister. I told Susanne it was a mistake to marry you—"

"Susanne was a grown woman."

"She was hardly grown! Seventeen is practically a child. And now look. She died, just like our mother, and her three sons are left in this wilderness—"

"It's not a wilderness."

She waved her hand in the air, desperation and fear squeezing her chest. "What do you call this place? There is no town, no neighbors. Nothing for miles but this sawmill."

He leaned forward, his voice tight and defensive. "You're right—there is no town, but, God willing, there will be. There is a mission four miles north of here, with a military fort just beyond that. There are trading posts—"

"Where are the boys, Mr. Cooper?" Nothing else mattered to her at the moment but the welfare of her nephews.

"They are safe and well cared for."

"How could they be safe here…?" She paused, realizing how fruitless her argument was. "I'm here to rescue them—"

"They don't need rescuing."

"I disagree."

"I can see that."

The river rushed past the building as Charlotte took several deep breaths.

Sawdust floated in the air and stuck to Abram's wild hair. He looked so different than the man she had met seven years ago at the Fireman's Ball. Why had Susanne fallen in love with him? Why hadn't she learned her lesson from Mama's ordeal? Mama had followed Father from the safety of New York State to pioneer in Iowa when Charlotte and Susanne were young girls. The hard life had taken a toll on Mama's health. Instead of listening to the doctor and going back to New York, Father had chased one scheme after another, and their mother had succumbed to an early death—just like Susanne.

Tears gathered in Charlotte's eyes and her chin quivered. She swallowed several times, trying to compose herself. "My sister left civilization, despite my objection, and she met an inevitable fate. I refuse to let you destroy her children in your plan to get rich quick— or to make a name for yourself—or...or whatever it is you're trying to do."

The tension fell from his shoulders and he looked at her as if she had struck him. "Is that what you think this is? I'm trying to get rich quick?" He raised his large hands, cracked and bleeding, and indicated his work-worn clothing and his scraggly beard. "Do I look like a man out to make an easy dollar?" His voice shook with an emotion as strong as hers. "I've poured my life into this mill, not to mention every last penny I've earned. Susanne and I mortgaged everything—"

"Including her life!" The words came out before she could stop them and she slapped her hand over her mouth. Pain filled his eyes—but at the moment her grief was so raw and fresh, she couldn't stop herself from continuing. "You're just like my father. You're filled with an insatiable desire for adventure and challenge. You don't finish anything you start, because you're always moving on to bigger and better things—to the detriment of your family—"

"This time is different." Abram ran his hand through his long hair, causing the sawdust to drift down to his shoulders. "Little Falls will rival any town on the Mississippi. Susanne believed in my vision—"

"Of course she believed in you. She saw the best in everyone—" A sob choked off her words and she turned from him lest he see the tears she could no longer contain. How could her sweet sister be gone? Her short life was snuffed out far too soon and her babies had lost their mama. Robert, the oldest, had just turned five, Martin would be three, and the baby, George, was not quite a year old. The boys had been without a mother for three months. Though Charlotte could never replace Susanne, she would honor her sister's wishes and do her best.

She finally looked back at Abram. Susanne had been sick for months before she died. She should have gone to a city doctor, yet he had failed to leave his scheme behind to take her. That thought strengthened Charlotte's resolve. "You can do what you will with your life, but Susanne's boys deserve better than this, and I intend to give it to them. It's what she wanted."

Abram was still a young man, not much older than Charlotte at the age of twenty-five, yet the weight on his shoulders and the anguish in his eyes made him look much older. The fight was gone from his stance as he studied Charlotte. "Do you have the letter she sent you?"

Charlotte nodded and opened the door. Susanne's

wishes were as plain as could be. As soon as he saw the letter, he would agree, and Charlotte could get the boys ready to move.

She left the sawmill and walked across the board plank to the riverbank. Her trunk sat next to the house and she quickly opened it and found the stack of Susanne's letters bound in red ribbon. She had put the letter on top, knowing Abram would want to see it, and rightfully so.

"Here." She stood and handed it to her brother-in-law. "This is the letter she wrote right after Robert was born."

He took the letter and scanned the paper, his brow furrowed.

Charlotte had the words memorized by heart. "'Now that I'm a mother, I understand how much you sacrificed to provide for me after Mama and Father passed away. If anything ever happens to me, I can't think of anyone I'd trust more to take care of my children.'" It was quite common for a family member to take over the responsibilities of child care when a father was widowed—especially when there was no one else to help. Surely that was what Susanne had had in mind.

Abram handed the letter back to Charlotte. "She didn't ask you to take them to Iowa—"

"Of course she did." Charlotte glanced at the letter to make sure she had given him the right one.

"I'm afraid this trip has been a waste of your time." He closed the lid of her trunk and effortlessly hefted it to his shoulder before she could stop him. "You'll have to wait here until the stagecoach returns. Until then, you'll sleep in my room and I'll bunk with my employees in the room across the hall."

He turned to grab the doorknob but she reached out and put her hand on his arm. "Please, Abram. Let me take them back to Iowa."

He stopped and glanced down at her gloved hand. It looked pristine next to his dingy work shirt. "The children are staying at the mission. I will take you to see them before you leave." His eyes were filled with a warning. "But I will not let them go to Iowa."

Charlotte's chest rose and fell with her disappointment, but she wasn't surprised by his declaration. Somehow she would convince him that sending the boys to Iowa was the best thing for all of them.

Somehow.

Abram pushed open the door to his home, cringing at what his sister-in-law would think of the dirty interior. It had been three and a half months since Susanne had died and she'd been sick for several months before that. The house was in need of a good cleaning—especially since five men now occupied the premise.

"I'll haul this up and put it in the room you'll use." He stepped over the threshold and couldn't help but look to see her reaction.

Charlotte's brown eyes trailed over the main room and she lifted the hem of her fancy green traveling gown, as if she didn't want it to get soiled.

He didn't blame her. It was filthy—but when Susanne was alive, his home had made him proud. A large fireplace dominated one wall and modest furniture was spread around it. Four glass windows, a rare treat in Minnesota Territory, looked out at the river. Susanne had kept them shining, just for him—yet now they were dull with grime, just as his soul felt dull with grief. A shelf with Susanne's books was near the desk in the corner and several muddy rugs were tossed about the room in no particular order.

A chicken ambled in from the kitchen and he winced. Caleb must have left the back door open again. It cackled at them and Charlotte squealed.

Abram balanced the trunk on his shoulder as he pushed the chicken toward the door with his boot.

"I was under the impression that this was the house." She glanced around the room once again, a wrinkle wedging between her eyes. "Have we mistakenly entered the barn?"

He couldn't help but goad her. "Hopefully only the chicken wandered in. We've been known to attract a few skunks and weasels, too."

Her eyes grew wide and he tried not to smile. Instead he cleared his throat. "As soon as I get your trunk to your room, I'll rustle up some supper."

"Aren't we going to see the boys?"

"It's getting too late tonight." Abram started up the stairs.

"Why did you wait?"

He paused and turned. The agony on her face twisted his heart. "Wait for what?"

"To tell me Susanne had died."

He frowned. "I wrote to you immediately."

She pulled a letter out of the pile she still held in her hands. "This didn't arrive until three weeks ago—almost three months after she died."

He readjusted her trunk on his shoulder. "Look at the date at the top of the letter. You'll see it says July sixteenth, the day after her death."

She glanced at the piece of paper and shook her head. "There is no date."

He hadn't put a date on the letter? She couldn't blame him for the oversight. Right after his wife had died, he'd barely been able to put two thoughts together. "It must have been lost in the mail."

"Didn't you wonder why I hadn't come until now?"

"Frankly, I didn't think I'd ever see you again, Charlotte—and neither did Susanne. Not after the way you treated us when we said we wanted to marry."

Anguish passed over her brown eyes yet he couldn't help but say what he had wanted to say for the past six years. "You broke Susanne's heart when you didn't give us your blessing and when you never once inquired about our marriage in your letters. Until her death—" He choked on the word and didn't have the heart to tell her that Susanne had wept on her deathbed over their broken relationship. "She carried the pain with her until the end."

Tears fell down Charlotte's cheeks but Abram didn't wait for her response. Instead he continued up the stairs.

He stopped at the top and took several deep breaths. He had always hoped to convey to Charlotte how much she had hurt Susanne, but it didn't make him feel any better. If anything, he felt worse.

With a sigh, he opened the door to his left and stepped into his modest-size bedroom. It had a large bed, a bureau, a rocking chair, the boys' cradle and a washbasin. He had packed up all of Susanne's things, except her Bible, and put them in a trunk, which sat at the foot of the bed. It had been too painful to have the memories surrounding him.

Abram set down Charlotte's trunk and then rubbed

his whiskers as he surveyed the dust in the corners and the bedding that hadn't been washed for weeks. Dirty clothes hung from the back of the rocker and the foot of the bed.

The room needed some fresh air. He went to the single window looking toward the river and opened it, thankful for the mild November weather.

With another sigh, he gathered up his clothing and piled it near the door and then threw the bedcovers over the sheets, hoping Charlotte wouldn't come into the room until after dark.

He stood for a moment, rolled his shoulders and looked toward the ceiling. "Lord?" It was more of a question than a statement. "Why did you let Charlotte come? Don't I have enough trouble to deal with already?"

He snatched up his clothing and strode out of the room and downstairs.

Charlotte stood with her back to the stairs, a handkerchief hovering near her face.

He moved past her and went through the kitchen and into the lean-to, where Susanne had kept her washtubs. He dumped his clothes in the corner, planning to get to them later. After Susanne's death, Abram had devoted almost every waking moment to his business. It had been the only way to deal with his pain, but the housework had slipped.

Charlotte entered the kitchen as he came back in. She was out of place with her extravagant dress and perfectly styled hair. She looked nothing like Susanne, who had been short and blonde. Charlotte had dark brown curls and she was tall and slender—almost too thin for his tastes. Her face would be pretty if it wasn't scrunched up in disapproval all the time.

He went to the cupboard and pulled out the coffee beans and grinder. "Feel free to take off your hat and gloves. We're not going anywhere soon."

She didn't move but her eyes roamed this room, as well.

Abram assessed it as he ground the coffee beans, trying to see what she would see. The kitchen was a generous room with a long table, a cookstove and a large cupboard. Susanne had spent hours in this room preparing meals for him and the children. She hadn't been a very good cook, but she had tried—he'd give her that. When he was able to hire his first laborer, she had taken on the extra responsibility without complaint. She had often told him she'd learned her work ethic from her sister, who had been forced to provide for them after their parents had died.

He continued to turn the grinder, uncomfortable with Charlotte's perusal. "Have a seat. I'll get the coffee boiling and then fry up some bacon."

She took a handkerchief from her handbag and wiped the bench.

He tried to ignore her as he fried the bacon and tended to the coffee—but it was almost impossible. Her presence filled the room, just as it had years ago when he'd first met her and Susanne at the Fireman's Ball in Iowa City. He had actually noticed Charlotte first, with her tall, dark looks—but as soon as he had met the sparkling Susanne, his attention had been stolen.

Neither one spoke as he prepared the simple meal. When it was ready, he went to the front door and clanged the large triangle dinner bell.

The waterwheel was no longer spinning, which meant Caleb and Josiah would hear the call. Harry and Milt were delivering lumber to Fort Ripley, so they probably wouldn't arrive back until after dark.

He went into the house and found Charlotte had finally removed her hat and gloves and sat with her back rigid as she waited for the meal to begin.

What would his laborers think of the pretty young woman in his home? Single females were so scarce, having one at his table would be a rare treat. If this one wasn't so unreasonable, maybe they'd enjoy having her.

Caleb and Josiah rushed in through the back door, as if they had been waiting for the call—and they probably had been. Both men drank up Charlotte's presence like men dying of thirst.

"Boys, this is my sister-in-law, Miss Charlotte Lee." Abram set four mugs on the table. "Charlotte, this is Caleb and Josiah."

Caleb bowed and offered her a dimpled smile, his green eyes shining with appreciation. "It is a pleasure to meet you, Miss Lee." If his easy demeanor and gregarious personality couldn't charm Charlotte, then nothing would. "I don't believe I've ever met such a lovely woman in my life."

Charlotte dipped her head ever so slightly with embarrassment. "Thank you."

Josiah pushed Caleb to the side in a great show of aplomb, his curly black hair falling over his forehead and into his dark eyes. He also bowed, unwilling to be outdone. "Lovely does not do you justice, Miss Lee. Gorgeous would be a more appropriate description."

This time her cheeks filled with color—yet still she did not smile. "I'm pleased to meet you," she said.

Undeterred, the young bucks took a seat across from Charlotte at the table, still vying for her attention with compliments.

They were in their late teens and had come to Abram fresh off their family farms back East. Eager and energetic, they reminded Abram of himself when he'd left his parents' home in Michigan eight years ago. He had been full of confidence and invigorated with optimism. Raised by a man who had founded the successful town of Cooper, Michigan, Abram had set out to make his father proud and start his own town. But it had been much harder than he'd realized and the reality of the obstacles had almost crushed his spirit as he went from Michigan to Iowa to Minnesota Territory.

Father had died before Abram could prove himself—and then Susanne had died. The only two people who had ever believed in him, and he had disappointed them both.

Now he must succeed for his sons.

"Shall we say grace?" Abram asked.

Charlotte closed her eyes and inhaled a slow breath. Her face lost all trace of grief and became almost serene.

Abram dipped his chin to pray. "For this meal, and our lives, Lord, we are eternally grateful. Amen."

"Amen," echoed the others.

Abram opened his eyes and watched as Charlotte opened hers. Their gazes met for only a moment before Caleb and Josiah nabbed her attention again. They reached for the platter of bacon at the same moment and then handed it to Charlotte as one, grins on their faces.

Charlotte suddenly seemed quite interested in them. "Maybe you gentlemen can help me."

They looked at each other, their grins growing.

"We'd love to help," Caleb said.

Abram picked up the coffeepot and poured the steaming brew into his blue-speckled mug. The aroma filled his nose and made his stomach rumble. He had stocked the pantry and cellar with a bountiful harvest, but he had little time to prepare a decent meal. For weeks all they had eaten was bacon and coffee. But with his appetite, he hardly cared.

"Could one of you take me to Susanne's children?"

The coffee sloshed out of Abram's cup and pooled on the table. "What?"

Josiah and Caleb grinned. "Yes," they both said at the same moment.

"No," Abram said with force. "I'll take Miss Lee when I'm ready." He wanted to be there when the boys met their aunt for the first time, and it would be impossible to go this evening.

Charlotte let out a sigh and then took two pieces of bacon off the platter.

The woman was definitely determined.

Here, at least, was something they had in common.

Yet a niggle at the back of his conscience suggested Charlotte wasn't completely out of line in asking to take his boys. Susanne had never spoken an unkind word about her sister, and it didn't surprise him that she'd want Charlotte to help raise the boys—but surely she didn't want Charlotte to take them away from Abram. She wouldn't want them separated by four hundred miles—which only left one solution.

If Charlotte wanted to help care for the boys, she would have to stay in Little Falls.

He hated to even contemplate such a thing, but the idea was there nonetheless.

Chapter Two

Charlotte walked up the steep stairs, a lantern in hand, ready for bed. She was exhausted from a week of travel, but she didn't know if she would sleep. The house her sister had written about was not what Charlotte had anticipated.

She could overlook the filth and the farm animals roaming about, but it was the sparse furnishings and lack of amenities that had surprised her. Susanne had boasted about how well Abram provided for her—yet Charlotte had not seen anything other than the bare necessities.

Charlotte pushed open the door on the left and shone the lantern into the interior. It was just as filthy as the rest of the house—and cold.

She set the lantern on the bureau and crossed the room to close the open window. If Abram thought he could mask the stale smell, he was wrong. What the house needed was a thorough cleaning, and no amount of fresh air would change that.

The room looked toward the west, where the Mississippi flowed under the light of a brilliant moon. Charlotte leaned against the window frame, hugging her arms about her waist, and allowed the weight of her grief to sting her eyes with tears. Would the pain ever subside?

She glanced around the room. A small cradle sat in one corner and Susanne's Bible lay on a table next to the bed, but nothing else marked her sister's presence.

Charlotte put her hand over her heart and sank down to the mattress. "Susanne, you had so many hopes and dreams." She had written to Charlotte about their plans for Little Falls and their growing family. They had been living in Little Falls for three years, yet what did they have to show for their work? Had Susanne really believed Abram would build a town? How long would she have waited for him to succeed?

Forever, because Susanne believed in her husband and his vision. That was why she had left with him even though Charlotte had begged her to stay. The day they'd left Iowa City, without saying goodbye, Charlotte had mourned as if Susanne had died.

It had been just as painful as the day Charlotte's fiancé, Thomas, had left Iowa City to go west in pursuit of gold. He had gone without saying goodbye and she had never heard from him again. She had half expected Susanne to never write, but thankfully her sister had kept up a steady correspondence.

Charlotte didn't bother to change into a nightgown.

She locked the door and lay on the bed, curling up in a ball. Tears wet her cheeks and hair, and stained the pillow beneath her head. The last thing she recalled before falling asleep was the scurry of mice along the floorboard.

* * *

A rooster's crow pulled Charlotte out of a fitful dream. Thomas had been calling to her, and when she'd raced toward him, he'd run away, taunting her to catch him if she could. She opened her eyes slowly and blinked several times before she recalled where she was.

A knock came at her door.

"Breakfast is ready." Abram's voice sounded just as stiff this morning as it had yesterday.

She wished her stomach wasn't growling so she could stay in her room and not face him. Instead she got out of bed and looked at her reflection in the dusty mirror above the bureau. Her hair stuck out in disarray, her eyes were still gritty from the late-night tears and her dress was wrinkled. She tried to smooth down her curls and tucked some wayward strands behind her ear, but it was no use.

She checked inside her shoes for uninvited critters and, finding none, slipped them on and then unlocked the door. The smell of fresh bacon and coffee wafted up the stairwell. Was that all these men ate and drank?

Charlotte descended the stairs and entered the kitchen. This time there were five men at the table instead of three.

Two older men glanced up at her arrival, their coffee cups halting midway to their mouths. One had stringy gray hair and was missing all his teeth. The other had thick red hair and a freckled complexion.

The one without teeth stood and then the other followed, their eyes a bit round.

"Milt and Harry, this is Miss Charlotte Lee." Abram set the coffeepot down on the table.

The men nodded a greeting as she found her seat.

Caleb and Josiah immediately began to tease her and try to draw her out, while Abram sat at the head of the table, his attention on his meal. His hair was in need of a cut and his beard should either be trimmed or shaved completely. She could hardly remember what he looked like without all that mangy hair. She did recall that he was handsome, and she clearly remembered the first time she'd seen him at a ball in Iowa City.

He had walked into the hotel with an air of confidence few men his age possessed, and he had immediately caught her eye. It had been a year since Thomas had left, and she had been wary of romance, but when he had asked her to dance, she had accepted. The moment he spoke of his dream to prospect a town, she knew right away that he was like Thomas and her father, and couldn't be trusted. After the dance she had tried to forget him, but it was impossible to ignore him when he came to call on Susanne.

Yes, he was handsome, but that was the only thing she had understood about Susanne's infatuation, though it wouldn't have been enough for Charlotte to make her heart vulnerable.

The meal finished and Abram rose. For the first time since she'd entered the room, he offered her his full attention. "I'd like a word with you outside."

"Are we going to the boys?"

He put on his hat and coat and then stepped toward the back door. "I'd like you to see something."

She didn't bother with her own hat or coat, which were in her room, but followed him out the door and into a barren yard. The bright morning sunshine almost blinded her with its brilliance—yet the air was much colder than she had thought. She wrapped her arms about her waist and allowed her eyes to adjust.

Goats grazed nearby, munching on brown grass, while chickens waddled around and a pig snorted from a pen closer to the barn.

Abram walked with a steady purpose up a gentle hill toward the east, away from the river and sawmill. A small grove of leafless birch trees stood off a ways with a white picket fence nearby.

As soon as Charlotte realized his destination, her feet slowed. "Are you taking me to Susanne's grave?"

He continued to walk. "Yes."

Part of her wanted to see her sister's final resting place—but the other part wanted to run in the opposite direction.

Abram entered the small graveyard and stopped beside Susanne's headstone. A clump of wildflowers, wilted, yet not completely dry, lay on the grave. Had he brought them recently?

Charlotte slowly walked through the gate and stopped just inside the fence.

"It isn't much." He swallowed, putting his hand on the dark granite. "I had to send away for the stone, but I was pleased when it arrived." It had Susanne's name, birth and death recorded in simple letters. Nothing more. But it must have been expensive.

A lump gathered in Charlotte's throat and she put her hands to her lips, holding back the tears that threatened to spill.

Abram turned to her, his shoulders slumped. "I know what you've always thought of me, but despite my shortcomings, Susanne somehow found a man to love." He looked back at the headstone. "I never deserved her, and

I told her that often. But she treated me like a king and made me very happy." He put his hands in the pockets of his tattered work coat. "Maybe Susanne didn't dream of settling a town before she met me, but she wanted it as much as I did when we came here."

Her sister had been just as optimistic as Abram—even if misguided and unrealistic. If Susanne hadn't been in love, maybe she would have understood the dangers of life with a man like Abram.

"As her husband, you should have taken better care of her." Charlotte's voice caught as she looked at the lone grave. "When she became sick, you should have brought her somewhere with a competent doctor, instead of leaving her here to die." Father had done the same thing and they had lost Mama.

"The military doctor came from Fort Ripley and he said there was nothing left to do."

"A military doctor? What does he know of female complaints?"

"I did the best I could—"

"I didn't get to say goodbye." A sob escaped her throat and she turned her face away from Abram, clutching the picket fence for support. "Not when she left Iowa and not when she died." Her body trembled from the cold and grief.

He was quiet for several moments and then his coat enveloped her shoulders. "I'm sorry for your loss."

Charlotte squeezed her eyes closed as the weight of his compassion weakened her knees. She longed to share her grief—yet years of heartache and disappointment forced her to bear it alone.

She wiped her tears with her handkerchief and slipped

his coat off her shoulders, handing it back. "Thank you, but I'm fine."

He took the coat and draped it over his arm but didn't put it on. "Susanne and I wanted to build this town for our sons," he said softly. "She wanted them here—"

"But don't you realize things have changed—"

He held up his hand to stop her. "I know it seems impossible, but I believe this place will one day be a great city. It's a legacy Susanne and I wanted for our sons."

"You don't really think you'll succeed—"

"I do."

She closed her eyes, tired of the unabashed optimism in his gaze—so like the look her father and Thomas used to have.

He cleared his throat. "Why don't you stay here to help raise them?"

She opened her eyes and stared at him. "Here? But I have a business and a home in Iowa City." She had made a living as a seamstress for eight years, since her father had died.

"You could be a seamstress here."

"I have friends there." Though not many since she devoted so much time to her work and had resigned herself to being an old maid.

"You could make new ones here."

"There isn't even a town here."

"I'll have one built soon."

"How soon? A year, five years, ten? By then the boys will be grown, if they survive this place."

"A year," he said. "This place will be a real town in one year's time."

She shook her head. "A year?" There was nothing

but trees, and hills, and tall, dead grass. "How will you build a town in one year?"

"More settlers are coming into the territory and speculators are arriving in droves at St. Anthony Falls, which is only a hundred miles southeast of here. If I had one or two investors, we could begin construction on more buildings immediately."

"Buildings do not make a town."

"What does?"

"People. Teachers, preachers, doctors—"

"There are teachers and a preacher at the mission, and the military doctor is at Fort Ripley—"

"No. Here. To make this place a town."

"If I had a teacher, a preacher and a doctor living here, would you consider this a real town?"

"Not just a teacher, but a school. And not just a preacher, but he must have a church—a separate building from the school. And there must be at least one doctor in town." She looked at the empty woods. "And then, yes, I would say it is a town—or at least a good start."

Abram took a tentative step toward her. "Then this is what I propose. Stay for a year and help me take care of the children. I'm confident I'll have a teacher, with a school, a preacher, with a church, and at least one doctor by November first of next year. But if I don't—" He swallowed. "You may take my boys back to Iowa City with my blessing."

Charlotte stood speechless.

He studied her closely. "It's my only offer. If you refuse, you will have to return to Iowa City alone, immediately."

"Why?" She shook her head. "Why are you giving me this option?"

"Because." He paused and looked down at his weathered hands. "I know how much you want to be with the boys. And—" he let out a sigh "—I'm sure Susanne would want it, too."

"But I can't stay here for a year."

He looked up, a challenge in his eyes. "Why not?"

"I already told you. My business."

"Is there no one to do the work for you—at least for now?"

Of course there were people who could take over for now—but one year? More important, could she survive in a place like this for one year? Her sister hadn't, and her mother hadn't. What made her think she could? Charlotte never took risks. She had learned long ago that nothing good came from taking risks. She was content to stay in Iowa City, unmarried, and be a seamstress for the rest of her life. It was safer that way.

"Why can't I take them with me and bring them back if you succeed?"

"I have no desire for them to leave Minnesota Territory. If you're worried about a living, I would pay you to keep my house." He studied her as if gauging whether or not she could do the work. "If you think you could manage."

Manage? Hadn't she been the one to care for Susanne all those years? "Of course I could manage."

"Then you'll stay?"

Charlotte wrung her hands. "Why a year? Why not six months?"

"That's impossible." He shook his head. "Six months from now is the first of May. I couldn't build a town over the winter. I need the spring and summer—at least until September first of next year."

Charlotte quickly calculated. "Ten months."

He rubbed his beard, as if in thought. "If I found the right investors, I think I could do it in ten months."

Was she mad to say yes and take a risk? But what choice did she have? She wanted to care for Susanne's boys. They were all the family she had left. Her house in Iowa City was locked up and her customers could find other seamstresses until her return. There was nothing to stop her but fear.

She spoke quickly, hoping she wouldn't regret her decision. "Yes."

He became still. "Yes?"

She glanced at Susanne's grave. She wasn't doing this for Abram; she was doing this for her sister and her nephews. She could give up ten months of her life to ensure that Susanne's boys returned with her to Iowa City.

And maybe, just maybe, she could make Abram realize how foolish his dream was and she'd return to Iowa much sooner.

Abram stared at his sister-in-law, suddenly unsure of the agreement they had just made. He had set out to convince her to stay on as his housekeeper, yet now he had agreed to send the boys with her if he couldn't build a town. What had he been thinking? What if he didn't succeed? How would he live without his boys?

Yet the truth had been evident since Susanne had died and he had sent the boys to live at the Belle Prairie Mission. This settlement was no place for growing boys without a woman to care for them. Charlotte's sudden appearance seemed like an answer to an unspoken prayer—even if it meant living under the same roof with her.

No matter what, he would have a teacher, a preacher and a doctor living in Little Falls within ten months. Miss Charlotte Lee would go back where she came from, and at that point, the population would boom and there would be other women available to hire as a full-time housekeeper. *If* he succeeded.

"Are we going now?" she asked.

"Going where?"

"To get the boys."

He shook his head, still a bit unsettled by the sudden shift in his plans. "Not today. I have another lumber order I need to deliver to Fort Ripley on Monday and I only have today to work on it. We'll go for them tomorrow."

She shivered and wrapped her arms around her body.

"You should get back inside," he said, leaving the graveyard.

"I'll go after them," she said, keeping up with his long-legged stride. "I'll hook up the wagon and fetch them myself."

"No. The boys have been through enough change these past few months already. I want to be there when you meet them."

"Abram, I've waited five years to meet the boys—"

"And you can wait one more day." He hated to sound so heartless but she had to understand that there was work to do, and only so much time in a day to get it done. "Use today to get the house ready."

By the set of her shoulders he could see she didn't like his answer, but she had little choice.

"See that dinner is ready by noon," he said. "And then bring us a light lunch in the midafternoon. We'll work until dark, so have supper ready at eight. You'll find everything you need in the pantry and root cellar under the lean-to." He inspected her fashionable gown and recalled how she had responded to the chicken and the dirt yesterday. "Do you think you can manage all that?"

She didn't respond but set her mouth in a firm line and veered off toward the house like a soldier marching into battle.

Susanne claimed she had learned how to work hard from Charlotte, but he wondered if his wife had been stretching the truth. From her neatly pinned hair to her polished boots, Charlotte didn't look as if she had ever lifted a finger in her life. Could she keep his home and provide care for his children?

There was only one way to find out.

Abram put his hands in his pockets and walked with determination to the mill.

On Monday morning he would make a trip to St. Anthony Falls and talk with several men who were interested in investing in his town. There had been dozens of men who had come to look over the area since Abram had bought the sawmill and property in 1851, but he had turned each one down, determined to make a go of it himself. After three years of barely getting by—and now his deadline to produce a town in ten months—he had no other options. He needed to find financial partners whether he wanted to or not.

Charlotte opened the lean-to door and entered the house. After five long years she had hoped to meet her nephews. One more day felt like an eternity.

She stood just inside the lean-to with her hands on her hips and looked at the stack of dirty clothes, the cobwebs in the corners and the dirt on the floor. The housework loomed in front of her like a battlefield. She must strategize an attack or it might overwhelm her—and that was the last thing she could allow. She would prove to Abram that she was more than capable of taking care of his home.

She walked into the kitchen and inspected the greasy stove, the stack of dirty dishes and the mouse droppings. Her mother's chore rhyme ran through her mind: wash on Monday, iron on Tuesday, mend on Wednesday, churn on Thursday, clean on Friday, bake on Saturday and rest on Sunday. Since today was Saturday, and she would never think to bake in such a filthy kitchen, she would spend the remainder of the day cleaning and then start fresh on Monday morning with the wash.

She went to her room, changed into a work dress and apron, tied a red handkerchief around her hair and then set to work pumping water into a large kettle. At least she didn't have to sit around all day and fret about Susanne's boys. She enjoyed staying busy. It was a way to feel in control.

She scoured every surface in the kitchen, including the ceiling, with hot water and lye soap. When that was done, it was time to prepare dinner. She did a quick inventory of the pantry and was surprised at the abundance it contained. Flour, sugar, coffee, dried apples and dried beans. The root cellar was just as impressive with fresh eggs, milk, venison and a barrel full of salt pork. There were several bins of recently harvested vegetables, as well, so she picked out some potatoes, carrots, rutabagas and radishes.

She could make a nice stew with biscuits and dried apple pie for supper. But for dinner she didn't have time to produce much, so she decided to fry up some bacon.

If it was good enough for supper and breakfast, then it should be good enough for dinner, too.

Charlotte removed the last piece of bacon from the grease when the back door opened and Abram walked in with his crew.

All five men stopped and looked around the immaculate kitchen. The root vegetables were sitting on the worktable, washed and waiting to be diced up for the stew, while the dried apples were soaking in a bowl of water on the cupboard.

Charlotte's hands were chapped from being in soapy water all morning, but she met Abram's gaze with a bit of triumph. Of course she could manage a house!

He glanced at the handkerchief on her head and then his gaze traveled around the room once again. Disbelief showed on his face. "It hasn't looked this clean in here since before Susanne became sick."

The reminder of her sister brought a stab of grief to Charlotte's heart and her moment of triumph evaporated.

She placed the heaping platter of bacon on the table.

All five men looked at the platter, their faces sagging in disappointment.

"Ah, Miss Lee! Bacon again?" Caleb asked.

"I thought we'd have us a real meal now that you're here," Josiah said, pushing his curls out of his eyes as he slumped against the door frame.

Abram's appreciation dimmed and his eyes filled with irritation. He glanced at the vegetables, but before he could say anything, she grabbed the coffeepot and nodded toward the table. "There will be stew, biscuits and hot apple pie for supper. This was all I had time to prepare for now. Sit up to the table and eat the bacon while it's still hot."

They started to come into the kitchen but she held up her free hand. "Clean your boots off in the lean-to. I won't have you tracking up this floor with mud. And wash your hands in the basin I set up out there." She offered them a challenging look. "If I'm to serve food in this house, I'll be serving it to clean hands."

"You going to let her talk to you like that?" asked the one with freckles named Harry.

All the men looked at Abram to see what he would do. He stared at Charlotte for a moment and then nodded for them to do as she said. "It's Charlotte's kitchen for the time being, so we'll abide by her rules."

She suppressed an urge to smile as she filled his mug with coffee.

The men came back into the kitchen, each taking their seat, no one saying a word.

They ate their bacon in silence, though Caleb grimaced a time or two and looked at the waiting vegetables fondly.

Milt, Harry, Caleb and Josiah all stood when they were finished and waited for Abram, who took a final swig from his coffee mug. He tilted his head toward the door. "Go on without me. I'll be there in a minute."

Caleb glanced at Charlotte. "Thanks for the meal." He dipped his head. "I mean no disrespect, but I hope it's the last bacon we see for a long time."

Charlotte appreciated his candor. "I'll bring you a special treat this afternoon at the mill. Do you like doughnuts?"

His face lit with a grin. "Boy, do I!" With a holler

and a jig, he made his way out of the house, followed by the others.

Abram set his coffee mug on the table and stood.

Charlotte began to clear the dirty dishes and tried to ignore him. Why hadn't he left with the others?

"There's something you need to know."

She stopped stacking the plates and looked at him.

He swallowed and glanced down at the table, adjusting the fork near his plate. "I don't exactly know how to tell you this."

Apprehension wound its way around her heart. "What?"

When he finally looked at her, deep sadness etched the corners of his eyes. "Right after Susanne died, a sickness went through the area and Robert became ill. The military doctor was sent for, but Robert's fever became so high, he—" Abram swallowed and looked down at the table again. "When he got better we realized the fever had taken his hearing."

Charlotte clutched a tin plate. "He's deaf?"

Abram nodded. "I'm afraid so. It's been over three months now, and the doctor said if he was going to regain his hearing, it would have happened by now."

Her legs became weak and she took a seat. "What does this mean?"

"It means we'll need to learn how to communicate with him."

"You mean sign language?"

Abram nodded.

"Who's teaching him? Are you learning—"

"Just leave it be for now." He put up his hand to silence her questions. "You'll learn more tomorrow when we see him."

Charlotte sat in silence, though the questions continued to whirl in her mind.

Deaf. Five-year-old Robert.

"I need to get to the mill. I just thought I should tell you so you're prepared."

Charlotte looked up at him but had nothing to say.

Abram walked out of the kitchen and left her to mourn yet another loss.

Chapter Three

On Sunday morning Abram rolled out of the bottom bunk while it was still dark. He shivered in the cold and glanced out the window at the end of the long room.

Snow fell gracefully from the black sky, brushing against the windowpane and gathering in the corners.

Winter always frustrated Abram. Once the river stopped flowing, his saw would stop, too, and so would his income. Of course the snow and cold would come eventually, but he had hoped and prayed it would hold off a bit longer. At least until he had come back from St. Anthony. The trail would be difficult to travel now and the drop in temperature would make it more uncomfortable. But it wouldn't stop him from going. He'd leave before the sun was up the following morning.

He pulled his cold denim pants over his long johns. They felt grimy against his skin, but he had nothing else to wear. They would have to do for now.

The other men continued to snore, so he tried to be quiet as he pulled on his shirt and buttoned up the front. He didn't want to disturb them on their one morning off. All four of them had gone to Crow Wing village, about twenty-five miles north on the river, the night before, and they had crawled into bed in the wee hours of the morning. He wished they would come to church with him at the Belle Prairie Mission, but none of them had any interest—especially after a night of carousing.

Abram grabbed his boots from the end of his bed and tiptoed toward the door. He would see to the Sunday morning chores, like he did every week, and leave the rest of the afternoon and evening chores to his men so he could spend the day with his sons.

The hallway was dark and no light seeped from beneath Charlotte's door. She had worked hard yesterday and had gone to bed as soon as the dishes had been wiped after supper.

He slid past her room and down the stairs, hoping not to wake her, either.

He'd never seen someone clean the way she had. No wonder she'd gone to bed early. There was not a nook or cranny of the main floor that had not been touched. She had even taken Susanne's books off the shelves and hand-dusted each one. The place practically glowed. While he had sat next to the fireplace the evening before, after Charlotte had gone to bed and the men had left for Crow Wing, he had admired the way the firelight danced on the shiny windows again. She had outdone herself—and he sensed it was to prove him wrong.

But that didn't bother him one bit.

The kitchen door was outlined with light and Abram could smell the first hint of coffee on the cold morning air.

Charlotte?

He pushed open the door and found her standing in front of the cookstove in a fresh yellow dress, snug against her slender waist and belled out around the bottom. She wore a large apron and had her hair done up in a fancy knot. She stood with one hand on her hip and the other flipping a flapjack in a frying pan. Her right foot was tapping and he heard the soft sound of her humming "Oh! Susanna."

A smile teased his lips as he paused over the threshold, surprised at how nice it felt to have a lady in the house again. The breakfast table was already set with a butter dish, a pitcher of cream and a little bowl of white sugar. Six plates were set with a fork and a mug beside each.

Everything looked homey and snug. Warmth curled inside his chest—but then a pang of guilt rocked him back on his heels, stealing the smile from his face. What was he thinking? This was Susanne's kitchen. How could he feel good about another woman in her place?

Charlotte grabbed the plate of flapjacks and turned to put them on the table. She glanced up and her brown eyes registered surprise at his appearance. "Good morning."

He cleared his throat and mumbled, "Morning."

She turned back to the stove and flipped another flapjack, glancing over her shoulder. "Eat up while they're hot."

He took his place at the head of the table, his mouth watering at the smell of fresh coffee and the sight of steam rising off the flapjacks.

"Will the others be down shortly?" she asked.

"They've only been asleep for a couple hours. I don't think we'll see them anytime soon."

She brought the coffeepot from the stove and set it

on the table. "They're not going to the mission with us today?"

He shook his head and reached for the flapjacks. "No."

She put her hand on his arm to stop him. "Where were they all night?"

It felt strange to have her hand on his arm, so he pulled out of her grasp. "They went to Crow Wing. It's a trading center north of here."

"What do they do there?"

"I don't ask and they don't tell." Crow Wing had a reputation for being lawless. It was a mecca for transient fur traders, trappers and Indians. At any time, there were usually about two hundred people living there and very few things were off-limits. He was sure his men had enjoyed themselves.

Charlotte crossed her arms and looked at him with disappointment. "You let them do this?"

"They're grown men. What am I supposed to do?"

"Tell them to stop."

He took a flapjack off the top of the stack and put it on his plate, his stomach growling. He almost closed his eyes to inhale the warm scent but refrained—only because she was watching. "I can't tell them what to do."

Her foot began to tap again but this time she wasn't humming. "Well, I can." She marched around the table and out of the kitchen, her skirts swaying.

Abram scrambled up from the table. "Charlotte!" He raced out of the kitchen and through the dark room just as she opened the front door. "What do you think you're doing?"

"I'm reforming your employees." She reached for the triangle dinner bell.

His eyes grew wide. "They'll skin you alive! They've only been asleep for a couple hours and this is their one morning to sleep in."

She closed the door and marched across the room to the stairs. "This is the Lord's Day and I won't live in a house with four men who don't honor Him."

He reached for the dinner bell but she pulled away. Instead of grab the bell he grabbed her wrist. "I'm warning you, Charlotte. I don't know what they're capable of if woken up right now. They won't be happy."

She pulled her arm away and raced up the steps. He chased after her, but before he could stop her, she charged into the room and began to clang the bell.

"Everyone up! Wake up!" The bell drowned out her words and echoed in Abram's ears. "Breakfast is on the table. Get dressed and ready for church."

Caleb jumped out of his bed as if there was a fire, his eyes enormous. He stood in his red long johns and stocking cap. "What's wrong?"

Josiah groaned and threw his pillow across the room. It hit Charlotte right in the head. Her eyes registered surprise—and then anger. The bell stopped clanging for a moment and Abram thought for a split second that Charlotte would throw the heavy dinner bell at Josiah's head in return.

"Wake up!" Charlotte said instead, this time with more force. "I'm surprised at you men. Is this how you spend your hard-earned money?"

Harry sat up, a scowl on his weathered face, while Milt looked at Charlotte through the hair hanging in his eyes.

Caleb sank back to his bed, holding his head between his hands and moaning.

Charlotte crossed her arms and glared at the men. "I made breakfast and it's still hot. If any of you ever expect to eat a warm meal at my table again, I'd advise you to get dressed and come down immediately."

Harry stood and fisted his hands. "Last I heard, you were an employee of Abram's, same as us. Seems to me that he should be the one making the rules around here."

Charlotte turned and faced Abram. "You said it's my kitchen for now. Therefore, I make the rules. I say they eat now or I don't serve them again."

Panic swelled in Abram's gut. If he wanted Harry to stay, he couldn't take Charlotte's side—yet, if he wanted Charlotte to stay, he had to give her power over her domain.

"I say we show the lady some respect," Caleb said, grimacing as he reached for his shirt and pants off the floor. "If she went to the trouble of making us breakfast, the least we can do is come to the table on time."

Abram sighed in relief.

Caleb nudged Josiah. "Get out of bed and come eat Miss Charlotte's breakfast."

Josiah's black curls were in a mess on his head. He sat up and ran his hands through his hair. The look he cast Charlotte suggested she had lost all appeal in his eyes.

Milt didn't say anything but he also started to fumble for his clothing.

It was Harry who narrowed his eyes and glared at Charlotte. "I won't let no woman tell me what to do." He flopped back into his bed and pulled the covers over his red hair.

Caleb, Josiah and Milt all looked at him—and then at Charlotte—but none of them went back to bed.

Charlotte turned from the room, the dinner bell firmly in hand.

Abram was thankful a disaster had been averted—though for how long, he wasn't sure.

He followed Charlotte down the stairs, admiring and disliking her backbone all at the same time.

When the men were assembled around the table, and Abram had said grace, Charlotte poured each of them a cup of coffee. Their eyes were bloodshot and they didn't bother to hide their yawns. No one said a thing as Charlotte picked up Harry's plate, cup and fork and put them back in the cupboard.

"I'll expect each of you to join us at church today, too," Charlotte said, taking her place at the table.

Josiah's black eyes filled with horror. "Now, look here, Miss Charlotte—"

"What would your mothers think if they knew you weren't attending church?" Charlotte took a flapjack off the platter and put it on her plate. "I want you to make your parents proud."

Caleb, Josiah and Milt ate the rest of the meal in silence.

Abram did, too.

Charlotte was the only one who seemed to have something to say.

The wagon rumbled over the uneven road toward the north and the long-awaited meeting with her nephews. Charlotte huddled inside her coat, a cloud of air escaping her mouth.

The prairie was draped in a thin blanket of snow with patches of brown grass showing through. A large bluff rose up in the east, covered with leafless trees, now stark against the white landscape.

Caleb, Josiah and Milt sat in the back of the wagon, their heads bobbing up and down as if they had fallen asleep, and perhaps they had. None of them looked happy about going to the mission this morning.

Abram gripped the opening of his coat with one chapped hand while the other held the reins.

"Don't you have mittens?" she asked.

He glanced at her and she was reminded again of how blue his eyes were, especially now in the bright sunshine glinting off the fresh snow.

"The pair I have are worn through. I was planning to buy a new pair in St. Anthony."

"You don't need to do that. Buy me some yarn and I'll knit new ones for everyone in the house." She loved to keep her hands busy with sewing and knitting. "If you buy some wool, I'll also sew you a new coat to match."

He glanced down at his threadbare coat and sighed. "I wish there was enough time to make it before I meet with investors. I'd probably make a better impression if I didn't look so destitute."

She couldn't make him a new coat by tomorrow, but she could at least wash a pair of his pants and a nice shirt this afternoon so they were dry in the morning. She would have to break her Sabbath rest to do the work, but maybe this one time would be okay—though it might help her cause if he went to St. Anthony looking like a pauper. If others saw how poor he was, they would realize it was foolish to invest in his town.

As tempting as the thought might be, no self-respecting housekeeper would let him go the way he looked.

The moment the mission came within sight, Charlotte sat straighter. She didn't realize she was clutching her hands together until her cold knuckles hurt.

A commodious house sat off to the left, with a New England–style barn just behind it. The building across the road served as a church and a schoolhouse.

"This is a manual labor school," Abram said as he turned the horses into the mission yard. "All the children are given chores to help pay for their education and teach them about farm life. The Ayers built the mission in the late 1840s for the fur traders and Indian children in the area."

He stopped the wagon just outside the house and then jumped down to secure the reins to the porch. He walked around the wagon and offered up his hand to Charlotte just as the front door opened and a middle-aged woman stepped outside.

"Mr. Cooper." She looked over the group and her gentle smile turned into a look of surprise. "You've brought guests. How nice."

Charlotte put her hand inside Abram's strong grasp and their gazes met for a split second. She stepped out of the wagon holding her voluminous skirts with her free hand, but the moment her foot hit the earth, she removed her hand from his hold and began to rearrange her skirts.

"Mrs. Ayers, may I present my sister-in-law, Miss Charlotte Lee?"

Mrs. Ayers stepped off the porch and extended her hand to Charlotte. Her kind eyes crinkled at the edges. "It's a pleasure, Miss Lee. Welcome to Belle Prairie."

Charlotte shook her hand, her insides quivering.

and he took one pant leg in hand. "They look brand-new, Charlotte. I don't know what to say."

She slipped the needle and thread into her sewing basket. "You don't need to say anything. I'm only doing my job."

"No. You went above and beyond your job." He studied her, as if gauging whether or not she had done it out of kindness or duty. "Either way, thank you."

She couldn't meet his eyes but simply nodded and closed her sewing box.

He rubbed his beard for a moment and then walked over to the stove, where he closed his eyes and inhaled. "There's nothing like waking up to the smell of coffee. Before you came, I was the one who made it every morning."

"Even when Susanne was alive?"

Abram glanced over his shoulder with a knowing smile. "Unlike you, Susanne was not an early riser."

Charlotte smiled to herself. How could she forget? She had practically dragged her sister out of bed every morning of her life...until she had eloped with Abram.

A stilted silence fell between them.

Abram reached for a speckled mug as Charlotte stood and took a clean towel from the drying rope she'd strung over the stove the night before. She folded it on the table, laid Abram's pants on top, then hooked a wooden handle to one of the heavy irons and lifted it off the stove.

"Would you like me to do that?" Abram reached for the iron, his hand covering Charlotte's on the handle. "Susanne's arms used to get tired when she ironed."

Charlotte didn't let go, too stunned to move. She was so used to taking care of herself, the thought of someone else easing her burden made her feel helpless, which she tried to avoid at all cost. "That won't be necessary." She gently tugged the iron out of his grasp. "My arms are strong from my seamstress work."

Abram awkwardly turned to the stove and filled his mug. He walked around her and took a seat at the table.

She swallowed and glanced at him, her insides feeling a bit shaky with him watching her. "I'll have breakfast ready within the hour. I imagine you have work to do in the barn and then you'll want to get an early start."

He took a slow sip of his coffee, apparently in no rush. "The men should be up soon to take care of the animals." He paused. "I actually came down early to make a request."

She ran the hot iron over the first pant leg. "Oh?"

"I could use a haircut before I go."

Charlotte stopped ironing. "You want me to cut your hair?"

"Would you?"

She had cut her father's hair, after her mama passed away, but she had never touched the head of another man, not even Thomas's. Somehow it felt...intimate. "I don't know—"

"I haven't had a cut since Susanne died." He put his hand to his head and tugged on a long strand for emphasis. "I want to make a good impression in St. Anthony— and I'm afraid George might be scared of me with all this hair."

"You do look a bit like a bear."

He smiled at her and she returned the gesture. It was the first time they had ever shared a lighthearted moment.

Their smiles disappeared, as if they had the same thought at the same time.

"The boys' hair is in need of a trim, too," Abram said quickly, toying with the handle of his mug. "Do you think you could add it to your list of duties?"

Speaking of the boys reminded her of the idea she wanted to discuss with Abram.

"I have a request of my own."

He took a sip of his coffee and looked at her over the rim of his mug. When he set it down he let out a contented sigh. "This is good coffee, Charlotte."

His compliment made her blush, though she couldn't understand why. She turned from him and set the cool iron on the stove, unhooked the handle and then hooked it to the other hot iron waiting. Maybe her cheeks were warm from the stove.

"What kind of request?" he asked, taking another sip of coffee.

She cleared her throat and set to work on the other pant leg. "This past year, two men began a school for the deaf in Iowa City. I read an article in the *Iowa City Reporter* about their school. It sounds very promising."

Abram set down his mug. "What are you getting at?"

"I believe Robert is too young to attend, but someday I hope to send him there—"

"Of course I want the best for Robert, but I think the best is to be had here, at home."

"And I think he needs an education."

"I would never deny him an education."

She stopped her work. "How will he get it, if you don't send him?"

"He'll get it right here, when we have a school."

"But how will a teacher communicate with him?" Helplessness weighed down her shoulders. "How will *we* communicate with him? He must be terribly frustrated and alone right now."

Abram ran his hands through his hair. "We'll learn sign language."

"How will we do that?"

"We'll make it up if we have to."

Charlotte set the iron on the stove. "Wouldn't it make sense to teach him the same signs they use at the school in Iowa City? Maybe they have a sign language book. I'll ask them to send one if they do."

"That's fine—but I have no desire to send my son away. I'll find a teacher who uses sign language if I have to. I'll do whatever it takes to keep him here."

"Like build your town?"

"Exactly." He indicated his head with a bit of frustration. "Will you cut my hair now?"

She exhaled an exasperated breath. "Only if you shave your beard."

"Why do you always have conditions and counteroffers?"

She crossed her arms and tapped her foot. "Why are you so stubborn?"

"I don't want to shave my beard when it's getting cold. My face is liable to freeze if I don't have a beard."

"I'll knit you a scarf."

"Why don't you like the beard?"

Why not, indeed? Was it because a small part of her wanted to see if he was still as handsome as he had been the night of the Fireman's Ball? The thought sent heat coursing through her—heat of embarrassment and guilt. She shouldn't think that way about her sister's widower. "You can trim it, can't you?"

He rubbed his beard, as if sad to see it go. "I suppose I could give it a little trim. I'll go get my comb and shears."

While he was gone, Charlotte quickly ironed his shirt and folded it next to the trousers.

Abram returned, set the comb and shears on the table, and then began to unbutton his shirt.

Charlotte put up her hands, her eyes wide. "What are you doing?"

"Taking off my shirt."

"Why?"

"I always took off my shirt when Susanne cut my hair."

She shook her head quickly and grabbed the towel from the table. "Please keep your clothes on and put this around your shoulders. I have no interest in seeing you without your shirt."

His blue eyes twinkled with mischief and Charlotte was reminded of how charming he had been when he'd courted Susanne.

He sat at the table and set the towel on his broad shoulders with a chuckle.

Maybe it wasn't just his good looks that had attracted her sister to him.

Charlotte forced the thoughts from her mind and stepped up to the job. Her hands hovered over his head. Father's hair had been thin and greasy. Abram's hair was thick and wavy. It looked as if he had washed it recently, too.

She took a deep breath and ran the comb through his hair. She allowed her fingers to slip through the thick waves and assess how she wanted to cut them.

He sighed and his shoulders relaxed.

Charlotte paused, aware of how her touch had just affected him.

"Nothing too short," he said. "I like to keep a bit of insulation on top."

She picked up the shears, and with a quick snip, the first lock of hair fell to the floor.

Charlotte worked for several minutes, combing and cutting until she was satisfied. When she was finally finished, she stepped back and admired her work.

"Well?" He turned his head this way and that. "What do you think?"

"I think your beard looks even worse now."

He grinned and stood, holding the towel so the hair clippings stayed inside the fabric.

"Here—" she reached for the towel "—I'll take care of that."

"Then I'll go see what I can do about my beard." He grabbed his clean clothes and left the kitchen.

After she swept and threw the cuttings outside for the birds, Charlotte came back into the kitchen and began to make scrambled eggs and sausage for breakfast. Everyone would soon be awake and they'd want to be fed.

She set the table for seven—recalling that she would not be serving Harry at her table. If he couldn't come down for Sunday breakfast, she wouldn't serve him the rest of the week. He could take a plate to the barn.

The door opened and Charlotte turned from the hot stove.

There, standing in the doorway, was a handsome stranger—or so she thought for a brief moment. Abram looked like a new man. He had kept his beard but trimmed it close to his face. He wore his clean pants and shirt, tucked in, and had wet his hair and combed it into submission.

He smiled and the effect was stunning.

"I look that good?" he teased.

The room suddenly felt overly warm. She realized she was staring and wanted to spin back to the sizzling sausages, but if she didn't acknowledge his transformation, she suspected he would tease her incessantly. "You look fine."

He cocked a brow and swaggered into the room. "Just fine?"

At that, she did turn back to the stove, taking a deep breath to steady her thoughts. "Where will the men sleep while you're away?"

"The men?"

She looked back at him—she couldn't help it. "Yes."

He raised his hand to stroke his beard, but finding it gone, he rested his hand on his chest instead. "Why can't the men sleep in the house?"

"It wouldn't be decent."

"But it's decent when I'm here?"

"As my sister's husband, you're an acceptable chaperone. With you gone, tongues could wag."

"What tongues?" He looked around, a bit bewildered. "No one is close enough to care."

"I care." She flipped the sausages one at a time with a fork. "They'll need to sleep in the barn or somewhere else while you're gone."

"I doubt they'll like that idea."

"That may be so—"

The door opened and Harry and Milt walked into the kitchen.

Harry ignored Charlotte, while Milt nodded a halfhearted greeting. They both stopped when they caught sight of Abram.

"What'd she do to you?" Harry asked, his eyes filled with horror.

Abram touched his jaw and paused. "I thought I'd get cleaned up to go to St. Anthony."

Harry shook his head and exited the house, Milt behind him.

"I don't think Harry will be happy with the idea of sleeping in the barn," Abram said.

Charlotte indicated a plate sitting on the cupboard counter. "He can eat out there, too."

Abram groaned. "Maybe I'll take him with me to St. Anthony. Let the two of you cool off a bit."

Charlotte glanced outside, where Harry and Milt were entering the barn. Harry appeared to be just as stubborn as her. She doubted either one would cool off soon.

Abram stepped into the office of Cheney Milling Operation and inhaled the familiar scent of pine. The office stood on the eastern banks of the Mississippi at St. Anthony Falls, where dozens of men had built sawmills on wooden stilts in the water. Numerous mills crowded the piers and sawed thousands of feet of lumber a day. Mill owners were bringing in a fortune as the population increased, making St. Paul, St. Anthony and Stillwater thriving towns.

Over the years several prospective investors had traveled through Little Falls and longed to harness the power at the largest waterfall north of St. Anthony, but Abram had said no. One of those men had been Liam Cheney, owner of a successful sawmill here in St. Anthony.

Abram nodded at a clerk who stood behind a high counter. "Is Mr. Cheney available?"

The mousy clerk peeked at Abram behind his round spectacles. "Whom shall I say is asking?"

Harry had stayed outside, having no desire to sit in on the meeting, so it was just Abram. "Mr. Abram Cooper."

The clerk looked him up and down and then turned to walk into an office behind the counter.

A few moments later the office door opened and the clerk stepped out, followed by Mr. Cheney, a tall, slender fellow with a large mustache. "Mr. Cooper, what a pleasant surprise. Will you come into my office?"

Abram took off his hat and walked around the counter. "Thank you for seeing me."

Cheney slapped Abram's back. "Always willing to meet with a competitor."

Abram glanced around the large office overlooking the Mississippi and the dozens of men Cheney employed. He would hardly call himself a competitor with his four employees and simple sawmill.

Cheney took a seat behind a large oak desk and indicated a chair for Abram. "What brings you to St. Anthony, Mr. Cooper?"

Abram found it hard to ask for help. Seeking investors made him feel like he was admitting defeat—but he had no choice. He would do it for his children's sake. "I've reconsidered your offer to invest in my sawmill."

Liam Cheney didn't say anything right away. Instead he studied Abram from behind heavy brows. He indicated his office and the mill outside. "As you can see, I invested here—and I must say I'm not disappointed."

Abram's chest felt heavy at the news. "So your offer is no longer good?"

"My initial offer is no longer valid. However…" He leaned forward and placed his forearms on the desk. "I just met a man who is interested in investing in a sawmill. Since he was too late to invest in St. Anthony, he asked if I knew of any other promising locations."

Abram leaned forward. "What did you tell him?"

"I said the territory is very big and there are several prospects, but I did not mention Little Falls, since you had so adamantly refused my offer." Cheney leaned back again, this time steepling his fingers together as if sensing he held the upper hand. "He and I are planning an exploratory trip next week—but I didn't plan to stop in Little Falls." He paused. "Should we?"

"Who is this man?" Abram had devoted three years of his life and all his worldly possessions to his endeavors at Little Falls. He didn't want to hand it over to just anyone.

"His name is Timothy Hubbard. He and his wife just arrived from Moline, Illinois, with their three children. He told me he has several friends and family back home waiting for him to send for them. He's not only willing to invest, but he'll bring ready-made citizens in the bargain."

Abram sat for several moments, feeling like a poor beggar. Just looking around at the success Cheney had found at St. Anthony made Abram frustrated that he had turned down Cheney's offer two years ago. The sounds of men shouting orders and saws cutting lumber seeped through the walls in a muffled taunt.

Maybe it wasn't too late. Maybe he could have the same success.

"Well?" Cheney asked. "Is it worth our time to stop and look around Little Falls?"

Abram stood and extended his hand. "I believe it will be."

Cheney also stood and shook Abram's hand. His face became serious. "I feel it only fair to tell you we're looking at several possible locations to invest, and more than one has already caught our eye. I don't know if it's too late to convince Hubbard that Little Falls is the place to invest."

Abram was proud of Little Falls, as humble as it was, and he was convinced it was the best place to build a town on the Upper Mississippi. "You get him there and I'll do the convincing."

Cheney offered a shrewd smile. "I like your attitude."

Abram slipped on his hat, not wanting Cheney to think he was desperate. "And I feel it's only fair to tell you I'm meeting with several prospective investors while I'm in St. Anthony. I just hope you and Hubbard aren't too late when you come."

Cheney's smile fell and Abram nodded farewell. "Good day."

Abram turned and strode out of the office, his back straight and his head high, though inside he was shaking. He did plan to meet with several investors, but none had shown the avid interest that Cheney had.

Harry stood outside Cheney's office building, leaning against the wall. He was almost twice Abram's age and the deep lines in his face suggested he'd had a tough life. But he was a hard worker and had been the first to come to Abram looking for a job.

"Let's head over to Thompson's Mill," Abram said. "I have a feeling the answer will be no, but we need to ask."

Harry pushed away from the wall and came alongside Abram, his hands in his pockets.

"I don't like that Lee woman," Harry said. "She's not good for the mill or Little Falls."

Abram glanced up. "I'm surprised it's taken you this long to comment."

"If she hadn't come, you wouldn't be here—" Harry scoffed at their surroundings "—begging for handouts."

"I'm not begging for handouts. I'm seeking business partners—"

"Because she threatened you."

"She didn't threaten—"

"She's too high-and-mighty for the likes of us," Harry continued as if he hadn't heard Abram. "She'll eventually guilt the others into believing her way and she'll do it by threatening not to feed them."

"Harry, you have to try to see things from her perspective." Abram could hardly believe he was defending Charlotte. "She's doing what she thinks is best."

"She's going about it the wrong way." His jaw clenched and his eyes filled with bitterness. "I don't want her preaching to me, or threatening to make me go hungry, just because I won't do what she says."

"She still feeds you and in time—"

"In time, nothing. I won't play her games."

Abram stopped on the muddy path and looked Harry in the eyes. "Keep in mind that Miss Lee is my sister-in-law, and a guest in my home, not to mention a lady."

"She's your employee first and foremost." He looked Abram up and down, disgust on his face. "You'll let her get away with anything, because you don't want her taking your boys away."

"She can't take them without my blessing."

"No—but you're afraid she's right, and Minnesota Territory is no place for them, so you'll cave if she makes demands. You're letting her get away with too much because you're afraid of her."

Abram wanted to laugh at the accusation but the truth was that he had always been a little afraid of Charlotte. From the moment he had made his intentions known about Susanne, years ago in Iowa City, Charlotte had been a force to reckon with. Susanne had respected her older sister, and when Charlotte made it clear she didn't approve of Abram, he thought Susanne would bend to her sister's wishes. Thankfully, Susanne had found the courage to walk away from Charlotte—but there was always a part of Abram that believed Charlotte was right way back then, and he wasn't good enough for Susanne. He had fought the fear every day of their marriage, and when Susanne died, it had slapped him in the face.

Even now he was afraid Little Falls wasn't good enough for his boys…and maybe he wasn't enough for them, either. Would time prove Charlotte right again?

"Harry, I want you to listen carefully." Abram's breath fogged the air in front of his face. "Stay clear of Charlotte. If I find out you've even looked at her funny, you'll have to leave."

Harry stared at Abram, his thoughts imperceptible within his gray eyes.

Chapter Five

Charlotte sat at Susanne's desk, her head resting on her folded arms. The letter to the Iowa School for the Deaf was half written beneath her weary arms.

With the boys taking a nap, and the clean laundry freezing on the clothesline outside, she had tried to sneak in a moment to write the letter before starting supper. But the lure of sleep had won.

It had been horrible timing for Abram to leave. The boys didn't know her, nor did they trust her. Robert refused to eat what she had prepared for breakfast and threw a tantrum, causing George to cry. Nothing she did had soothed either of them.

Martin had eaten his breakfast without complaining, but when Charlotte had asked him to clear his plate, he refused. She had lost her patience and scolded him, and he'd begun to cry.

Charlotte had almost thrown her hands up in defeat, but she wouldn't give in—not now, not when she had come so far and wanted so badly to be a part of their lives.

Though she and the boys were upset for the remainder of the morning, she had managed to get the beds stripped and the laundry under way before it was time to prepare dinner.

Caleb, Josiah and Milt had eaten their dinner quickly and then left the house without looking back—and Charlotte didn't blame them. George had cried through the whole meal.

Between doing laundry, trying to soothe George, disciplining Martin and communicating with Robert, she had worn herself ragged the rest of the afternoon.

She sighed and picked up her head. The November sun was already starting to fall toward the western horizon. If she wanted to have supper ready by the time the men came in to eat, she needed to get busy. The letter would have to wait until later.

Charlotte stood and stretched her aching back. Her hands were chapped and her feet were sore. She walked across the main room and into the kitchen, hoping she wouldn't wake the boys who were sleeping in the big room above her head. She would fry up salt pork for supper and serve it with pan gravy over boiled potatoes.

She grabbed several pieces of firewood from the box in the lean-to and began to stoke the fire when a shadow passed by the kitchen window.

Charlotte glanced over her shoulder and a scream lodged in her throat.

There, standing at the window, was a tall Indian. His black hair was collected in two long braids running over his shoulders and down his chest. Though he wore a white man's shirt and hat, he had large hoops in his earlobes and a buckskin jacket over the shirt. He stared back at her without expression, his black eyes like two dark pools of ink.

Charlotte slowly straightened from the cookstove. She was too far away from the sawmill to call for help and she had no weapons in the house, except a kitchen knife. Her thoughts immediately went to the boys who were asleep upstairs. She prided herself on being prepared in every situation—but right now she felt defenseless.

The man moved away from the window and toward the lean-to door. She raced to shove the crossbar in place to prevent his entry, but the door was already opening when she entered the lean-to.

Panic swept over Charlotte as he stepped into the house, his leather moccasins making no sound on the wood-plank floor. His eyes were hooded as he studied her.

Charlotte backed into the kitchen, her chest heaving. "C-can I help you?"

His solemn eyes traveled from her shoes, to her dress, to her hair. "Is Susanne here?" He spoke with a strange accent, foreign to Charlotte's ears.

This man knew Susanne? But how? Should she tell him Susanne was dead? She'd rather not invite conversation—but what else could she do?

"S-Susanne died."

Something akin to shock, and then sadness, permeated his countenance. If he had known Susanne, how did he not know she had died in July?

"Who are you?" he asked.

Perspiration gathered under Charlotte's collar. "I'm her sister, Charlotte."

"Charlotte." He let her name roll over his tongue, as if tasting it or trying it on for size.

She stood motionless, afraid to breathe or to speak again. Did he mean her harm?

"And Abram?" he asked.

Charlotte glanced out the window to see if there was anyone to call for help—but there was no one. She couldn't tell him Abram was gone.

Her eyes landed on the firewood and she was reminded of her task. "Food." She said the word quickly.

"Food?" His eyebrows came together in a quizzical expression.

"Would you like some food?" She remembered when she was a young girl and they had homesteaded in Iowa, an Indian had come to their door looking for food. He didn't leave until her mother had produced some. Charlotte took a tentative step toward the oven. "I can make cornmeal cakes."

He looked at her for a moment, confusion evident on his face, and then lowered himself into a chair at the table and nodded.

Charlotte quickly set a griddle on the stovetop and went to work mixing up the batter, glancing at him several times, though he didn't appear to be in a hurry to leave.

Before long she had fried up several cornmeal cakes and put them on a plate before him. She stepped back and waited, unsure what to do next.

He looked at his plate of food and then at her. "Will you join me?"

She shook her head, her stomach in knots.

He frowned again and then bowed his head and clasped his hands. "For this meal, and our lives, Lord, we are eternally grateful. Amen." His prayer was exactly the same as Abram's.

Charlotte stared at him, confusion clouding her mind. Clearly there was more to this man than she originally thought—but what was it?

George began to cry upstairs and the stranger's eyes wandered to the ceiling. He nodded to Charlotte. "Go ahead."

Charlotte didn't need a second invitation. She rushed out of the kitchen and up the stairs. Her mind raced with what she needed to do next. Should she sneak out the front door with the boys and go to the sawmill for help? Should she stay upstairs until the Indian left? Should she go back to see if he needed anything else, hoping he would leave sooner?

She opened the door to her right and three pairs of sleepy eyes turned at her arrival. She didn't want to alarm the boys—but she needed to keep them safe.

"Martin, will you please help Robert with his shoes? I'm going to change George's diaper."

Martin climbed out of his bunk and obeyed without complaint—so different from earlier in the day.

Charlotte offered up a prayer of thanksgiving.

George continued to cry until Charlotte put a clean diaper on him, and then the baby actually smiled at her, his brown eyes sparkling.

For a moment Charlotte stood in the boys' room and simply waited—but for what, she didn't know.

A tug on her dress made her look down into Martin's face.

"I'm hungry," he said.

"I know—"

Voices from below interrupted her words. Had the men come in from the mill for their supper? Relief washed over her—followed by a new fear. Would violence erupt in her kitchen?

She needed to get rid of the stranger, but she couldn't put Martin in charge of his brothers, and she couldn't explain to Robert and George that she wanted them to stay in the room—so there was only one thing to do. She motioned for the boys to follow her and put her finger to her lips to indicate silence.

She opened the door and listened.

It didn't sound violent.

Charlotte tiptoed down the steps, with the older boys close behind, and George in her arms—but she heard something that made her stop in her tracks.

Laughter.

With round eyes, Charlotte peeked into the kitchen and found the Indian still seated, with Caleb, Josiah and Milt sitting around him. He was regaling them with a tale about a fishing trip on Gull Lake.

Caleb glanced up and saw her first, but the others soon noticed her arrival and the Indian stopped talking.

He stood and offered a bow. "I'm sorry I startled you earlier. My mother's people call me Abooksigun—or Wildcat, but my father's people call me Benjamin Lahaye. My friends call me Ben."

"His flock calls him *Reverend*," Caleb said with a shine in his young eyes. "You probably like that, don't you, Miss Charlotte?" He looked at Reverend Lahaye. "Miss Charlotte made us all go to church on Sunday."

The reverend glanced at Charlotte and offered a simple nod. "Then she's accomplished more in just a few days than I have in two years."

The men thought this quite funny, but Charlotte did not join in their laughter. Embarrassment flared in her chest and she entered the kitchen on shaky legs. She set George in his high chair and clasped her hands so they would stop trembling. "A gentleman would have told me who he was and waited for an invitation to enter the house."

The reverend looked contrite. "I am sorry. I'm a circuit preacher, and when I came through the area Susanne used to insist I let myself in. Since I thought she was still here…" He paused and Charlotte felt the weight of his sadness. "After I learned about her death, I decided to let you decide for yourself whether you would trust me or not—before you learned who I was."

Charlotte felt chastised and even more confused. Surely he must understand how his presence had made her feel. She didn't answer him, but went to the pantry and took out enough ingredients to make cornmeal cakes for everyone.

Before returning to the kitchen, she paused and took several deep breaths. What if he had not been a friendly Indian? She had not even contemplated such a risk—but now that she had been faced with the possibility, her mind began to race with all the other dangers involved in settling a new territory. Wasn't that why she had been afraid for Susanne?

How was she going to survive ten months in this place? And how would she learn to parent with no previous experience and no other woman to help guide her?

The reality of her situation suddenly felt like a heavy burden she wasn't sure she could shoulder.

Abram burrowed deeper into his thin coat on Wednesday evening as he and Harry followed the Wood's Trail toward Little Falls. The wind had picked up, swirling snow across the path.

"It should only be about ten more miles," Abram said to Harry, who rode silently next to him.

Thick woods stood on either side of the trail and the Mississippi flowed to the left. If it had been nicer, Abram would have done some hunting to bring Charlotte fresh venison. No matter how tight his finances over the years, there had always been one thing he did well, and that was supply Susanne with a well-stocked larder. He had spent a great deal of time harvesting and preserving the large garden this fall, and he had salted and smoked the pig they had slaughtered—but with more mouths to feed, he would need more food.

"Rider." Harry drew to a stop and slowly put his hand over his pistol. There had been little cause for concern recently, but one could never be too cautious on the Wood's Trail.

A lone horseman broke through the swirl of snow and moved steadily toward them.

"It's Ben," Abram said, his muscles relaxing.

Harry didn't bother to respond, so they continued forward to meet the reverend.

Abram reached out and extended his hand to his old friend. "Ben. You haven't been through these parts since last spring. It's good to see you."

Ben squeezed Abram's hand and held on for a bit longer than usual. "I'm sorry about Susanne. I just heard. I would have come if I had known."

Abram nodded, trying to put on a good face for his friend, but the reminder stabbed.

An interesting light filled Ben's eyes. "I met Miss Lee." A hint of a smile appeared on his brown face. "A lively soul, that one."

"Lively is one way to describe her," Abram conceded. Stubborn, opinionated, plucky…all adjectives related to Charlotte.

Ben's gaze turned serious. "I think I scared her, though, and I'm sorry. Please convey my apology again."

No doubt his presence had created quite a stir.

Harry pounded his hands against his arms, as if to warm them, and Abram took the hint. "Come and visit us again soon. We have much to catch up on."

Ben nodded. "I'm going to St. Paul, but I'll stop by on my way back through."

They shook hands again and Abram nudged his mare into motion, dreading what he might find at home. How badly had Charlotte been scared? Would her bags be packed?

She couldn't leave now. If she did, the boys would have to go back to the mission, and that was the last thing he wanted.

The wind whipped off the cold Mississippi and chased them all the way home. When they finally arrived, they walked the horses toward the barn. Abram was eager to see his boys, but his horse needed to be rubbed down and fed.

"Go on," Harry said, nodding toward the house.

Abram knew voicing his thanks would make Harry uncomfortable, so he simply nodded his appreciation and picked up his bags and the box of staples he had brought for Charlotte.

The waterwheel was turning at the sawmill, which meant his men should be hard at work. Good. He craved a little time alone with his sons before everyone came to ask about his trip to St. Anthony.

He entered the lean-to and immediately smelled roasting pork and fresh-baked bread. Now that they had a good cook, he had splurged and bought cocoa powder, more dried apples and his favorite, molasses.

Abram set down the box and bags and walked into the kitchen. Charlotte had lit the wall lantern and the reflector plate illuminated the light into the room. George sat in his high chair, a wooden spoon in his hand, banging it against the table. Martin and Robert sat on the floor playing with jacks. And Charlotte stood at the stove frying potatoes, her left hand on her hip and her foot tapping as she hummed "Over the River and Through the Woods."

"Papa!" Martin saw him first and jumped up from his game. He raced to Abram's arms and Abram threw him high in the air. Robert's face glowed with delight, and Abram picked him up, as well. He tickled the boys and sweet laughter emanated from their lips.

Apparently, George approved of Abram's new haircut and trimmed beard, because he banged his spoon harder and said with a wet mouth, "Pa-pa-pa."

Abram set down the boys and kissed George's downy head. He glanced at Charlotte, who had turned at the commotion, her cheeks pink from the stove. "Hello, Charlotte."

She dipped her head, her dark hair shining under the lantern light. "I wasn't expecting you back so soon."

Abram slipped out of his coat and hung it on a peg in the lean-to. He came back into the kitchen rubbing his hands to warm them.

She glanced at his hands and then moved to the medicine cabinet and removed the jar of salve. "Do they hurt?"

He looked down at his red hands. They were cracked and bleeding in several places, but they had been worse. "I suppose."

She opened the jar and dipped her long fingers into the medicinal-smelling ointment. Without asking, she took his hands into hers and began to apply the salve.

Warmth quickly returned to his fingers and the tingling sensation raced up his arms and into his chest. Her touch, though platonic, felt far too good. Susanne's memory filled his mind and cold remorse replaced the warmth. He pulled away. "I've got it from here. Thank you."

Charlotte's brow crinkled at his abrupt behavior, but she silently wiped her hands on a towel and replaced the salve in the cabinet. "Did you buy yarn and wool for me to make mittens and coats?"

"Everything's in there." He tilted his head toward the lean-to, his voice a bit too gruff.

She nodded and then flipped the potatoes, steam rising from the frying pan. "I'll get to work on your mittens this evening."

"You've been busy while I was away." The kitchen was even more organized than when he had left, the boys' hair had been cut and they were wearing clean clothing. Several loaves of bread sat on the cupboard, cooling under dishcloths.

She removed the pan from the stove and scraped the golden potatoes onto a platter. Robert and Martin crowded close to her, and she had to put her hand up to keep them away from the hot pan. She pointed to the iron skillet and made a motion as if being burned and then said to Robert and Martin, "Hot. Danger. Stay back."

Robert seemed to understand the warning and he backed away, but Martin didn't obey and continued to crowd Charlotte.

"Aunt Charlotte told you to back away, Martin." Abram

stepped in and took the boy into his arms. "You must listen and obey what she says. She's trying to keep you safe."

Charlotte turned and he caught the look of appreciation in her eyes.

"Do you need any help?" Abram asked her.

She looked as if she would refuse him—but then she paused and offered a quick nod. "You may call the men in to supper. It's almost ready."

Abram did just that. He walked through the main room, marveling at the clean rugs and the polished furniture, and stepped out onto the front porch. He used the metal stick to clang the dinner triangle. When he was satisfied that his men had heard, he walked back into the kitchen just as Harry entered.

Charlotte glanced at him and then handed him a plate filled with roast pork, fried potatoes, bread and spice cake. "Bring the plate back when you're finished."

Harry's face turned crimson and he glared at Abram, as if demanding him to do something.

Charlotte didn't miss a step. She turned away from Harry and brought the platter of pork to the head of the table, where Abram usually sat.

"Don't you think it's time to invite Harry back to the table?" Abram asked.

Charlotte paused and studied Harry. "Do you plan to join us for breakfast on Sunday morning?"

Harry opened his mouth to offer a retort but Abram took a step between the two, as if to shield Charlotte from Harry's scathing words. "She's not asking much, Harry."

Harry narrowed his eyes at Abram then spun out of the kitchen and strode through the lean-to and outside.

Abram let out a breath and turned to face Charlotte. "I don't know why you insist on riling him up."

Charlotte brought the bread to the table. "I don't know why he insists on being so ungentlemanly."

"Charlotte, I'm warning you, Harry is not a man to be told what to do."

She paused. "Then why do you keep him here?"

"Because he's a good worker and good workers are hard to come by."

She stood firm. "I won't deny him food—but I will deny him a place at my table until he can show the Sabbath some respect."

It was a reasonable request, but she needed to realize things didn't always work the way she wanted them to.

But maybe that was the problem. Maybe Charlotte's life was full of events that didn't work out as she had hoped, and that was why she fought so hard to keep control.

Chapter Six

Charlotte sat near the main room window, allowing the afternoon sun to illuminate the dark green coat she held on her lap. She studied the seams with a critical eye, holding it up to look at the front and back one last time. Abram had tried it on the night before, but it had been tight around his shoulders. While the boys napped, she had taken out the seams and restitched them to allow for a better fit. Hopefully now it would be ready for him to wear.

Following Abram's trip to St. Anthony three days ago, he and Milt had been working up the hill from the house, clearing trees. Though he didn't complain of the cold, she had noticed him sit closer to the fireplace in the evenings, a shiver often shuddering through his sturdy frame.

Charlotte stood and glanced out the window toward the mill, as she often did. The water had frozen along the banks and, according to the men, would soon be frozen solid all the way across. The milling would cease and Milt, Caleb and Josiah would move on to the logging camp for the winter.

She slipped on her own coat, buttoning it tight up to her chin. She had come to enjoy the evenings around the fire with Josiah and Caleb, and had even grown to appreciate Milt, though he was much quieter than the other two. The looming winter felt gloomy with the thought of the men leaving. She wished Harry would leave with them, but according to Abram, the grizzly man stayed on through the winter. Hopefully he remained in the barn, like he had the past few days since returning from St. Anthony.

After putting on her bonnet, Charlotte draped Abram's coat over her arm and stopped at the bottom of the steps to listen for the boys. They should sleep for another hour or so, and she was anxious to get the coat to Abram as soon as possible.

Hearing nothing, she walked through the kitchen and picked up the hot pot of coffee and mugs, and then went out the lean-to door. The chickens were brooding in the henhouse, trying to stay warm, and the lone pig was grunting in the trough, his food probably frozen. Abram's mare stood in the corral, her breath blowing out in a cloud from her nostrils.

Steam poured out of the spout on the coffeepot, its aroma filling her with much-needed heat as her eyes roamed the gently sloping land toward the Mississippi. She was growing to love its beauty, though it did feel lonesome, especially when her gaze landed on her sister's grave. She offered a sad smile but was thankful Susanne had loved the Lord. It made Charlotte's loss a bit easier to accept. Someday, when Charlotte's earthly life passed, she would see her beautiful sister once again.

"Timber!" A loud cry came from the direction Charlotte was headed, followed by the crunch of breaking tree limbs. A thud reverberated through the cold woods and then there was silence.

Charlotte followed the well-packed trail through the snow, pushing aside branches that wanted to catch on her wide skirts.

A massive white pine lay on its side, large branches sticking up and out. Abram stood on the felled tree, his boots firmly planted as his ax flew back and forth, cutting limbs and branches off in quick order.

Charlotte watched for a moment, amazed at the agility and strength in his movements. His threadbare coat was flung on a nearby bush and he sweated with exertion, his face red and his muscles rippling under his flannel shirt.

Milt walked behind Abram, picking up the branches and limbs and stacking them in a large pile off to the side.

Abram glanced up and noticed her arrival. His ax stuck into the tree with a thwack and he leaned against the handle, breathing heavy. He nodded at her, his blue eyes sparkling in the sunshine.

The sight of him sent a tingle of awareness through her limbs. With a wobbly smile she raised the coffeepot in one hand and the coat in the other. "I thought you might need help keeping warm."

He looked over her offerings, a smile lighting his face. "I'll gladly take a cup of coffee and a warm coat." He jumped off the log and walked over to her, his boots crunching in the snow.

The sensation she felt upon seeing him grew stronger with each step he took. She quickly handed him the coat and turned to set the mugs and coffeepot on a tree stump.

Abram walked around the stump and slipped the coat on, an appreciative whistle slipping from his lips. "I've never owned such a fancy coat before. I don't dare wear it while I work."

"Nonsense," Charlotte said as she poured the coffee. "I made it for you to work in. It's hardly fancy."

He rubbed one rough hand over the sleeve. "I'm not joshing with you. This is a first-rate coat, Charlotte. I'll be proud to wear it."

Her cheeks grew warm at the compliment but she didn't want him to see the effect he was having on her. What would he think? More important, what would Susanne think? She grew cross at herself just thinking about her silly reaction. "I don't know who will actually see the coat on you. With winter setting in, it seems as though this place will be dead."

Abram chuckled.

She stopped pouring the hot liquid. "What?"

His eyes twinkled with mirth. "I'm just wondering why you have such a hard time taking a compliment from me."

She filled the second mug with coffee and wished she could come up with a reply that wouldn't reveal the true reason she was short with him—or, more accurately, with herself.

Thankfully, Milt placed the last branch on the pile and wandered over. He nodded a greeting to Charlotte and took the mug of coffee with a grateful dip of his head.

It would be best if she just walked away but something kept her standing there. Maybe it was adult interaction or simple curiosity. "This is the first time I've come to the top of the hill."

"This is where the town will sit," Abram said. "The land levels out here. And—" he set the mug on the stump and put his hands on her shoulders to turn her around "—when you look in this direction, you have a beautiful view of the river."

He removed his hands but she could still feel the weight of them on her skin.

"And look over there." He pointed to the east, where a road ran through the trees. "That's part of the Wood's Trail. It was created by the Red River Oxcarts and runs all the way from Pembina to St. Paul. That will be Main Street. And this—" he spread his arm out and indicated the cleared spot of land "—near Susanne's grave, is where your church will sit—at the end of Main Street."

"My church?" She turned quickly and looked up into his face. He was standing much closer than she had realized. "This isn't my church."

He took a leisurely sip from his coffee mug, his eyes smiling at her over the rim. When he lowered the mug he said, "It's the one you ordered."

"Ordered? I didn't order a church—"

"Sure you did. But I suppose it's not just your church." He took a final swig of coffee and set the mug back on the stump. "It's for Little Falls, and for my boys." He crossed his arms and looked over the land, a sense of triumph on his face. "This church is part of the legacy I'll leave them."

She felt herself being drawn into his dream and it scared her. She shouldn't allow herself to trust him, because nothing in her past had shown her it was safe. "For the sake of the boys, I hope you're right."

Abram studied her for a moment and then stepped back up on the log and started swinging his ax again.

Wood chips went flying. "Thank you for the coffee and the coat."

Milt finished his coffee, as well, and handed her the mug. "Much obliged, Miss Charlotte." He scurried off to pick up the branches that were rapidly falling to the ground.

Charlotte gathered the coffeepot and empty mugs and headed back toward the house. Abram's comments had stirred her but she was smart enough to put up a guard.

She must stay strong for herself and for her nephews. They were the ones most at risk, just as she and Susanne had been when they were children.

The following Friday morning Abram stood at the top of the hill and looked at the frozen Mississippi, his skin pinching from the cold. Charlotte had already rung the dinner bell, calling him and Milt to leave their work and come to the house. One more day and they would have the church property cleared. Yesterday, he had the men mill the trees they had felled. The last milled lumber of the year.

This afternoon, the sawmill stood quiet, frozen in place overnight. No doubt Caleb, Josiah and Milt would leave in the morning and head to the logging camp.

Abram walked down the hill and opened the back door just as Harry exited with his plate of vittles. He glanced at Abram, irritation lacing his eyes. "That woman's liable to drive a body crazy with her stubbornness. It's been five days and she still thinks she can manipulate me into going to church on Sunday." He kept walking, his back now to Abram. "It'll take more than a warm kitchen to force me to a place like church."

Abram stepped through the doorway and into the lean-to, the smell of biscuits and gravy warming him clean through.

"Like this, Robert." Charlotte's patient voice floated to Abram's ears. "Hold your fingers to your lips like this, and then I'll know you are hungry."

"He can't hear you," Martin said matter-of-factly.

"I know he can't hear me, but I still want to talk as if he can, so he feels he's part of this family. I'm showing him how to tell me he's hungry."

Abram entered the kitchen and found Charlotte bent at the waist, eye level with Robert, who sat at the table. Charlotte put her fingers to her lips and then pointed to the plate of food in her hands. "If you're hungry, point to your mouth. Don't scream at me."

Abram noticed the tears staining his oldest son's red face.

"And when you're thirsty," Charlotte continued, circling her fingers as if holding a cup, "put your hand up to your mouth as if you're drinking." She demonstrated to Robert and then took his cup off the table. She glanced at Martin, who watched her carefully. "You can do this, too, Martin, so Robert doesn't feel alone. We'll all do it, regardless of the fact that we can hear and speak."

Martin circled his hand, too, and brought them to his lip like he was drinking.

Robert watched his little brother and his blue eyes sparkled with recognition. He mimicked the movement and then pointed to his cup.

"Yes!" Charlotte cried. "Yes, you've got it, Robert!" She hugged Robert and then Martin. "You're both such smart boys."

"Papa!" Martin noticed Abram. "You must do this when you want Aunt Charlotte to give you something to eat, and this when you want something to drink."

Charlotte and Robert both looked his way, their faces beaming with success.

Abram grinned and put his fingers to his lips. "I'm famished. Let's eat."

Robert signed for food and nodded.

Caleb and Josiah walked into the kitchen from the main room just as Milt entered in from the lean-to.

"Dinner is ready," Charlotte said. "When all of you are washed up, we'll eat." As she spoke she made a sign as if she was washing her hands, rubbing them back and forth, and then put them to her lips for food.

Robert watched her closely, as if no one else was in the room. His face filled with such adoration and trust, Abram had to swallow a lump of emotion. For the first time in months hope shone on his son's young face. He jumped up from the table and raced to the pitcher and basin in the lean-to and was the first to wash his hands.

Abram glanced back at Charlotte. Her satisfied gaze warmed his heart and he smiled. "Thank you."

She nodded, as if embarrassed. "Susanne would be so proud of him."

"I think Susanne would be just as proud of you."

Charlotte nibbled on her bottom lip. "I hope so." She turned away and busied herself with putting the food on the table. "I hope we receive a book, or a pamphlet, or something from the deaf school in Iowa. I'm at a loss for what else I can teach him."

"You're doing well with what you have."

"It doesn't feel like it's enough."

"It is."

She moved around the kitchen with practiced ease, and Abram was suddenly very thankful she had come.

The others soon came to the table and Abram said grace. As they were about to eat, the sound of sleigh bells filled the air.

Abram glanced out the window and stood. "It looks like we have guests."

Charlotte also stood and, after glancing out the window, quickly set to work gathering extra plates and utensils and cups.

Abram walked to the lean-to and pulled on his new coat. He opened the door and waved to the arrivals.

Liam Cheney sat beside another man, presumably Timothy Hubbard.

Anticipation mingled with anxiety in Abram's chest as he walked out into the yard. When the team of horses came to a stop, he grinned. "Welcome to Little Falls," he said. "I didn't expect you so soon."

Cheney extended his hand. "We were eager to get here before the others."

"Others?" Abram asked.

"There was talk after you left St. Anthony," the other man said. "I'll wager we're not the only ones heading this way."

He hadn't expected to hear such heartening news.

"Abram Cooper, meet Timothy Hubbard, recently of Moline, Illinois."

Hubbard extended his hand. He had piercing blue eyes and a generous forehead. He wore a stocking cap, covering a balding head, no doubt, but his long beard more than made up for the lack of hair. His handshake was powerful and direct—two things Abram appreciated from a man of business.

"Let's get your rig stored away and then come in and join us for dinner. My…" He paused, unsure how to introduce Charlotte. She was more than a housekeeper. "My sister-in-law is one of the best cooks in the territory."

Hubbard's eyes filled with humor and a hint of healthy competition. "I'll be the judge of that. My wife just recently entered the territory, as well. Sounds like your sister-in-law may have a bit of competition."

After seeing to the horses, the three men returned to the house. Abram didn't miss the cursory glances or the scrutiny in Hubbard's eyes as he surveyed the house and barn and sawmill.

Cheney didn't, either. "Let's eat and then talk business, Hubbard." He chuckled. "I know you'll want to walk around and inspect everything—but I want to sample that food first."

They entered the house and Charlotte rose from her seat at the table.

"Charlotte, this is Mr. Cheney and Mr. Hubbard. Gentlemen, this is my sister-in-law, Miss Charlotte Lee."

"I'm pleased to meet you," Charlotte said. "Won't you join us?"

"I can't think of anything I'd rather do," Cheney said. "In the short time I've been here, I've already heard about your excellent cooking."

Charlotte glanced at Abram with surprise and he didn't bother to hide his pride. Her food was always outstanding, and he was eager to have his guests sit down and eat.

She sat, and the others followed.

Robert stood so quickly, he bumped the table and set

the silverware to quaking. He pointed toward the lean-to with animation and then made the sign for the two new men to wash their hands.

The table erupted in laughter—though Cheney and Hubbard didn't seem to understand the joke.

Abram grinned and motioned for Robert to sit. "Sit down, son. Guests aren't required to wash up." He shook his head and did the sign for washing. He glanced at their guests. "Robert lost his hearing a few months back, and Charlotte is teaching him sign language."

"Ah," Hubbard said with a laugh. "And we're being warned to wash up or Miss Lee will kick us out?"

"Where's the water basin?" Cheney asked good-naturedly. "I don't want to get off on the wrong foot with the cook!"

"She's liable to kick you out to the barn if you do," Caleb said with more of a warning than a joke. Again, everyone laughed, though he suspected Cheney and Hubbard didn't understand why they laughed so hard.

Charlotte's cheeks turned crimson but her eyes glowed with pleasure. "In the lean-to. And Robert is right. Everyone must wash up before eating at my table."

"My wife wouldn't have it any other way," Hubbard said. "Shall I wash behind my ears, as well?"

Charlotte offered a gracious smile. "That won't be necessary, Mr. Hubbard. The hands will do."

Abram couldn't take his eyes off her. Without even realizing what she was doing, she was making these two men feel as if they were already at home, and that would go a long way in securing a partnership with them.

She glanced at Abram and dipped her head when she caught him staring.

The men came back to the table and Abram was glad

for the diversion from his pretty sister-in-law. The last thing he needed was a romantic interest so soon after his wife's death—with his wife's sister, no less. Just the thought of it made him feel ashamed.

No. He needed to focus on building his town and securing a legacy for his sons. Nothing must stand in his way.

Nothing.

Chapter Seven

Charlotte sat in her favorite rocking chair near the fireplace, close to a lamp Abram had affixed to the wall. Her knitting needles clicked with a steady, soothing rhythm as she thought through Mr. Cheney and Mr. Hubbard's recent visit. After they had left, several other men had appeared, eager to inspect Abram's holdings.

The kitchen door creaked and Charlotte glanced up. Abram came through the door quietly but, upon seeing her, he stopped.

"I thought you would have gone to bed by now," he said.

"I'm almost finished with Robert's mittens." She held up the red mitten. "I wanted to get it finished tonight."

"Do you have all the supplies you need?"

"You bought me enough yarn to knit mittens and socks for an army." He'd also bought enough wool to outfit them with coats. Abram might have his faults, but Susanne had been right after all. He provided well.

Abram walked across the room and lowered himself into the rocker on the other side of the fireplace. He moaned slightly as his body folded into the chair. "Ah. It feels good to just sit."

She glanced at him but didn't allow her eyes to linger long. "You've been busy."

"Yes. But hopefully we've seen the last visitor for a while. I have work I need to get done, and since Caleb, Josiah and Milt are gone now, all the chores will fall on Harry and me."

Charlotte already missed the other men. They had left last Saturday morning, the day after Cheney and Hubbard had arrived, and though they had only been gone for three days, she felt their absence. After being alone for six years in Iowa City, she had quickly grown accustomed to a full house and hated to see them leave. Thankfully, she still had the boys...and Abram.

Charlotte glanced at the man beside her. His eyes were closed and he was breathing steady. She had often wondered how Susanne had endured the isolation of this place, but now she understood how the intimate company of a husband could fill almost any void. Though she and Abram did not have that type of relationship, it didn't take much for her to imagine how it would feel.

She sighed, silently chastised herself for letting her thoughts travel that path, and focused on finishing the mitten.

"I'm on my way," he said several minutes later.

Charlotte glanced up, half startled. "On your way to what?"

"Fulfilling my dream. Accomplishing what I promised I'd accomplish." He quietly watched her. "I think I'll have investors by the end of this year."

Charlotte didn't respond. Her heart was torn between disappointment that she might have to return to Iowa

City without the boys—and joy that he was starting his town.

"Hubbard and Cheney appeared more eager than the others," he said. "I have a feeling they'll want to act fast."

Charlotte tied off the last knot and snipped the loose end. He needed some response, but she was afraid her emotions would betray her if she said too much. "Congratulations." She stood and put the ball of yarn in her basket. "I'm tired. I think I'll go to bed."

Abram also stood. "What did you think of Hubbard and Cheney?"

"I think they were very nice," she said as she gathered her things.

"Do you think they'll be good partners?"

Charlotte clutched her knitting basket. "I'm probably not the best person to ask."

He studied her, his face half shadowed by the lantern, and the look in his eyes made her heart speed up.

She couldn't stand there anymore. "Good night, Abram." She moved around him and started up the stairs.

He followed her across the room and reached for her wrist as she took the first step. "Charlotte."

His gentle voice stopped her ascent. She glanced down at his hand, heat tingling up her arm.

"I'm sorry. I didn't mean to—" He paused and removed his hand. "I know if I succeed, it means you'll have to go back to Iowa alone." He ran his hand through his hair. "I just want someone to talk to. I used to discuss everything with Susanne, and I always appreciated her wisdom. Women tend to look at things differently than men. I'll have some important decisions to make soon, and I want to make sure I'm doing the right thing."

She removed her hand from the rail and turned slightly to look at him. "I wish I could help you make your decision—but you're right. If you succeed, I'll fail—"

"You won't fail."

"I'll fail at my reason for coming." And she would have to go back alone—which was the last thing she wanted. The boys deserved to be raised in a proper place, with good schools and hospitals, and comfort—the frontier was far too dangerous a place to grow up. "Good night, Abram."

Charlotte walked up the stairs and entered her room, closing the door behind her. The room was dark, so she set her basket on the floor and felt along the bureau until she found the matchbox. She pulled out a match and then struck it against the rough side. Sulfur filled her nose as the match lit. She removed the chimney from the lantern and lit the wick. Light filled the little room, sending shadows dancing into the corners.

Charlotte locked the door and then slowly undressed and put on her nightgown, shivering in the cold.

She heard Abram climb the stairs and enter the room across the hall where the boys slept. It comforted her to know he slept with them and could hear if one of them needed something in the night. Not once had he woken her up to see to the boys' needs.

His arrival in the room must have woken George, because the baby's whimpers were loud enough to travel across the hall and enter Charlotte's room.

George only cried for a few moments, and when his

whimpers subsided, the soothing sound of Abram's sing-ing filled the upstairs.

She stood for several moments next to the closed door and listened, surprised by the beauty in his tone. He must be exhausted, but he continued to sing, until even Char-lotte's eyes grew sleepy.

She brought the lamp to her bedside, putting it on the little table where Susanne's Bible lay. Charlotte had scrubbed this room, as well, and washed the bedding. She had placed one of the rag rugs next to the bed, and that was where she knelt to pray.

Outside her window, a wild land lay dormant, poised on the brink of growth. There would be much blood, sweat and toil poured into this town, and, if Abram was correct, it might one day be a real city with churches and schools and doctors. After seeing the interest on Hub-bard's and Cheney's faces, she began to fear that maybe Abram wasn't the one who was a dreamer. Maybe it was her, dreaming of a life in Iowa with her nephews—a life that might never come true.

A soft knock pulled her off her knees. "Yes?"

"It's Abram."

Charlotte took a step closer to the door, unwilling to open it in her nightgown. "What do you need?"

"I just want you to know something."

She waited, taking several deep breaths.

"No matter what happens, you won't fail," he said. "You've already accomplished a great deal since you've been here, and all of us are grateful."

She bit her bottom lip and watched the flame on the lantern flicker.

"It's too early to tell," he said softly. "I'm hopeful about Little Falls, but I'm also realistic. I've been involved in several town prospects that have failed, even when they looked this hopeful."

He was trying to make her feel better, and for that she was thankful, but *she* was also realistic and knew what was at stake. He might succeed, but that didn't mean he would be satisfied. The children would be at risk until they were old enough to care for themselves. "Good night, Abram."

The other side of the door was quiet until she heard his footsteps retreat into the boys' room.

Charlotte leaned her head back. She must not allow her heart to soften toward him. There would be nothing but heartache and devastation if she did.

A month after Cheney and Hubbard had visited, Abram sat on a stool in the darkening barn, a log of white oak balanced between his cold feet. He placed a metal froe against the wood and then pounded the froe with a handmade mallet until it sank into the log. He wiggled the froe and then pushed against it, causing the shingle to pull away from the log in a thin layer.

Making shingles filled him with memories of his childhood in Cooper, Michigan. How many times had he made shingles with his father? He used to sit beside Father hearing the steady tap, tap, tap of the mallet against the froe and the splitting of wood as they made each one.

Abram tossed the unfinished shingle on the growing pile. He still needed to smooth it out with the drawknife and round the edges a bit. The church would require hundreds of shingles, which he'd work on throughout the winter. It was a lot of work up front, but the shingles should last for seventy or eighty years. Maybe, one day, his grandchildren would have to replace them when he was gone.

"Looks like the stagecoach is here," Harry said, coming into the barn. His cheeks were chapped and his hair matted. He'd been sleeping and eating in the barn for over a month since Charlotte's arrival in early November. More and more, he braved the weather to spend his evenings at Crow Wing, and Abram wondered if the red cheeks were caused more by the cold or by the drink.

"I'll go out and meet Andrew." Abram rose from his stool and stretched his tight muscles. "I could use a break."

Harry took a leather saddle off the hook. "I think I'll head on out for the evening."

"Charlotte should have supper ready any minute."

Harry glanced over his shoulder and scowled at Abram. "I'll pay for a meal in Crow Wing. At least there I'm not forced to eat with the livestock."

"Would it hurt you to go to ch—"

"I wouldn't go if it was the last place on earth." He walked to the stall where he kept his gelding. "Don't ask again, Abram. I'm getting mighty tired of saying no."

"Maybe I'm hoping you'll get so tired, you'll finally say yes."

Harry continued to scowl. "You're getting as bad as that woman."

Abram buttoned his coat and slipped on the mittens Charlotte had knit for him, enjoying the simple pleasure of their warmth. "Come back alive, Harry." He paused and gave his employee a serious look. Several murders had happened at Crow Wing recently. "I need you."

"You mean you need my help."

Abram put his hand on Harry's shoulder and gave

it a brief squeeze. "No. I need you to come back alive because you're wanted here."

Harry pulled away from Abram's touch and snarled, tilting his head toward the house. "Not by everyone."

"Maybe if you gave her a reason to like you, she would."

"She's given me no reason to like her."

Abram wanted to sigh—instead he slipped out of the barn and walked up the wagon road toward the Wood's Trail.

The bright red stagecoach waited atop the hill with the driver, Andrew, lazily sitting in the driver's seat. The wheels had been replaced with sleigh runners, and made the conveyance sit lower to the ground. Andrew carried more than passengers in his coach. He also carried mail and gossip from one settlement to the next.

The side door opened and Timothy Hubbard emerged from the stagecoach. "Cooper!"

Abram hurried his steps and extended his hand. "What a nice surprise."

A lady sat in the stagecoach and Hubbard reached in and offered her a hand. She emerged, her hazel eyes soft and gentle around the edges.

"Mr. Cooper, may I present my wife, Mrs. Pearl Hubbard?"

"It's a pleasure to meet you, Mrs. Hubbard."

Pearl shook Abram's hand with robust enthusiasm. She wasn't a beautiful woman, nor was she homely. She was simply plain, though she had a friendly countenance. "It's my pleasure, Mr. Cooper. Timothy has told me so much about Little Falls, I've been eager to come see it for myself."

Abram suddenly felt self-conscious of his home.

When he showed it to prospective business partners, he didn't have a hard time selling its potential. But women were different. They weren't impressed with lumber output and available waterpower. They wanted churches and schools and gardens. Things Abram didn't have—at least not yet.

"We hate to impose," Pearl said, "but Andrew informed us that he won't be back this way until Monday morning, and since there's no hotel, we're at your mercy to house us." Her black hair dipped down her cheeks and slipped under her brown bonnet. "I hope you don't mind."

"Mind?" He offered her a smile, which he hoped conveyed his hospitality. "We'd have it no other way." Thankfully, Charlotte's housekeeping was immaculate and she was always at the ready to welcome anyone.

Pearl's face relaxed and she looked at Hubbard. "You were right. He's a very likable fellow."

Hubbard laughed. "Indeed."

"I've got a package for Miss Lee," Andrew said, handing down a small parcel wrapped in brown paper. "It's from Iowa. Was she expecting something important?"

Abram took the package. It looked and felt like a book. Could it be the book of sign language she'd asked for? Eagerness filled Abram with the desire to race to Charlotte's side and give her the early Christmas present. He could imagine the look of pure delight on her face already.

"Well?" asked Andrew.

Abram laughed and patted the nearest horse on the hindquarters. "And give you more fodder for your gossip mill?" He shook his head. "I think I'll leave you guessing."

"Wise choice," Hubbard concurred, his blue eyes filling with mirth. He took their carpetbags out of the stagecoach. "We've had our fill of news from St. Anthony all the way to Little Falls."

"I'll be back on Monday morning," Andrew called as he clicked the reins and the horses trotted north toward Crow Wing.

Abram led the way down the icy incline toward the house. Several snowstorms had come through in December, burying the house in drifts of snow. Smoke spiraled out of the chimney and frost etched the glass windows.

"Charlotte will be happy to have some female company," Abram said to Pearl. "She's been surrounded by men since she got here in November."

"I'm eager to meet Miss Lee," Pearl said, picking her way carefully along the slippery path. "Timothy tells me she's your sister-in-law."

"She is." How much did he tell her of their arrangement? "She came in November and only has plans to stay until I've established Little Falls and can find a permanent housekeeper."

"That's quite a sacrifice she's making," Pearl said. "She must be a wonderful woman."

The back door opened and the woman in question stuck her head out the door, George on her hip. She put her hand up to shield her eyes from the bright sunshine reflecting off the snow. "Do we have guests?" Her voice was filled with happiness and disbelief.

"Yes!" Abram said, anticipation mounting. "And a package you'll be happy to see."

"Guests *and* a package? I thought Christmas was next week." Charlotte opened the door wider, clearly glad to see Timothy Hubbard again, and especially his congenial wife.

Abram made introductions, including little George,

and Charlotte took their outerwear and hung it on a hook in the lean-to. "I have fresh-baked sugar cookies just out of the oven, and I'll have some hot coffee ready in a moment. Then we'll have a nice, long visit."

"I'd be happy to help," Pearl offered.

"I wouldn't hear of it," Charlotte said. She led them into the main room, where the two older boys were playing on the rug. "Sit by the fire and warm yourself."

The boys looked up, and upon seeing Mr. Hubbard, they both rose with smiles. "Mrs. Hubbard, this is Robert," Charlotte said, a hint of pride in her voice. "And this is Martin."

"Charming little boys."

Charlotte stood for a moment grinning, her hand on Martin's blond head. "Oh! The coffee. I'll be right back."

"Here," Pearl said. "I'll hold the baby if he'll let me."

"All right."

"I'll help you," Abram said to Charlotte. He wanted to give her the book in private, so he could enjoy her unreserved response.

Charlotte led the way and Abram followed, closing the kitchen door softly. She went to the stove and placed the coffeepot over the front burner. She looked almost giddy.

"I've never seen you this cheerful before," Abram said, enjoying the scene. "I'm happy the Hubbards are here—"

"Of course." She paused and turned toward him, the giddiness of the moment slipping from her face. "In all the excitement, I failed to realize what this means." She studied him, but he couldn't gauge her emotions. "He must be ready to make you an offer."

Abram wanted to see the joy return. "It means nothing of the sort. They could be here for any number of reasons."

Charlotte swallowed and reached for a platter.

The package! Abram took a giant step toward her, thrusting the package into her hands. "Here. This is for you."

She pulled back slightly, eyeing the package with a bit of surprise, and then she eagerly ripped off the paper. "It's the book of sign language!" She glanced up and the excitement had returned to her eyes. "It's here! Now I can teach Robert to my heart's content and we can all learn and have real conversations. I can ask him questions and he can ask me questions. There's no end to the possibilities." She opened the book and quickly began to scan the pages.

He chuckled. "Are you planning to learn it all in one sitting?"

"I'm looking for something..." she mumbled, her finger sliding down page after page.

"What?"

She didn't answer—but then she stopped and, when she looked up at Abram, tears filled her eyes. "I love you."

Abram's breath caught in his throat. "Pardon me?"

"I found the sign for 'I love you.'" She flipped the book around and showed him the diagram on the page. It was a hand with the pinkie, the forefinger and the thumb pointed toward the ceiling, while the ring and middle fingers pointed toward the palm.

She raced around him and flew out of the kitchen.

Abram frowned as he followed her back to the main room.

"Robert." She said his name but he didn't look up from the book he was studying on the rug.

Charlotte knelt and put her hand on his shoulder.

Robert turned and, seeing it was Charlotte, smiled.

She raised her hand, just like the diagram had said. "I love you, Robert."

He glanced at her hand and then her face, confusion tilting his brow.

Pearl and Timothy sat in the rockers near the fire, both watching Charlotte with interest. Timothy had no doubt told Pearl that Robert was deaf.

"I love you," Charlotte said again, making the sign with her hand, but this time she gathered Robert into her arms and hugged him tight, rocking him back and forth. "I love you so much."

Robert looked over Charlotte's shoulder at Abram, his face glowing.

Abram also made the sign for "I love you" and tears stung his eyes.

Robert pulled back and Charlotte placed her hands on his cheeks, but Abram couldn't see her face.

Robert slowly lifted his right hand and attempted to make the same sign Charlotte and Abram had made. He put his hand in front of Charlotte's face and then turned to Abram.

Abram grinned and knelt beside his son, gathering him in his arms, just as Charlotte had done.

Tears streamed down Charlotte's face and her hand came up to her mouth. "I think he understands."

Abram rocked his son and put his hand on the back of Robert's head. "Of course he understands. Love is a universal language."

They sat that way for several moments, until Charlotte stood and wiped her cheeks. "Look at me, going on like this. I'll have our refreshments ready in a moment."

"There's no need," Pearl said with a gentle smile. "This scene was all the sweet refreshment we'll ever need."

Charlotte laughed and they all joined in on her joy.

Abram held his son, but he couldn't stop looking at the woman who had made this moment possible. There was no doubt in his mind that Charlotte loved his children. The only doubt he had was how he would separate them once the town was built. Because, despite what he said, there could be only one reason for Timothy and Pearl's visit.

They had come to make him an offer, one he was sure he couldn't refuse, no matter how much it might cost him and his boys—and Charlotte.

Chapter Eight

The next afternoon, while the boys were napping, Charlotte and Pearl put on their outerwear and slipped outside for some fresh air.

"This place really is as beautiful as Timothy told me," Pearl said, taking a deep breath and exhaling a cloud of fog into the cold air. "I foresee a lot of hard work in front of us."

Charlotte had enjoyed Pearl's company immensely. Not only because it was a treat to have another female, but because Pearl was an authentic woman who had a keen sense of understanding and compassion.

"Have you and Mr. Hubbard prospected many towns?" Charlotte asked as she led Pearl up the hill, toward the town site.

"A few."

"Do you think this one will be the last?"

Pearl laughed and slipped her arm through Charlotte's. "It's always the last one, dear, and the best, and the most promising."

Charlotte frowned. "How do you continue to support him, when you know he'll grow tired of this place, too?"

"He won't grow tired of it, but eventually it will grow tired of him."

Charlotte stopped and faced Pearl. "What do you mean?"

Pearl offered Charlotte a gentle smile and then pointed toward the Mississippi. "Do you see that mighty river?"

Charlotte glanced at the frozen water. From this vantage point she could see the whole span of the river, including the high island that divided the west channel from the east, where the wing dam and sawmill were waiting until spring.

"The river is alive and well," Pearl said with respect in her voice, "and it won't be conquered easily. It's been my experience that the land, the water, the very air around us will fight as hard as it can to prevent civilization from harnessing it. There will be setbacks, both physical and financial, that will drain our men until they reach the very end of their abilities."

Our men.

"Some of them will give up," Pearl continued, "but some will stay and fight. Eventually, this land will be settled. What remains to be seen is how long it will take, and who will be standing at the end."

Abram and Mr. Hubbard stepped out of the barn at that moment, deep in conversation.

"How do you do it?" Charlotte asked Pearl, wrapping her arms around her waist.

"I love him."

Charlotte studied her companion. "That's it?"

"That's all there is to it. I love him, and I will stand beside him during the good and the bad. I'll encourage him and believe in him and do whatever it takes to help him succeed."

Charlotte let out a long sigh. "My mother and sister had the same devotion and both of them died standing beside their husbands."

"I'm sorry, Charlotte."

Charlotte pointed toward the town site. "My sister's grave is just over there, by the birch trees."

"Life is all about risks. Love is simply one of them."

It was a risk Charlotte wasn't willing to take—not again, not after being jilted by Thomas and disappointed by her father, time after time.

Charlotte glanced back at the barn and saw Abram and Mr. Hubbard walking toward them.

Abram's sparkling blue eyes gazed upon Charlotte and her pulse sped up at the sight.

"It's final," Mr. Hubbard said, coming alongside his wife with a grin. "I've made our official offer and Mr. Cooper has accepted. By this time next year, there will be a town standing on this very ground."

"Congratulations," Pearl said to both men. "This will be a merry Christmas, indeed."

Charlotte offered Abram the faintest smile. "Congratulations."

"Thank you."

Pearl caught Charlotte's eye and she nodded. "Now we shall see what happens."

The land was asleep beneath the winter winds, but what would happen once it woke up? Would it comply with Abram and his dream, or would it put up a fight and prevent him from having a teacher, a preacher and a doctor here by the first of September?

There was nothing to do but wait and see.

* * *

Charlotte stood with her hands on her hips surveying the table she had set for their Christmas meal in the main room. Yesterday, Abram had brought in a balsam fir and put it in the corner. Charlotte had shown the boys how to string popcorn and make stars out of paper. She'd baked gingerbread men and helped the boys hang them on the tree, savoring every moment, afraid it would be the one and only Christmas they would enjoy together.

Tonight, George and Martin sat on the rug near the Christmas tree looking through a picture book Charlotte had brought with her from Iowa. It was filled with Bible stories and illustrated with beautiful paintings. They had spent hours looking through the book over the past two months, asking her questions about Jonah and the Whale, David and Goliath, Daniel in the Lion's Den, and so many others.

Robert sat at Susanne's desk, making a necklace out of old buttons. He had gone through the box of buttons countless times, sorting and arranging them, picking out his favorites and then exchanging them for others. Finally, Charlotte had given him a needle and thread and shown him how to string the buttons together.

The lean-to door opened and the sound of male voices filled the festive air.

Charlotte took George into her arms, not trusting him to stay away from the fireplace or the Christmas tree without her supervision. "Martin, remember what I told you about not touching the tree."

Martin looked up at her, his blue eyes blinking, inviting her to trust him. "I remember, Aunt Charlotte."

Charlotte turned her attention to the kitchen. Had

Harry stayed home and decided to join them for supper? It couldn't be. He had left yesterday for Crow Wing and planned to stay with friends for several days. So who had come in with Abram on this bitter cold Christmas evening?

"Charlotte, we have a surprise visitor!" Abram said.

Charlotte entered the kitchen with George on her hip and watched as a man in a long buffalo robe strode into the room. His face was covered by a scarf and his eyebrows were white with snow and ice. It was his eyes that looked familiar.

"Charlotte, you remember Reverend Lahaye."

He took off his hat and scarf and offered her a handsome smile. "It's nice to see you again, Miss Lee."

Despite the reminder of their frightening introduction, she couldn't help but return his smile. "It's nice to see you, too, Reverend Lahaye."

"Please call me Ben." He rubbed his mitted hands together. "Brr. It's cold out there."

"Come warm yourself by the fireplace," Charlotte said quickly. "We're just about to eat."

"I'm sorry to interrupt your Christmas meal. I was working my way toward Crow Wing when the snowstorm overtook me. I barely found my way here."

"We're happy you've joined us," Abram said. "We wouldn't have it any other way."

Ben glanced at Charlotte and she smiled in agreement.

"Come." Abram patted Ben on the shoulder and then reached over and took George from Charlotte's arms. "Do you need any help, Charlotte?"

"Everything is ready."

Ben removed his coat and hung it in the lean-to with

his scarf and hat. He wore a suit much like Abram's, but his long brown hair remained in braids and he wore large hoops in his ears.

Charlotte took another plate, cup and set of silverware from the cupboard and followed the men into the main room.

They quickly found their seats, Abram said a prayer and then they began to eat. Charlotte had roasted a wild turkey Abram had shot, and she had made stuffing, mashed potatoes, corn-bread muffins, sweet potatoes and baked beans. For a special drink, she had made hot chocolate.

"The boys look good," Ben said. "How is Robert doing?"

Abram set down his fork and bent his hands, putting the backs of the fingertips together close to his chest. He curved them up and out, and then pointed to Robert. "How are you?"

Robert grinned and took his right hand, his fingers splayed, and tapped his chest twice with his thumb.

"Robert is fine," Abram said with a smile.

Robert made the same signs Abram had, but this time he pointed to Ben.

Ben, his eyes lighting up, awkwardly touched his chest just as Robert had. "I'm fine, too." He laughed and said to Abram, "He is doing well. I'm so happy."

Abram signed "thank you" and pointed at Charlotte. "We only have Charlotte to thank."

Charlotte warmed under his praise and looked at Robert to hide her embarrassment. The little boy smiled at her as if the sun rose and set on her face. She reached over and ruffled his blond hair and signed "I love you."

"If Charlotte hadn't come," Abram continued, "the

boys might still be at the mission and I wouldn't have investors."

"Investors?" Ben's eyes went wide with surprise. "I hadn't heard."

Abram quickly glanced at Charlotte, but she busied herself with putting mashed potatoes on George's plate.

"We'll draw up official papers after the first of the year, and then we'll incorporate into a town after that. Hubbard and Cheney have already petitioned the government for two thousand acres around the falls and will have a surveyor here sometime after the incorporation is finished."

"You're actually doing it," Ben said with a bit of awe. "I never doubted you—it's just exciting to see that your dreams are finally coming true."

The fireplace crackled and a log fell, sending sparks and smoke spiraling up the chimney.

"What are you building at the top of the hill?" Ben asked.

"A church for Charlotte."

"It's not for me," Charlotte protested, and both men looked in her direction. "It's for the town," she said a bit quieter.

Abram's blue eyes twinkled. "She doesn't think I'll have a permanent preacher here by September to take over the church, though."

"Why September?" Ben asked, looking at Charlotte.

"That's when she aims to go back to Iowa City." Abram supplied the answer, his tone a bit flat.

"You're not staying on here?" Ben asked, again looking at Charlotte.

"I have a business and a home waiting for me in Iowa City."

Ben glanced between Charlotte and Abram, his thoughts imperceptible.

The wind blew outside and the snow blasted against the house, rattling the windows.

"Would you be willing to be our preacher?" Abram asked their guest.

Charlotte held her breath, her fork stopped midway to her mouth. Was Abram about to have the first of her requirements in place?

Ben clasped his hands together and set them on his lap, his face serious. "I wish I could, Abram, but I've devoted myself to being a traveling preacher. I couldn't stay in one place, even if I wanted to." He glanced at Charlotte, his gaze soft. "As tempting as the proposition may be."

Something about the way he smiled at her made her sit a bit straighter. Was he insinuating that she could be a reason to stay? She wasn't insulted. On the contrary, she had never been more flattered. But she must not encourage him in any way. Though she admired him, and recognized his wandering was part of his calling, she could not live his way of life.

Abram cleared his throat. "I'll wish you well, then." He slapped Ben on the shoulder and pulled his attention off Charlotte. "If you happen to find someone who would be willing to pastor our humble church, please tell them to come."

"I'll do that." Ben picked up his fork and took a bite of the stuffing Charlotte had made. "This is the best Christmas feast I've ever eaten, Miss Lee."

"Thank you."

"What's this?" Abram asked, his brows coming together as he teased. "You accept Ben's compliments, but when I offer them, you blush and try to ignore me."

Her cheeks filled with heat and she reached over and wiped Martin's chin so she wouldn't have to meet Abram's eyes. What could she say?

"She won't let you compliment her?" Ben asked, his voice teasing, as well. "Is it because she's modest?"

"I think it's because she's embarrassed," Abram said with a chuckle. "But I don't know why. She's only the best housekeeper, cook and caregiver this side of the Mississippi."

"That's quite a compliment." Ben leaned back and openly admired Charlotte.

"Gentlemen," Charlotte said, rising from the table. "I think I'll check on the dessert."

Their good-natured laughter followed her into the kitchen, where the pumpkin pie was in the oven. She removed it from the heat and set it on the table, giving the pie, as well as her cheeks, a moment to cool down.

Abram's compliments did embarrass her, but not because she was modest. His words made her feel things she shouldn't feel and set her mind on paths it shouldn't follow. It was easier to ignore his compliments than to face her emotions.

She returned to the main room and they enjoyed their dessert, the men safely ensconced in a conversation about territory politics.

After supper was finished, Charlotte set a cloth over the table so they wouldn't have to look at the dirty dishes as they all sat around the fireplace. The candles had been lit on the tree, offering a warm glow, presents had been pulled out of hiding places and the boys waited with shining eyes.

Abram handed the boys each a gift. They unwrapped the brown paper with eager hands and exclaimed over their handmade wooden toys. For Robert there was a boat, for Martin, a little wagon, and for George, a set of blocks.

"Did you make those?" Charlotte asked, looking up at Abram from her rocker near the fireplace.

Abram nodded. "They're not much."

"They are gorgeous," Charlotte said. George sat in her lap and she ran her fingers over the smooth wooden blocks. "Well done."

"Thank you."

"Could you hand out my gifts?" She suddenly felt embarrassed, knowing her gifts would pale in comparison to Abram's.

Each of the boys opened their packages and found a scarf and hat to match their mittens. There was a set for Abram, as well.

"I know it's practical but—"

"But perfect," Abram said, wrapping his scarf around his neck. "I only wish there were more people around to see me."

Charlotte laughed at the silliness and shook her head.

Ben sat off to the side in a wooden chair.

Thankfully, she had made Abram an extra pair of mittens with her abundance of yarn, and had not given them to him yet. Instead, she stood and pulled them out of her knitting basket and offered them to Ben. "Merry Christmas, Ben."

His brown eyes lit with delight. "You didn't need to bother."

"It's my pleasure."

Ben slipped them on and held them up. "I'll think of you every time I wear them. I wish I had a gift for you."

"Your company is a priceless gift," Abram said quickly.

He stood and went to a chest in the corner where he kept several documents. "I hid Charlotte's gift in here."

"My gift?" Charlotte had not received a Christmas gift since Susanne had eloped six years ago.

"Of course." Abram removed a brown-paper package from the chest and handed it to Charlotte while taking George into his arms.

Charlotte took a seat and held the package for a moment. It didn't weigh much, but felt a bit bulky under the wrapping.

Nerves bubbled up in Charlotte's stomach as she felt all eyes upon her—especially Abram's. She untied the white string and slowly turned back a corner of the paper to reveal an ivory-handled brush, hand mirror, comb, shoehorn and nail file.

"It's a dresser set," Abram said a bit awkwardly, shifting George in his arms and sitting on the rocker next to her. "I picked it up in St. Anthony."

"When I first came?"

Abram shrugged, appearing nonchalant, but she could tell he was watching her closely to see if she really liked the gift. "I thought of you when I saw it."

"Abram has always been a generous soul," Ben added. "Thinking of others before himself."

"I wouldn't go that far," Abram said, though Charlotte had witnessed it several times. Even if he didn't have much, he still offered what he had.

"Thank you," Charlotte said, holding up the mirror. She turned it around and allowed Robert to see his reflection. The boy took the mirror and Charlotte ran her right hand over the top of her left hand. "Gentle."

"You're welcome," Abram said as well as signed. "I hope you like it."

"It's the first gift I've received since Susanne gave me a hair comb the year before you were married." She paused, but found it didn't hurt as much to talk about her sister. "I like it very much."

Abram was silent for a moment and she looked up at him. Sadness weighed down his brows. "I'm sorry you had to be alone all those years."

Something heavy and melancholy wanted to press in on Charlotte's good mood, so she quickly stood. "I'll go make some coffee. Does anyone want more pie?"

She left the room before anyone could answer and entered the dimly lit kitchen, afraid of the emotions swirling inside her head and heart. It was so much safer holding Abram at a distance—but when he spoke with such compassion, she wanted to pull him close and allow him to heal her wounded soul.

"Charlotte?" Abram entered the kitchen, worry edged between his brows. "Is everything all right?"

She quickly turned toward the stove and pulled the coffeepot to the front. "I'm fine."

"Are you sure?" His voice was close—too close.

She moved away and turned, forcing a smile on her face. "I'm just missing Susanne a bit more than usual this evening. I'll be fine."

He took a step closer to her. "I'm sorry about what I said. I didn't mean to dredge up bad memories."

She held up her hand. "It's fine, Abram. Truly."

He studied her for a moment and then reached out and took her hand.

The gesture captured her by surprise and she took a step back, her legs pressing against the table.

"Thank you, for everything. I know it hasn't been easy,

but I don't know what we would do without you. I mean that."

Pleasure coiled inside her stomach and it took all her willpower not to melt into his arms.

"You're welcome."

"Merry Christmas, Charlotte."

She gently extracted her hand and put it behind her back, wrapping her fingers into a tight ball, trying to hold on to the feeling of his touch. "Merry Christmas, Abram."

He smiled and then left the kitchen, closing the door softly behind him.

Charlotte sank to the chair, her legs weak and her heart beating an unsteady rhythm. She put her face in her hands and took several deep breaths.

No matter what the cost, she must deny her growing feelings for Abram.

It was the only way she would survive until September.

Chapter Nine

March 15, 1855

Today was finally the day. The winter had passed and spring was proving to be warmer than usual. Abram walked over to the kitchen window and looked out at the pale morning. Patches of dirt showed through the snowbanks, confirming an early thaw, though one could never be too sure in Minnesota.

"All of your pacing is making me nervous," Charlotte said from her place at the stove.

Abram turned away from the window and took the cup of coffee she offered him. "I can't help it. I'm a bit nervous myself." The letters of incorporation had been signed, the partnership made legal, with Abram retaining five-twelfths of the business, Hubbard with four-twelfths and Cheney the remaining three-twelfths. They had called it the Little Falls Company.

"You? Nervous?" She glanced at him as she filled three glasses of milk for the boys.

His sons sat at the table finishing their breakfast, unaware of how important this day was for all of them.

"I didn't know you could get nervous," Charlotte said, handing Robert and Martin their milk.

"Of course I can get nervous." He looked out the window again, though it could be several hours before Hubbard arrived with the land surveyor. "You should have seen me on my wedding day." He belatedly realized how insensitive his words were, and the look on Charlotte's face confirmed it.

"I didn't have the pleasure of attending your wedding, if you recall," she said, helping George sip from his cup.

Thankfully there wasn't anger behind her words anymore—just regret. After four and a half months, they had come to a quiet truce over the past and had fallen into a formal, if somewhat stilted, relationship. Something had happened on that long-ago Christmas night, and since then Charlotte had held him at a distance, for which he was grateful. He had left the conversation feeling shaky and unsettled, and had resolved to never put himself in such an intimate situation with her again.

It was best to treat Charlotte like his housekeeper and nothing more.

Abram sighed. "I suppose I'll get the chores started." Usually he enjoyed the work, but today he felt too distracted. "There's no telling when Hubbard will arrive, or if I'll have a chance to get any real work done today."

The morning passed quickly. When Abram was finished with his chores, he went to the church, which had taken on shape over the long winter months. Susanne's grave was now in a real graveyard next to the church. The exterior of the building had been shingled and sided, but there was no door or windows to fully enclose the space.

When he heard Charlotte ring the dinner bell, he put down his hammer and nails and left the church behind, glancing down the Wood's Trail for a sign of Hubbard and the surveyor.

Abram walked into the house and hung his things on the hook in the lean-to. He washed his hands with the fresh water in the basin and entered the kitchen. Martin was singing a Christmas song, though Christmas was long over, while George was banging something on the table, talking in his gibberish, and Charlotte was giving Robert instructions about setting the table. She still spoke audibly, even as she signed.

Abram entered the kitchen and she glanced up. "Any news of our guests?"

"Not yet," Abram answered, signing back. "I expected them long before now." He sat at his place and reached over to remove the spoon from George's hand.

A movement outside the window caught Abram's eye. "It's Hubbard." His heart pounded as he stood and opened the door. Two wagons pulled into the yard, both loaded with men. "What in the world?"

Charlotte joined him at the door. "Who are all those men?"

Abram grabbed his coat. "I don't know."

"Should I put more plates on the table?"

"You might have to put out more tables."

She laughed. "I'll at least get some coffee on."

Abram walked away from the house and met the wagons when they came to a stop. Timothy Hubbard drove the first wagon, his cheeks ruddy and his eyes shining. "Good afternoon, Cooper."

"Good afternoon." Abram glanced at the men in the

wagon. "I didn't realize you were bringing an entire town with you today."

Hubbard secured the reins to the dashboard and jumped out of the wagon. He indicated a slightly smaller man with spectacles. "This is Mr. Ingalls, the land surveyor. And these men—" Hubbard indicated at least a dozen men piling out of the wagons "—are our new laborers."

"Our what?"

"They've come to clear roads, build bridges and construct buildings. People are pouring into St. Anthony this spring, and they're looking for work. There are more where these men came from."

"What buildings will they construct?"

"The company store, for starters, and my house. Mrs. Hubbard gave me explicit instructions to build on the land up the hill from here."

The men were lifting out boxes of tools, carpetbags and bedrolls from the backs of the wagons. Many of them had started to look around, as if trying to figure out where to begin.

"Where will they stay?" Abram scratched his head. Why hadn't Hubbard made these plans known to him? He would have found some way to prepare.

"I suppose some could stay in the barn—or even up at the church. It looks like it would be suitable enough to sleep in for now. In no time at all, there will be more options."

"What about food?"

"The men will be getting regular paychecks. Perhaps Miss Lee would be willing to provide meals for payment—like a boardinghouse."

Abram glanced at the house, where Charlotte was watching from the window. What would she think of that? She had her hands full with the demands of his home and children. Could she cook for a dozen more people?

"Where should we start, boss?" One of the men came up to Hubbard, his box of tools in hand.

Hubbard looked at Abram, a grin on his face. "Well? What do you think, boss?"

A dozen men stared at Abram, waiting for direction. In this moment he would set himself apart as boss—or he would hand that title over to Timothy Hubbard. As principal owner of the company, the position should fall on Abram's shoulders.

"First, you can all come in and warm yourselves with some coffee and meet my sister-in-law, Miss Lee. After that, we'll start clearing Main Street and Hubbard will take a few of you over to his house site, and you can get started there."

Hubbard nodded. "Sounds good to me."

Abram directed the men to put their things in his barn for now, and a couple of them took the horses in to rub them down and give them some oats. When they finished, Abram led them to the house, hoping Charlotte would be amiable to the new plans.

Charlotte opened the door before they reached the house, a cautious smile on her face.

Several men in the group whistled under their breath.

The response unsettled Abram. She stood in a blue-gingham dress, tight at her waist and belled out from her hips. Her dark hair was held up in a snood, and her brown eyes surveyed the oncoming crowd behind thick lashes. She was a beautiful woman and he wasn't surprised the others noticed—but he was suddenly aware that, from this moment on, he would have to share her attention with all these men and many more who would come after them.

"Who's the pretty lady?" one of the men asked from the back of the group. "Is she your wife, Mr. Cooper?"

Abram didn't answer the question immediately, but waited to address the group until they stood before Charlotte. "Gentlemen, this is my sister-in-law, Miss Lee." He watched them eye her up with appreciation. "Charlotte, Mr. Hubbard has brought these men to work on the town."

Her dark brows arched. "They'll be staying?"

"I hope I haven't inconvenienced you, Miss Lee," Hubbard said, his charming smile falling into place. "The company intends to pay you, and each man will offer a stipend for his meals."

"Meals?" Charlotte blinked at Hubbard. "You expect me to cook for all these men?"

"I—"

"Charlotte." Abram put his hand on her elbow. "May I have a word with you?" He led her back into the house as he spoke over his shoulder. "Everyone come in and have some coffee. Miss Lee and I need a few minutes alone."

"I wouldn't mind a few minutes alone with her," said someone from the group.

"Now, men." Hubbard turned to face the laborers. "I won't tolerate any disrespect."

Abram and Charlotte walked into the house, where the boys were eating their meal. Hubbard and his men followed, and Abram showed them where the coffee cups were while Charlotte stood with her arms crossed.

He touched her elbow again and led her into the

main room, closing the door behind him. "Charlotte, I had no idea Hubbard was bringing those men with him. I'm sorry."

"Am I really expected to cook for them? That wasn't part of the deal, Abram."

"I realize that, and I hate to ask it of you, but I'll see that you're paid well." He thought quickly. "You could use the money to build a dress shop for yourself in Iowa City and make a real business out of your seamstress work."

"A real business?" She dropped her arms.

"That's not what I meant." He was bungling this whole thing. "I'm simply saying you could profit a great deal from this endeavor. And it wouldn't be permanent. I'm sure there will be a hotel and a restaurant built before long, not to mention a boardinghouse or two."

She studied him for several moments. Excited conversation floated in from the kitchen and he knew the men were anxious to get started. *He* was anxious to get started. But they needed to settle this business before suppertime or they'd all be in a mess.

"I don't have any other options, Charlotte." He put his hand on her arm. "You'd be doing me a favor."

She glanced down at his hand—but didn't move away from his touch. She swallowed and nodded. "All right."

He bent to look her in the face. "If anyone can do it, you can, Charlotte." He wanted to kiss her cheek, or pull her into a hug, or do something else to show her how much he appreciated her willingness to help—but he refrained, remembering his resolve to keep his distance. Instead he squeezed her arm and then let her go.

Together, they reentered the kitchen and Abram nodded at Hubbard.

It was time to get started.

Charlotte opened the oven door and a wave of heat bathed her face with the fragrance of baked bread. She normally enjoyed the smell, but this was her third batch today, and she had one more to go. The kitchen felt overly warm and sweat dripped from her brow.

George stood next to a kitchen chair, his face red, tears streaming down his cheeks. His bottom two teeth looked like small pearls on his swollen gums. The poor little boy was running a fever and his nose was draining—but she had to get this last batch of bread in the oven before she could take care of him. She had sixteen men to feed, plus the three children and herself.

"I'm sorry, Georgie," she said. "Your ginger tea is almost ready."

"Aunt Charlotte," Martin called from the main room. "Robert needs you."

"Tell Robert to wait a moment," Charlotte shouted above George's cry. "I'm busy."

"But he hurt himself," Martin called back.

"Is he bleeding?" Charlotte pulled the second loaf of bread from the oven and set it on the cupboard.

"No."

"Then tell him to wait."

Charlotte took out the third loaf and then closed the oven door. She used her towel to flip the bread pans over onto a cutting board.

George's wails escalated.

"Oh, baby." Charlotte left the bread and picked up George. She bounced him as he laid his head on her shoulder, his tears and drool staining her dress. She touched his forehead. "You're burning up." She went to the cupboard where she had George's ginger tea cooling. She lifted the ginger root out of the tea and mixed in a little sugar so the baby would drink it. "Here you are." She put the tepid liquid to his lips. "This should help your fever."

Thankfully, he sipped the tea, but a hiccup escaped his mouth, causing the tea to drip onto her dress, and the tears to start all over again.

Robert's muffled cries met her ears at the same moment.

The lean-to door opened and Abram blew into the house, pushing the door closed behind him. His hair and beard were coated with snow and ice. "Fickle weather. April first and we get a snowstorm." He walked into the kitchen and glanced at Charlotte. "What's wrong with George?"

"He's teething." Her words were strained and exhausted. "And Robert just hurt himself." She glanced out the window for the first time all afternoon. "When did it start snowing?"

"You didn't notice?"

For reasons unknown to her, tears sprang up in her eyes and she choked on her words. "I've been busy."

"Here." He took off his coat and hung it on the peg. "I'll take George and see what I can do for Robert."

"You're busy."

He took the baby from her arms. "I'm never too busy to help my family. Is this ginger tea?"

Charlotte used her apron to wipe her eyes and nodded. "It should help with the fever."

Abram left the kitchen and Charlotte put the last

batch of bread into the oven. She sat at the table and started chopping carrots to put in the stew. Her eyelids felt heavy and her back ached. For over two weeks she had been cooking and cleaning up after Abram's laborers, and there was no rest within sight. Already, four extra men had joined the original group, simply showing up and asking for work. One of them, Nathan Richardson, had immediately set to work on building a large hotel on Main Street, north of the church.

Within two weeks several roads had been cleared, and the construction of the Hubbards' home, as well as the company store, had begun. Charlotte had stepped outside on several occasions and glanced up the hill toward the town site, but she hadn't had time to leave the house and get a closer look. There was always another meal to prepare.

The knife slipped, slicing her left forefinger. For a second she stared at it and didn't feel a thing, but then the pain came and blood pooled at the surface. Charlotte could handle many things—but blood was not one of them.

She moaned as she jumped up from the table and grabbed a towel off the cupboard, her hands shaking. She pressed it to her pulsing wound, her stomach feeling woozy and her head spinning. The cut was deep—much too deep. How would she stop the bleeding?

"George is sleeping," Abram said as he stepped into the kitchen. "He fell asleep the moment I—" He paused. "Charlotte, what's wrong?"

She swayed and he rushed to her side, placing his arm around her. "What happened?"

"My finger." A cold sweat broke out on her forehead and her legs buckled.

Abram lifted her off her feet and brought her to the table, where he gently lowered her to a chair. He glanced at the knife. "Did you cut yourself?" His eyes grew wide. "Did you lose a finger?"

She shook her head, hating her weakness. "No— but it's bad."

"Let me see." He knelt in front of her and took her left hand, tenderly unwrapping the towel.

She caught a glimpse of blood and had to look away lest she lose her breakfast.

"Charlotte."

She swallowed back the nausea. "What?"

"You hardly broke the skin."

"It's gushing blood."

"Look." He held up her hand. "It's already stopped bleeding."

She tried to look—but couldn't make herself do it.

He began to chuckle. "I had no idea you were so queasy around blood." He still knelt before her, his blue eyes sparkling with mirth. "Imagine that. The indomitable Charlotte Lee afraid of a little blood."

"It wasn't a little blood." She swallowed and then forced herself to look at her hand. Sure enough, it had stopped bleeding.

She met his gaze and the nausea was replaced with an altogether different feeling in the pit of her stomach. One that scared her even more—attraction.

Charlotte sat straighter and tried not to look into his eyes. "Well...maybe I overreacted just a bit."

He tilted his head back and laughed. "You almost fainted! I thought you cut off your finger."

"It could have been serious." She lifted her chin—

but a smile played about her lips. "I can't believe how insensitive you're being."

He continued to rock with laughter. "I'm sorry, Charlotte—but I never expected you to be so..." He paused and his face sobered as he studied her with care. "So in need of rescuing."

Warmth filled her at that look and she suddenly realized, for the first time in her life, that she had never once allowed someone to rescue her. She had always prided herself on not needing anyone—but at the moment, with the reminder of his strong arms around her, she found she had enjoyed it.

She blinked and stood, almost knocking him over, and went to the cupboard where she kept scraps of cloth to wrap wounds. "I should bandage it, just in case."

She couldn't look at him—not right now. She didn't trust herself to keep her emotions in check. No matter how hard she tried, she couldn't control the tender feelings he stirred within her. The only thing she could control was the distance she kept between them.

Charlotte pulled a strip of white linen from the box and started to wrap it around her finger.

"Do you need help?" he asked, close to her elbow.

She kept her back to him. "No, thank you."

The lean-to door opened again and Charlotte turned to find several men walk into her kitchen, their bodies covered in snow.

"It's not fit for man nor beast out there," Nathan Richardson said.

"Come on in and warm yourself," Abram invited.

Charlotte breathed a sigh of relief at the interruption. "I'll put on the coffee."

The men filled her kitchen and poured over into the

main room. Eventually all sixteen of them came into the house, except Harry, who remained in the barn.

For hours, they laughed and joked, some of them pulling out decks of cards and cribbage boards, others drinking coffee and telling stories.

The house shook with the intensity of the wind. It screeched and hollered like a panther, whipping around the eaves and threatening to blow in the windows. Charlotte kept the coffee cups full and tried to make supper with everyone in her way.

"We're in for a three-day snowstorm, mark my words," one man said as he dealt a round of cards to half a dozen others sitting at the kitchen table. "No one'll be working in this weather."

Charlotte glanced at Abram, who stood by the window, one hand in his pocket, the other holding a steaming cup of coffee. He turned at the remark and caught her gaze. "I hope you don't mind company for the next several days."

Mind? Already her ears were ringing from the compliments and ardent attention. How would she survive three full days with all these men?

Chapter Ten

Abram felt like a caged tiger. He'd seen one once, when the circus had come to Cooper, Michigan. It had paced in its cage, running its shoulder blades against the metal bars that held it captive, snarling his fangs at the crowd. Abram had wondered what would happen if one of those bars gave way—and now, as he paced in his kitchen for the third day, he knew what would have happened. That tiger would have sprung out of its cage and run as far and as fast as his legs would have taken him, knocking down anything that stood in his way.

"Abram."

Abram jumped at the sound of Charlotte's voice. "What?"

She looked surprised but she didn't cower—not like he did when the tiger had roared at him as a child. "The boys are ready for bed. Would you like to help me tuck them in?"

Abram rubbed the back of his neck and nodded. He followed her into the main room, where Robert, Martin and George were being entertained by the card tricks Mr. O'Conner was teaching them.

"It's time for bed," Charlotte said as she signed.

"Ah!" Martin's bottom lip protruded. "Not again."

"Do the lads have to go to bed?" Mr. O'Conner asked, stacking his cards together. "Their laughter brings a bit of sunshine on these drab days."

"I'm afraid they do," Charlotte said. "But tomorrow is another day."

"Come, Martin." Abram took his son's hand and then touched Robert's shoulder.

"Good night," the men called from all corners of the house.

Charlotte led the way up the stairs with a lantern, her voice low as she spoke to George. The wind blew with such force, it drowned out her words.

She pushed the boys' bedroom door open and set the lantern on a little bureau against the wall.

George was asleep almost before Charlotte laid him in his crib and Robert went about his nightly routine as if nothing was different. But it was Martin who looked at the window with large, frightened eyes as Abram buttoned his nightshirt. "Papa, that storm scares me."

Charlotte left George's side and went to Robert to help with his buttons.

"What about it scares you?" Abram asked.

"The noise."

"Why does it scare you? What do you think makes the noise?"

Martin's little shoulders came up in an attempt to cover his ears. "Angry cougars and bears."

"Do you think cougars and bears would be out in this storm right now?" Abram shook his head. "They're just as scared of the noise as you. It's the wind that makes that noise as it howls from the north. And soon, it will be done and the quiet will return."

"Shall we say our prayers?" Charlotte asked, her hand signs shadowed by the lantern.

Abram nodded and he knelt beside Martin's bed, while Robert and Charlotte knelt by Robert's bed.

Robert signed his prayers first and then, when Charlotte said, "Amen," it was Martin's turn.

"Dear God." His small voice could barely be heard over the storm. "Please make the storm stop, and please protect the cougar and the bear tonight—but please don't let them eat me if we should ever meet. Amen."

Abram looked over his shoulder and caught Charlotte's eye and they shared a smile.

"Papa," Martin said, climbing into his big bed. "Can you sing to me until I fall asleep, so I don't have to hear the scary noise?"

Abram glanced at Charlotte, who was tucking Robert into bed. His oldest son's eyes were already closed, unaware of the noises in the night.

"And, Aunt Charlotte, will you rub my cheeks?" It was something Martin loved, and Charlotte never refused. She nodded and sat on the edge of Martin's bed, near his head, and began to stroke his cheek. Martin burrowed into his pillow with a sigh.

Abram had never sung in front of Charlotte, though he suspected she heard him singing to the boys on occasion. He felt a bit self-conscious, but he couldn't say no.

He also sat on Martin's bed, near his son's feet, and began a slow, melodic lullaby his mother had sung to him as a child. The song had several verses, and spoke of a young bird flying alone at night, scared of all the night sounds, but finding its way home safe and sound to his parents.

When the song came to an end, Abram looked at his sleeping son and then up at Charlotte. She was watching Abram in the dim light.

"That was beautiful," she whispered.

She was beautiful, sitting near his son, her slender fingers on his rounded cheek. "Shall we go back downstairs?" he asked before his thoughts went any further.

She nodded and they gingerly left the boys' room, Charlotte holding the lantern. The hall was shadowed and the noise downstairs was muffled against the storm. Charlotte stood for a moment at the top of the stairs, as if she didn't want the moment to end, and he didn't blame her.

The first night of the storm, all the men had stayed up late playing cards, the second night they had regaled each other with tall tales, but tonight, with tempers short, how would they amuse themselves?

Charlotte took a deep breath and then turned toward the stairs.

Abram wanted to call out to her and tell her to wait. But for what?

They descended the stairs and Pierre LaForce rose from one of the rocking chairs. He met Charlotte at the bottom step and stood beside her—too close for Abram's comfort. "Some of us have decided to have a dance, *mademoiselle.*" He was a handsome young Frenchman, as far as Abram could tell, with dark eyes that held a hint of superiority and defiance. He'd been flirting incessantly with Charlotte since the first day of the storm, trying to get her to laugh or smile, speaking to her in English and French.

"Dancing?" Charlotte looked a bit surprised at the suggestion.

"That's a great idea," said another. "I call the first dance!"

"I got the second."

"Third!"

Soon all the men were clamoring for a dance with Charlotte—and Abram didn't like the thought of all those men with their arms around her. "No."

"No?" Pierre crossed his arms. "And why not, *monsieur*?"

"It's late and Charlotte is tired."

"Are you tired, Miss Charlotte?" Pierre asked. "Or would you like to *danser*?" He swayed, as if dancing, and smiled at her.

Charlotte looked at Abram and then back at the eager men. If she said no, he suspected a riot on their hands. But if she said yes, no doubt she'd have to spend the next several hours taking turns with every man in the house. Even if they didn't know how to dance, they wouldn't give up a chance to hold her. He saw how they all admired her while she went about her work. She'd already turned down two marriage proposals.

But the look in her eyes suggested that none of that mattered. "One dance each," Charlotte said with a good-natured smile. "And not a single more."

There was a round of cheers as the men scrambled to move the furniture to the outside edges of the room. Someone produced a mouth organ, another grabbed a set of spoons, and together they played a lively Virginia reel. The men lined up, half of them taking the female side and the other half taking the male side. A caller shouted the steps and Charlotte was pulled into the dance by

Pierre. She laughed as she sidestepped and do-si-do'ed, while the others clapped and shouted.

Abram stood by the kitchen door, watching everyone carefully—especially Charlotte. Her cheeks turned pink and her face glowed, making her lovelier than ever.

As soon as the reel ended, the mouth organ spilled out a waltz and everyone paired up, another man taking Charlotte in his arms. She was swung around the room, her blue skirts swirling and swishing as she moved. Those who didn't dance simply watched, their eyes shining at the sight of her.

Charlotte danced on and on, without a break. When one of the men approached her for a second dance, he was hauled away by the others and tossed out into the snowstorm. He came back in, laughing and wiping snow off his face.

Abram didn't move from his spot, leaning against the kitchen door frame, his arms crossed.

As he watched Charlotte, he was slowly transported back to Iowa City and the first time he'd seen her. He had walked into the dance at the hotel, new in town, just barely twenty years old. The first woman in the room to catch his eye had been Charlotte—not because she was the first he'd laid eyes on, but because she was the first that had fully captured his attention. She had been dancing, much like she was tonight, with one partner after another. The lights had been dim, the orchestra loud and the sight breathtaking.

He had been determined to get a dance with her that evening, and had moved into her line of sight. When she had looked at him, he had been captivated by her beauty. When he'd asked for a dance, she had cautiously agreed. He'd told her a little about himself and his dream to one day build a town, but the more he'd talked, the more she had pulled away. He'd wondered at her behavior, but hadn't had time to ask before the dance had ended and she'd walked away. And when he had shown up on her doorstep to court Susanne, she had treated him like a villain.

But those days were in the past. As he watched her now, understanding her in ways he hadn't then, he wondered if he would have handled the situation any differently. Yet—if he had—he might not have married Susanne and had his sons. He would never give up the years he'd had with his wife. She had filled his home with joy and had given him the belief he needed to follow his dreams.

No. He would not have changed a thing and he felt horrible for even entertaining such thoughts.

"You're the last one, Cooper," Nathan Richardson called. "What'll it be? A waltz? A reel?"

Charlotte turned, breathing hard, her eyes bright and full of expectation.

He wanted to dance with her—but something inside him warned against it. The one and only time they had danced together had led to disaster, and he suspected this time would be the same—but in an entirely different way.

"I think I'll let Miss Lee have a rest." Abram shoved away from the door frame. "We should all turn in for the night. As soon as the storm ends, I want all of you back to work."

Groans filled the room and several men called out their displeasure at the announcement.

Abram glanced at Charlotte, expecting her to be relieved, but he was surprised to see disappointment on her features.

"Good night, gentlemen," Charlotte said, tearing her gaze from Abram. "I'll let one of you bank the fires and turn out the lights."

"Good night," the men called back.

"Shall I escort you to your room?" Pierre asked with another bow.

"That won't be necessary." Abram took two steps and was by Charlotte's side. "I'll see her to her room—and I'll wait outside her door until she has it locked."

Pierre laughed at Abram and then lifted Charlotte's hand to his lips. *"Bonne nuit, mademoiselle."*

"Shall we?" Abram asked her.

She lifted the hem of her gown and turned toward the stairs. He followed her up, leaving the noise behind.

She climbed the steps slowly and then turned left at the top of the stairs. She opened the door and took a step into her room.

"Good night, Charlotte," Abram said.

She paused and looked at him over her shoulder, a question in her eyes. "Why didn't you want to dance with me?"

The hall was dark, with only a swath of light seeping up the stairwell, but he could see her features clearly—or maybe he just had them memorized.

"I did want to dance with you," he said quietly.

She turned fully, her skirts swishing with the movement. "Then why didn't you?"

He took a step closer to her—and then paused, his heart pumping harder than it had in years. What was happening to him? Why now, after all this time, was he recalling the night he had met her for the first time? Why was he asking what might have been? He didn't want to know what might have been. Things had worked out exactly as they should have. God knew what Abram needed then—and He knew what Abram needed now. And it wasn't Charlotte.

He took a step back again—feeling foolish. "Good night, Charlotte."

He turned and opened his bedroom door before he could embarrass himself further.

The mid-May sunshine warmed Charlotte's shoulders as she stood in front of the church with George on her hip, scanning the new downtown. Half a dozen store buildings were under construction, and dozens of men were clearing more lots. The old oxcart trail actually resembled a street now—or at least, it promised to resemble a street. Tree roots protruded from thick mud and deep wagon ruts ran in chaotic patterns, crisscrossing from one side to the next.

A second main road had been cut perpendicular to Main Street. Abram called it Broadway. It started east of town, crossed a bridge that had been built over the deep ravine edging the downtown, and continued west toward the river. Additional side streets were being cleared even now, with saws and shouts of "timber" reverberating through the air. Sixty men worked for the Little Falls Company and they used nineteen oxen and eight horses—all of them housed in Abram's barn at night.

Abram stood beside Charlotte, holding Robert's and Martin's hands. He turned to Charlotte with excitement sparkling in his blue gaze. "What do you think?"

Charlotte tried to find something nice to say about

the disorderly mess. "A lot of work has been done in eight short weeks."

"You're right, and there's a lot more to do." He pointed to the large brown house across the road from the church, behind an empty lot sectioned off for a store building. "The Hubbard house is almost ready. Pearl and the children plan to move in next week."

A smile lifted Charlotte's lips. "It will be good to finally have her in town." It had been several months since Charlotte had visited with another woman and she was eager for the company.

"Look over there." Abram guided Charlotte and the boys up the road and pointed to the northwest corner of Main Street and Broadway, where a rough-lumber frame promised to be a substantial building. "Nathan Richardson is calling it the Northern Hotel. It's supposed to be the largest hotel north of St. Anthony."

"It's quite impressive."

Abram looked down at his boys. "Would you like to see where your school will be?"

They both nodded enthusiastically and Abram led them to the plot of land designated for the school. They stood across the road to watch the men cutting trees.

Martin let go of Abram's hand and was about to dart across the road before Charlotte reached out and put her hand on his shoulder. "Stay close. It's much too dangerous over there."

"Those men wouldn't see you," Abram said, taking Martin's hand once again. "You must not bother them."

Martin blinked as a large tree fell to the ground.

"Now that the sawmill is running again," Abram said to Charlotte, "I can make the lumber for the schoolhouse."

"Have you had any success finding a teacher yet?"

"Hubbard has a young woman from Moline in mind. He wrote to her, but she hasn't replied."

"And a preacher?"

"Nothing—yet."

Yet. He had only three and a half months to find someone, but with the way everything was progressing, it looked as if he might very well accomplish what he had set out to do.

"I'll show you where the company store is being built." Abram guided them west toward the river and pointed to a building under construction. Another road ran behind the store and down the hill toward Abram's home. The road had been named Wood Street and went directly between Abram's house and barn as it continued along the river.

"What do you think?" Abram signed to Robert.

Robert's blue eyes shone. "I like your town, Papa."

"This is your town, too. I made it for you and Martin and George."

"Mine?" Robert signed, his eyes growing wide.

"Yes."

Charlotte was happy for Abram, but daily struggled with the sadness of leaving the boys behind. She needed something to look forward to, and had made a big decision. "I've had a letter from an acquaintance back home." Charlotte blurted the statement. "Andrew just brought it this afternoon."

Abram gave her his full attention. "Is it good news or bad?"

"I inquired about a building."

"A building?"

"I decided to take your advice and open a dress shop when I return to Iowa City."

She waited for him to say something, but he just watched her, his thoughts imperceptible.

"I told the proprietor to have the building ready for me by the second week of September," she added.

He glanced around the town, squinting as he rubbed the back of his neck. "I've been so busy lately, I kind of forgot about our agreement."

Forgot? How could he forget? The thought plagued Charlotte every waking moment.

"I suppose you wouldn't consider staying on here?" he asked.

She paused for a moment. "I have a life in Iowa City—one I need to get back to as soon as possible." And there was a part of her, despite Abram's success, that feared for the boys. There was still so much that could go wrong for Abram. Every cent he made was poured back into the Little Falls Company, and he was no better off financially than when she had arrived. If anything, he was more in debt. She needed to have a steady income and a life for the boys, if they should ever need her. "There was a small building that came up for sale," she went on. "With my earnings, I decided to purchase it."

Abram nodded, but didn't meet her eyes. "Congratulations."

She smiled down at Robert, realizing they had stopped signing—but it was probably for the best. No need to worry him over something that was still months off. "I need to get back to the house to start supper preparations. If my calculations are correct, I'll be serving sixty men tonight."

"Sixty-one men," Abram amended. "And two women.

We had a family arrive today, and I told them to come down to the house for supper."

"Two women?" Charlotte looked around the town, her eyes wandering over the rough streets, looking for traces of another female.

"Well, a woman and a—" Abram faltered, and for the first time since Charlotte had known him, his cheeks filled with a bit of color.

"A what?" Charlotte asked.

"I suppose she's a woman, too." He nervously rubbed the back of his head, tilting his hat forward. "It doesn't really matter. I said they could come a little early to meet you. After the men get inside, I think there will be too much commotion, especially when they get a look at—" Again he stopped and looked embarrassed.

"When the men get a look at what?" Charlotte asked.

Abram repositioned his hat. "Never mind." He reached down and lifted Martin into his arms and then tossed him in the air. "I should probably get back to work. Hubbard and Cheney are coming to town tomorrow and there are several things I need to do before then." He was rewarded with a giggle from Martin and then he lifted Robert and did the same. After setting him down, he kissed the top of George's head. "See you at supper." He waved as he strode off toward the company store.

Charlotte directed the boys toward home and pondered his strange words.

They took Wood Street and approached the house from the north. Charlotte marveled at how much it had changed since the first time she'd seen it over six months ago. The actual house and barn hadn't changed, but the landscape around it had. No longer did it look like a lonely farm in the middle of the wilderness. Now it looked like a house in the midst of a growing community, albeit a fledgling one.

What did this town hold? Would it flourish, as Abram envisioned, or would it die like so many other towns built on lavish dreams and fanciful imaginings?

Charlotte descended the incline toward the house. The snow was all but gone, except for a few shadowed places around town.

Movement caught her eye and she glanced over at the barn, where Harry was making shingles with the froe. He sat just outside the barn door on a stool, pounding the froe into a log. His job hadn't changed much since the town's construction began. He still took care of Abram's animals and the chores around the farm. He didn't go to Crow Wing as much as before, because a ramshackle saloon had been built to the south of town, near the riverbank. Several men who had previously spent their evenings by Abram's fireplace now went to the shanty saloon and played cards and did other things Charlotte would prefer not to think about. She had asked Abram why he didn't have the place pulled down, but he simply said the lot had been purchased by a proprietor, and there was little he could do about the business he chose to run.

Harry glanced up as she and the children passed by, and he glared at her.

Like always, a knot of regret pinched her stomach. After all these months, nothing had changed between them. Instead of being a light in the darkness, she had pushed him further into the recesses of sin.

Lord, how do I remedy the mistake I've made?

No ready answer arrived. Should she invite him to eat with them again? The Bible admonished Christians to practice hospitality—yet, if she gave in now, would Harry think her weak?

The afternoon sped by, as it usually did while she prepared supper. She scraped the bottom of the vegetable bins and came up with just enough potatoes to boil and serve with the roasted venison. She would serve it with gravy, fresh-baked bread from that morning and the last of the dried apples made into pies. Abram had placed an order from St. Anthony, and Mr. Hubbard was bringing a wagonload of supplies with him in the morning.

As she placed the last potato in the pot to boil, she glanced out the window and saw two women walking down the road from the town site.

It had been over four months since Pearl Hubbard had visited, and the sight of dresses and bonnets outside her door almost brought tears to Charlotte's eyes. She quickly tucked her wayward hair into her bun and then wiped a towel across her damp forehead. She wasn't as presentable as she would like to be for a first meeting but, at the moment, she just wanted female companionship.

Charlotte flung open the lean-to door, a smile on her face, and was greeted by two of the loveliest women she had ever seen.

The mother was the first to extend her hand. Her mouth lifted in a beautiful smile, accentuating her high cheekbones and crinkling the edges of her pretty green eyes. "Hello, I'm Mrs. Perry, and this is my daughter, Maude. Mr. Cooper told us to come early."

"Yes! Yes, of course." Charlotte practically pulled the women over the threshold. "Please come in."

The ladies entered and Maude offered Charlotte a smile almost identical to her mother's. "It's a pleasure to meet you, Miss Lee." She wore a pretty green bonnet, which matched her eyes. Her honey-blond hair curled out around her face. "Mr. Cooper was kind enough to invite us for supper. We hope we aren't intruding." The girl's cheeks held a becoming blush, and when she mentioned Abram, the blush deepened.

"Of course you're not intruding," Charlotte said. Yet somehow she felt that Maude Perry's arrival in Little Falls would intrude a great deal into the life Charlotte had been living these past six and a half months.

Miss Maude Perry would cause quite a stir. And, if Abram's reaction was any indication, she had already impressed one gentleman.

Suddenly, Charlotte wasn't so sure she craved female companionship after all.

Chapter Eleven

The evening sun slipped behind a bank of clouds, threatening to send another June rainstorm. Abram strode south on Kidder Street from the company store, where he now had an office, and crossed over toward Wood Street and home. His head pounded and his eyes felt gritty from exhaustion. Charlotte would have his supper warming on the back of the stove, no doubt, since he had missed suppertime once again.

The swollen Mississippi rushed past the riverbanks, lapping over the edges in a few places. The sawmill was working at full capacity, with Harry managing the daily operations—and still, they were not producing enough lumber to meet the demands of the growing community.

The boys had asked him to be home early tonight but, like every night for the past month, since Hubbard had moved to town full-time, he had been called from one thing to the next, until he realized the sun was setting on another day. Judging by the time, the boys would already be asleep.

Abram pushed open the lean-to door and walked into the quiet kitchen. Now that the large Hubbard home was built, most of the laborers ate and slept at their house. On last count, Hubbard said they had nineteen men living with them. About half a dozen men still came to Charlotte for their meals, but they were usually cleared out by the time Abram came home. All the other men in town ate at the shanty saloon, though Abram imagined the food wasn't much to speak of.

Abram washed his hands in the basin and then entered the kitchen, where he lifted the waiting plate and took off the cloth to reveal chicken and dumplings. He sat at the table and ate in silence, expecting Charlotte to enter the kitchen at any moment.

But she didn't.

By the time he was finished, the sun had set completely and the kitchen was dark.

He put the dish in a pan of water on the stove and walked through the door into the main room.

Charlotte sat in her rocking chair, looking out the window, her chin in her hand. The sewing project in her lap was apparently forgotten as dusk had settled.

"Would you like me to light a lantern?" he asked quietly.

She glanced up, a smile gracing her lips. "Abram. I didn't hear you come in."

He returned the smile, forgetting his headache for a moment. "May I sit with you?"

"Of course."

He struck a match and lit the lantern behind her chair. Light illuminated the room, sending shadows over her face.

"Thank you for keeping my supper warm." He blew out the match and lowered the chimney back onto the lantern. "I wish I could have been home in time to see the boys before they went to bed."

"Tomorrow I'll bring them to the store so they can see you for a bit."

"I would appreciate that." He sighed and sat in the other rocking chair, resting his head against the back. "My days are so full, and I don't get to everything that needs to be done."

She folded her sewing project and set it in her basket. "What things are consuming your time right now?"

The simple question eased a thousand worries. Already his shoulders felt lighter and he could breathe easier. He longed for someone to share his burdens, even if it just meant an ear to listen. "I need to start improving the dam to get more waterpower. We've had several people interested in building businesses along the riverbanks. A gristmill, a cabinet shop and another sawmill, for starters." He rubbed his hands over his eyes. "The company store just opened, but it's a mess. It will take me weeks to get it organized." He lowered his hands and looked at her, his greatest burden at the front of his thoughts. "And I can't find time to work on the schoolhouse, which is the most important building in town right now."

"Why? You have two and a half months before September first."

"Hubbard received a letter from Miss Helen Palmer today, the young lady from Moline who was asked to be our schoolteacher." He paused and watched her carefully. "She'll be here the last week of August, and she wants to start school immediately."

Charlotte glanced down at her hands, her bottom lip coming between her teeth as she nibbled it.

"I just need a doctor and a preacher—"

"I know," she said softly.

Abram didn't want to think about September or Charlotte leaving. He'd rather think about the here and now. "Pearl wants to have a dance. She's estimated about twenty families have recently moved to town and she thought it would be good to get everyone together."

"When?"

"Tomorrow night. We're going to have it here, in the barn. Now that the livestock are being housed at the Hubbards' new barn, Harry will get everything ready, and Pearl said she'd bring refreshments if you're willing to provide coffee."

"I'm always willing to provide coffee." She smiled and it lifted another weight off his shoulders, but then he saw the sadness hidden behind her smile.

She stood and he followed. "I think I'll turn in," she said.

Without another word, she crossed the room and went up the stairs.

He watched until her feet disappeared and then he dropped into the chair, his headache returning with a vengeance.

Why did he feel as if he was failing, while all his dreams were coming true?

A knock at the door made him frown. He pulled himself out of the rocker and opened the door.

Three familiar faces stared back at him and he grinned. "Milt! Caleb! Josiah!"

They exchanged hearty handshakes. "Come in," Abram said.

"What happened?" Caleb asked, stepping into the

main room. "We leave a farm and return to a metropolis!"

"Is that Caleb?" Charlotte appeared on the steps once again, a genuine smile on her beautiful face. "Oh!" She raced across the room and took Caleb's hand. "I've missed you all so much."

"Missed them?" Abram asked. "With all those men in the house this winter?"

Charlotte shook Josiah's hand and then Milt's, and received exuberant smiles in return.

"If I would have known we'd get such a welcome," Caleb said with a twinkle in his eye, "we wouldn't have stopped in Crow Wing on the way down the river."

"You didn't!" Charlotte put her hands on her hips.

Caleb laughed and shook his head. "Nah, I'm just teasing. We came straight back."

"We heard there was commotion in Little Falls," Josiah said. "Looks like we came just in time."

"Actually, you're about three months too late." Abram slapped his back. "But I'm happy you've come."

"Harry still here?" Milt asked, eyeing up Charlotte.

Abram nodded. "He's in the barn." Actually, he was probably at the shanty saloon, but Abram wasn't in a hurry to tell the others about the place.

"Ah, Miss Charlotte," Caleb chastised. "Still as stubborn as ever?"

Charlotte glanced down at her hands. It was clear she felt bad about Harry.

"Harry's even more stubborn than Charlotte," Abram said. "It's the man's own fault."

"It's not entirely his fault," Charlotte conceded, finally looking up.

Abram wrinkled his brow but he didn't comment.

"I reckon we should mosey on out and see what there is to see," Caleb said. "Where do the men spend their evenings?"

"Do you have to leave?" Charlotte asked. "Why not stay? I could make coffee and find something for you to eat. We'd love to visit."

Caleb glanced at Josiah and Milt, and they both nodded. "You got yourself a deal!"

Charlotte grinned and went to the kitchen, Milt and Josiah following.

Caleb held back and looked at Abram with a serious expression. "I half expected to see a wedding ring on Miss Charlotte's finger when we walked in."

"A wedding ring?" Abram frowned. "Why?"

Caleb tilted his head and suddenly he didn't look as young as before. "You're a man. She's a woman."

Abram shook his head. "There's no future for Charlotte and me. She'll be heading back to Iowa City to start a dress shop soon." It was ludicrous to even think about marrying Charlotte. In her eyes, Abram was irreparably flawed and he would never change. He could spend the rest of his life trying to convince her otherwise, but she would doubt him and his intentions forever.

No. He had no wish to consider a future like that... yet the thought of never looking into her beautiful brown eyes again filled him with a hollow feeling he didn't like.

Charlotte stood in front of the mirror in her bedroom and looked at her reflection. She wore a gown made of dark blue silk. The bodice fit perfectly over her slender waist and the skirt belled out a little more than her day dresses with the extra petticoats. The sleeves were short and she wore a long lace shawl over her shoulders. Her hair was up, with large, chocolate-colored ringlets dripping down her back and over her shoulders.

It felt good to dress up and to anticipate a real dance with real music. Harry had been busy cleaning out the barn all day, and Pearl had arrived early to set up the refreshments. She'd also brought their housekeeper, a young Indian woman named Rachel, to care for Robert, Martin and George, as well as the Hubbards' three children.

A knock at the door startled Charlotte from her reverie.

"Miss Charlotte," Rachel called through the closed door. "There's a gentleman downstairs to escort you to the dance."

A gentleman? Charlotte pinched her cheeks and then lifted her long white gloves off the bureau. She glanced at the ivory-handled dresser set Abram had given her at Christmas and her heart did a little flip. "Thank you." She pulled on the gloves and opened the door, wondering who had come to escort her. Abram?

Charlotte peeked inside the boys' bedroom, where the children were playing. "Good night. Don't hesitate to find me if you need anything."

Robert caught Charlotte's eye and he ran his hand over his face. "Beautiful."

Charlotte smiled, touched her hand to her chin and then out toward him. "Thank you." And then blew him a kiss.

She closed the door, lifted the hem of her gown and walked down the narrow steps. She caught sight of a pair of male feet at the bottom of the stairs and then she saw his legs and torso—and then his face, and a pang of disappointment almost stole the joy out of the evening. "Hello, Mr. LaForce."

Pierre LaForce was a handsome man—but he wasn't Abram.

He bent at the waist and offered a dashing bow. "*Mademoiselle*, you are most radiant. May I have the pleasure of escorting you to the dance?"

Several other men rushed into the house at that moment, their hair slicked down, wearing what were probably their best clothes.

"What is this?" Pierre asked. "I am first."

"Miss Lee, you can't allow LaForce to escort you," Nathan Richardson said, his hand over his heart. "It's simply not fair. We all worked hard to get here before him, but he cheated."

"Cheated?" LaForce lifted his nose in the air. "We agreed the first man to get here would have the honor of Miss Lee's company."

"We tried getting here as soon as possible," said another man, "but Mr. Cooper and Mr. Hubbard wouldn't let us off a minute sooner than usual. Pierre must have snuck away early."

Pierre simply grinned at Charlotte. "There is nothing more important than a beautiful woman—so I took my chances and left work early. But please do not tell."

"What'll it be?" Mr. Richardson asked, stepping next to Pierre. "A cheater or me?"

"Or me?" asked another as he stepped forward.

"I got here the same time Richardson did," said yet another.

Charlotte put up her hands, a giggle on her lips. "Let's all go together."

That seemed to please no one, especially Mr. La-
Force, but Charlotte insisted.

They left the house by way of the lean-to and crossed
Wood Street toward the barn. Already, the lanterns had
been lit, with several strung from the ceiling. Three
men sat in the corner on hay bales, playing their fiddles.

Charlotte entered the barn on the arms of Mr. La-
Force and Mr. Richardson, and was greeted by dozens
of familiar faces. The Hubbards were there, as well as
Mr. and Mrs. Perry and their daughter, Maude, who
was already dancing.

Besides these two families, there were over a dozen
more, but only three marriageable ladies in attendance,
Charlotte included. The rest were matrons who had
come to town with their husbands.

Charlotte scanned the barn but did not see Abram, and
her disappointment mounted. Where was he? She had
seen so little of him these past few weeks, she missed
his company and had looked forward to spending time
with him all day.

Mr. LaForce took the first dance, a lively schottische.
He twirled Charlotte around, teasing her until he won
a smile. As soon as the dance finished, she was swept
away by the vibrant Mr. Richardson, who told her of his
adventures walking to Little Falls from a logging camp
sixty miles away.

An hour passed and still Abram did not appear. Between each dance, she glanced around the barn to look
for him. The evening stars began to sparkle and a gentle
wind blew through the open doors, cooling Charlotte's
warm skin.

Finally, Charlotte begged for a break and her dance
partner made her promise to dance the next song. She

went to the refreshment table and took a cookie. As she nibbled on the flaky delight, she watched Pearl and Maude and Mrs. Perry twirl around the dance floor. There wasn't a woman, no matter how old, sitting on the sidelines watching. Everyone was in the hands of a dance partner, their cheeks pink and their faces filled with joy.

A movement near the door caught Charlotte's attention and, for a moment, she didn't recognize the man who stood there. His clean-shaven face was a sight to behold—and transported Charlotte back to Iowa City, to the Fireman's Ball, when he walked in, looking very much the same as he did tonight, with his smooth skin, brilliant blue eyes and charming smile.

Though now he looked more mature and handsome, if that was possible. He wore the evening coat Charlotte had made for him over the winter months. It fit him perfectly and set him apart from most of the men. He stood taller than everyone and would be hard to miss... even if she hadn't been looking for him.

Charlotte waited for him to look her way, but his eyes were trailing the dance floor, following Miss Maude Perry.

The fiddlers ended their song and began another. Mr. O'Conner appeared at her elbow. "I'm ready for that dance, lass."

Charlotte set down her cookie and, like the night at the Fireman's Ball, hoped Abram would look her way and ask her to dance.

She effortlessly stepped into the waltz, glancing toward Abram once again to see if he'd noticed her. But his eyes were not on Charlotte—he was already dancing with Maude.

The two of them together were stunning. He, tall and

dark. She, small and fair. As they danced, they smiled at one another, and Maude's pleasant laughter could be heard above the fiddler's music.

A tinge of jealousy colored Charlotte's perspective and all of a sudden the entire evening felt dull. Seeing Abram and Maude reminded her of when she'd seen Susanne dancing with Abram during the Fireman's Ball—but it wasn't jealousy that clouded her thoughts that long-ago night. It had been fear. A completely different feeling.

Or was it so different? Jealousy was only fear masquerading in a different costume. But why was she afraid of seeing Maude and Abram together?

She didn't want to even contemplate the answer.

"Lass, I believe I'm your dance partner," Mr. O'Conner said. "Would you mind focusing on me?"

"Pardon me." Charlotte directed her attention away from Abram and back to Mr. O'Conner, her cheeks filling with heat.

Another hour passed and Charlotte moved from one dance partner to the next, but Abram did not approach her. He danced with Mrs. Hubbard and Mrs. Perry, and then again with Maude—but still he did not ask Charlotte.

Her feet began to hurt and disappointment wedged its way inside her chest, though she tried to hide it from her dance partners. Eventually she didn't feel like dancing anymore and excused herself.

She left the barn and walked toward the privy, so no one would follow her, but she wound her way around the outbuilding and moved past the house and continued on to the river.

A bright moon cast shadows on the ground, illuminating the sawmill. The river rushed past, pushing and tumbling like a young child just released from school.

Charlotte stood on the riverbank and wrapped her arms around her waist, uninterested in returning to the dance to watch Abram from a distance. She didn't know why his behavior troubled her so, when it shouldn't matter whether he danced with her or not.

Maybe she was disheartened because Abram was getting close to achieving his goals and she would be leaving in September without the boys. The schoolhouse was framed and the shingles had been put in place. Half of the siding was tacked on the sides of the building. All he needed was a preacher and a doctor—which seemed almost too easy at this point.

She sighed and took a seat near the water. It was already the middle of June. Abram had two and a half months left to complete her requirements—and she had two and a half months to figure out how she would say goodbye to her nephews…if it came to that.

Chapter Twelve

Abram smiled down at Miss Perry. "It's been a pleasure dancing with you, again, but I'm afraid the others will string me up a tree if I ask for a third dance."

Miss Perry laughed, but she had no witty comeback or reply—not like Charlotte would.

He bowed toward Miss Perry and then turned away, just as Charlotte slipped out of the barn. Several men exited to watch her departure and Abram felt compelled to step outside to make sure she was safe.

He had tried not to notice her this evening, but it had been impossible. She was breathtaking in her blue gown, her hair done up in shiny curls. His only defense against the churning feelings inside was to keep his distance from her, which had been hard to do, especially when he was conscious of her every move, her every partner and her every glance in his direction.

It was almost as if she'd wanted him to notice her—yet he couldn't fathom why. He and Charlotte had developed an understanding, and even a fondness for one another, but he suspected that it had more to do with the children than it did with him.

He watched Charlotte skirt around the privy and move on toward the river, as the other men returned to the barn.

Abram followed Charlotte's path and stood near the corner of his house, watching her by the riverbank for several minutes.

She stood, looking out at the river, and then she sat, her shoulders bent forward. What was she thinking about? Was she contemplating her return to Iowa City? Or...was there any hope that she might consider staying in Little Falls and starting a dress shop here?

But what would be the point of her staying? They couldn't go on as they had been.

Or could they?

No, it was a pointless thought. Charlotte had no desire to make a life for herself in Minnesota Territory. She already had one in Iowa City and she was probably itching to return and pick up where she had left off.

A group of men walked by the house, on their way south, no doubt to the shanty saloon. The men were coming into town so quickly, Abram didn't have time to get to know them, and he suspected that many of them were drifters. Several were probably running from the law as was common in frontier towns.

Wood Street had become quite a thoroughfare, which made Abram apprehensive. He didn't like so many people coming that close to the house—especially when Charlotte was out there alone in the dark.

He pushed away from the house and walked toward her.

Charlotte sat on the grass to the south of the mill, her skirts billowed out around her. The moon shadows played with her figure, giving her an ethereal appearance. She was a stunning woman—both inside and out. In the months he had come to know her, he saw what Susanne had often talked about. Charlotte wasn't afraid of hard work and she was a good teacher. She had taught herself sign language and then taught it to all of them, even to some of the men who came to the house, so they could communicate with Robert.

She was fiercely protective, and confident, and loyal—all things he valued. She was also witty and smart and she had a tender heart. He suspected that if she ever trusted someone enough, she might let down her guard to reveal more of her inner beauty—and that would be a sight to behold.

The water rushed past in a soothing melody and it mingled with the distant sound of the fiddlers' music.

Abram took a seat next to her.

She startled and turned. "Abram."

"I didn't think you should be alone this far away from the barn."

"I didn't think you even noticed I was there." She looked down, her vulnerable words tearing apart his resolve to keep his distance.

Maybe it was time he and Charlotte spoke plainly with one another. "Of course I noticed you were there." He touched a dangling fringe on her shawl. "How could I not?" Dare he admit the truth? "You were the most beautiful woman in the room."

He waited, holding his breath.

She kept her eyes lowered to her hands as she played with a wrinkle in her gown. "Why didn't you want to dance with me?"

He let out the breath on a long sigh. "Why do you

have such a hard time accepting my compliments, Charlotte?"

She looked at him, her eyes filled with determination. "Why won't you dance with me, Abram?"

Could it be that the answer was the same for both questions? He couldn't dance with her because holding her at a distance was much safer than holding her in his arms. Was that how she felt about his compliments? Was she refusing to accept his praises because she was trying to guard her heart?

They continued to sit on the riverbank, but neither one said a word. The music spilled out of the barn and light illuminated the backyard. Beyond that, Little Falls sat up on the hill, overlooking the Mississippi, growing from a seed of a dream.

His town, his legacy, was taking shape before his very eyes. He wished his father and Susanne could see it—but somehow it didn't matter anymore. This had truly become a gift for his boys and it felt good to live out his dream in front of them—and Charlotte.

"I do appreciate your compliments," she finally said. "I just— Sometimes I'm afraid if I let myself trust you…"

"Charlotte." He hoped he wouldn't regret his next move but he needed her to understand he was a man she could trust. He moved closer to her and lifted her hand in his.

She didn't pull away—of that he was grateful—but neither did she look at him.

"I don't know why you've always distrusted me—but I promise you have nothing to fear."

She finally looked at him and he saw tears gathering in her eyes. One slipped down her cheek.

"What's this?" He lifted his hand and moved away

the tear. It glistened on his fingertip under the glowing moon.

"I wish I could believe you, Abram."

"Why can't you?"

She opened her mouth but at that moment another tear slipped past her eyelid and trailed down her cheek. She reached up with her free hand and wiped it away. "I've been hurt far too many times." She paused, as if gauging whether or not to continue. "My father was responsible for my mother's death because of his insatiable desire to follow one dream after another. But—" She stopped again.

"Charlotte, whatever it is, you can tell me."

"I don't know if Susanne ever told you about Thomas."

"I don't believe so."

"Thomas was my fiancé. I believed, with all my heart, that he loved me and that together we could build a life in Iowa City. He knew about my fear of leaving civilization, and my desire to care for and protect Susanne, but he still loved me and asked me to marry him. A week before the wedding, he disappeared. When I went to his parents to find out where he went, they said he was chasing gold out West." She took a deep breath and let out a weary sigh. "He didn't say goodbye or even write to explain. He just left me alone, brokenhearted."

She looked up at Abram. "When I met you, and we first danced, you told me all about your hopes and dreams, and I saw the same tendency in your heart. It made me angry and afraid." She removed her hand from his hold. "I wanted to stay as far away from you as possible because I believed you would follow in my father's and Thomas's footsteps."

So that was why she had turned a cold shoulder toward him—but couldn't she see he wasn't her father or Thomas?

"When you started calling on Susanne, I tried to convince her to stay away from you—because I wanted to protect her." More tears appeared and this time she didn't wipe them away. "I thank God that we were able to resume correspondence—but when I learned she had died, just like my mother, I—" She choked on the word and put her face in her hands. Her curls cascaded down her cheeks. "I blamed you, Abram—and...and I blame you still. I want to blame Susanne, but she was blinded by your charm and couldn't see the truth, as I could." She looked at him, disillusionment in her eyes. "I have to guard myself against the pain you're capable of inflicting—and that scares me more than anything in this world."

Anger set in, hot and fiery beneath his skin. "I never set out to blind Susanne. I fell in love with her, and she with me."

"But you had nothing to offer her—didn't you see that this life was not fit for her?"

Nothing to offer. He still had nothing to offer.

"I tried to make both of you see," Charlotte said. "I knew what would happen, if you had only listened. You married too fast."

"We married quickly, because of you." There, he'd finally admitted the truth. "You pushed us toward eloping, Charlotte. The very thing that hurt you most is the thing you created by your stubbornness and unwillingness to bend. You thought you were doing the right thing, but you were only creating more strife—just as you're doing with Harry."

She inhaled.

"You can blame Susanne and me for running away and leaving you alone, but you should ask yourself what part you played in the whole ordeal. Susanne and I didn't know the outcome—I didn't know much of anything, except that I loved her." He stood and looked down at Charlotte. "I'm not ashamed of having a dream and taking a risk. I'm not ashamed of asking Susanne to marry me and bringing her here. I blame myself for many things—but I never set out to hurt her, or anyone else."

"Of course you didn't." Charlotte also stood, desperation in her voice. "You didn't plan to hurt Susanne, just as you don't plan to hurt your boys—but I'm afraid you will, Abram, in time, just as my father did." She swallowed hard. "You'll become tired of this town when it starts to become more work than play. I can already see it happening. You'll start getting an itch inside and you'll look toward the horizon to see what new adventures await, if you haven't already."

His jaw became hard and he took several deep breaths. "Maybe it's time you went back to Iowa City."

She shook her head, tears and pain in her voice. "I wouldn't go back now—not when the boys need me. I won't leave until there is a school for Robert to attend, and a doctor to see to their needs, and a preacher to help bring hope to the desperadoes filling the shanty saloon—including Harry."

Her stubbornness knew no bounds.

"Fine," he said. "You can stay and watch me prove you wrong."

Her shoulders loosened and she leaned forward, her eyes desperate. "I wish you would, Abram. I really wish you would." With that, she turned and walked toward the house.

Abram resisted the need to chase her and convince her now, in this moment, that she was wrong. That he wasn't a villain and that if she'd let him, he would do whatever it would take to win her approval and heal her heart.

Because despite the fact he told himself it didn't matter what Charlotte thought, it always had—more now than ever before.

The following three weeks slipped by much as the weeks before and Charlotte found the months of June and July to be the most beautiful of all in Minnesota. Wildflowers grew in a profusion of pinks, purples and yellows along the riverbanks, wild strawberries filled the untouched plots of land and wildlife teemed on and above the water.

She stood outside in the sunshine, a cloudless sky hanging overhead, and draped the last bedsheet on the line to dry. Her gaze wandered up the hill toward the town and she couldn't help but wonder where Abram was and what was occupying his time. He worked from sunup to sundown, and sometimes even later. There were mornings, like this one, when he left the house before she was awake, and evenings when he came in hours after she went to bed.

After the dance they had barely spoken to each other, or seen each other for more than a moment or two—and she was grateful. After spilling her heart to him, and revealing the depths of her mistrust, she didn't blame him for his anger.

She stopped and wiped her hands on her apron as George toddled around her basket and Martin played with her clothespins, using them like little soldiers. Robert sat off by himself, under a large oak tree, its leaves unfurled and sheltering him from the sun, holding a book Charlotte had ordered for him. It was full of maps from around the world, and filled with colorful paintings from different countries, showing clothing and food and culture. She had found in him an insatiable desire to learn, and she wanted to seize that curiosity and to use it to propel him on to great things. Already, he had learned how to read three- and four-letter words, and was proving to be a bright young boy.

"Yoo-hoo! Miss Lee!" Mrs. Perry appeared at the head of the old wagon road, which was now dubbed First Avenue and ran from the mill up to the Hubbards' new home and beyond. Mrs. Perry waved her hand to attract Charlotte's attention. "Do you have a minute?"

Charlotte had grown used to neighbors stopping in to chat. In a town with only a few dozen women, they had quickly banded together and formed a tight-knit group. "Of course. I'm just finishing."

Mrs. Perry came down the hill, her cheeks flushed and her green eyes shining. She wore a pretty dress and her hair was styled in a neat twist. Her appearance never failed to impress Charlotte, who stood in a work dress, her apron and bodice wet and stained from laundry.

"I couldn't wait to tell you the news." Mrs. Perry placed her hand on Charlotte's arm, breathing hard.

It seemed every day brought some news or another—usually on the lips of Mrs. Perry, who had proved to be a woman of many words. Of interest recently was the arrival of the first newspaper, the *Northern Herald*, which had started printing the very day it was assembled. Before that, it had been the arrival of Mr. Hall, the first attorney in town.

"Would you like to come in for coffee?" Charlotte asked. "I made molasses cookies."

"No, no." Mrs. Perry shook her head, her hands moving to her hips as she panted. "I want to share the news and then scoot over to Mrs. O'Dell's house to tell her. These sorts of things have a way of spreading fast, and I do so enjoy being the first to share them."

Charlotte smiled to herself, wondering why Mrs. Perry hadn't gone into the newspaper business herself. If this news was so important that the woman wouldn't stop for cookies, it must be serious. Charlotte rested her hand on George's head as he toddled past. "What is it?"

"A second hotel is going up—the American Hotel—and I've heard there's already competition between the builder, Mr. Allen, and Mr. Richardson."

That was the news she was so eager to share? "Already? Neither hotel is even ready to be occupied."

"No, but they're both vying to hold the first real ball in town, so they've hired more men to complete their buildings, and the first to finish will host the ball."

"How nice."

"Oh, and maybe I should have led with this news, for it affects us all," Mrs. Perry said, almost breathless. "A Dr. Parker has arrived and purchased the store building on Main Street, across from the church building. He just put out his plaque today and has advertised his services to one and all in the *Northern Herald*. It's a relief to know we aren't dependent on the military doctor any longer."

"A doctor?" Charlotte wrapped her arms around her waist.

"He's brought a young wife and baby along with him. I'm eager to get over there and see what I can learn about them. I'll be sure to fill you in." She let out a contented breath and clasped her hands together. "There, I think that's all I have for now." She started off with a wiggle of her finger. "Happy wash day, Charlotte."

Charlotte lifted her limp hand and waved back.

A doctor.

Now all Abram needed was a preacher, and to finish the school.

The boys played contentedly in the warm sunshine, their blond hair shimmering and their cheeks tan. George looked up with his brown eyes and gurgled at Charlotte. He lifted a wooden clothespin toward his mouth and chewed on it as he waddled over to Martin and the band of soldiers marching through the grass.

"Hey!" Martin jumped up and reached for the clothespin in George's mouth. "Aunt Charlotte, George took one of my soldiers and he's eating him!" He wrestled it away and held it upside down as drool dripped off the end. "Eew! You put slobber all over my soldier, Georgie."

George giggled and clapped his hands.

Martin frowned at his brother but went back to his game, crowding around the clothespins, so George couldn't get to them.

Charlotte glanced at the sun and surmised it to be about ten o'clock. With two boardinghouses and a new restaurant in town, she no longer offered meals to laborers. Milt, Caleb and Josiah now worked for the Little Falls Company and boarded at a different home, so she rarely saw them. Abram ate all his meals away from home now, except supper, which she always kept on the back of the stove for him. It was just her and the boys most days—and she had over an hour before she'd need to prepare their dinner.

"Come, boys." She took off her apron and touched up her hair, signing to Robert, who glanced in her direction. "Let's go look around town." She longed to find Abram, and not just to discover how accurate Mrs. Perry's information had been. She and the boys had seen so little of him recently, she would use any excuse to seek him out.

Chapter Thirteen

Abram lifted his hammer, a whistle on his lips, as he pounded the next piece of clapboard siding on the schoolhouse. He had finally found some free time and would use it to make progress on the school.

"Cut the next piece at exactly twelve feet," Abram called to Caleb, who was measuring and cutting the siding.

Another week of work on the outside and the school would finally be enclosed. The shingles were all in place, and the copula built, ready for the school bell, which should arrive any day. After the siding was finished, they'd start on the inside. Next month, when Cheney came to visit, Abram would request funds for a blackboard, desks and schoolbooks. In about five weeks' time, their new teacher would arrive and school could start.

Abram let out a satisfied sigh and hammered the next nail into the wall.

Now, if only he had a preacher to fill his church, he'd have everything in place to keep the boys.

Which meant Charlotte would leave, probably for good.

He stopped whistling as he lifted the next nail into place.

It was such a long journey from Iowa City to Little Falls, Charlotte would likely never return—though maybe, one day, if Robert wanted, he could go to the deaf school in Iowa City. But that was so far in the future, Abram preferred not to think about it.

He aimed at the nail but missed, hitting his thumb. "Ow!" He put his throbbing thumb in his mouth, tasting the metallic flavor of the nails.

"It's been a while since you've done that," Caleb said with a grin. "Mind preoccupied?"

"Give me more nails." Abram took a handful from Caleb and slipped them into the pouch at his waist. He positioned the next nail and hit it square on the head.

A slender shadow with a full skirt fell across the siding and three smaller shadows hovered around it.

His family.

A smile tilted his lips as he turned to look at them, shading his eyes with his hand. "This is a pleasant surprise. What brings the four of you downtown?" He signed the question, but Robert was too busy looking around to see Abram.

Charlotte's gaze swept over the school and then rested on him, and his heart did a little leap. She looked pretty today, her hair windswept and her cheeks pink. He had been doing a good job keeping his distance, but it felt good to have her close again.

"Mrs. Perry visited and said a doctor has moved into town," Charlotte said.

Abram sobered. "It's true."

"How long have you known?"

"Just found out this morning."

Charlotte was silent for a moment as she nibbled her bottom lip.

Martin held a clothespin in his hand, which meant it must be washing day. With all the work lately, he had lost track of time.

"Do you have any leads on a pastor?" she asked.

"Not yet. Hubbard has sent out several letters and has a few prospects, though." The truth was, he hadn't heard a word from any of the preachers Hubbard had contacted, but he was hopeful.

Charlotte looked at George and put her hand on his plump cheek, a sad smile on her lips. "I think we'll look around town and then go visit Pearl for a bit."

Abram stood and hooked his hammer in the tool belt on his hip. "I'd be happy to show you around." The schoolhouse could wait for one more afternoon. Charlotte wouldn't be with them forever.

Charlotte placed her free hand around Robert's shoulder and pulled him closer to her side. She didn't answer immediately—but then, why would she? They'd hardly spoken in weeks.

Her words from the night of the dance still taunted him, especially on days when the work became so wearisome he'd give anything to go back to the simplicity of operating his small farm and sawmill. He had dreamed of a great city but, like all dreams, it required hard work and dedication. Things he thought he had in great supply but realized were lacking when he needed them most. If he'd had a wife at home to lean on and share his burdens, he suspected it might be a different story. He longed to let the cares and worries melt away at the soft and comforting touch of a wife's hand—but it wasn't to be.

She looked up at him and nodded. "I'd like that."

Abram inhaled a breath of fresh air and nodded. "I would, too. Just give me a moment." He unhooked his tool belt.

"Abram!" Hubbard appeared across the road. "Can I have a word with you?"

Abram paused and glanced at Charlotte, disappointment tightening his chest.

"Go ahead," Charlotte said. "We'll see you tonight." She took Martin's hand and turned toward the Hubbard home.

Timothy Hubbard crossed the road, tipped his hat at Charlotte and then nodded at Abram. "Let's head over to the company store."

Abram handed his tool belt to Caleb. "Keep going until I get back."

"Actually." Hubbard's jaw was taught. "That's one of the things we need to talk about. Cheney wants all work to stop on extraneous ventures—including the schoolhouse—until we have more cash flow."

"Extraneous ventures?" Abram sighed, knowing it was useless to argue. He took his tool belt back and nodded at Caleb. "The men could use your help on the gristmill roof. Why don't you head over there?"

Caleb didn't ask any questions, but moved around Hubbard and walked south toward the old wagon road leading to the sawmill and new gristmill.

Abram and Hubbard crossed Main Street and followed the road leading to the company store. The square building had a false front, large plate-glass windows and a green-and-white-striped awning already in place. Besides the church, Abram's farm and the Hubbard home, it was the only finished building in town.

They pushed through the front door and were met

by the jingling of a bell. The new store manager stood behind the long counter. Having him in place had freed up some of Abram's time, but had allowed Abram to take on more work elsewhere.

They walked through the disorganized merchandise and went to the back room where Abram's desk sat littered with paperwork. In their company agreement, Hubbard saw to the accounting and bookwork, while managing real estate sales. Abram was in charge of the sawmill, the new gristmill and the company store. Paperwork was the last of his worries, so it continued to pile up on his desk.

Abram hung his tool belt on the back of a chair and sat behind his desk. "What's going on?"

Hubbard took a seat and let out a weary sigh. "I just returned from St. Anthony, and Cheney was livid."

"Livid? Why?"

"I brought the books with me and he pored over them for hours, questioning every decision we've made. He noticed I had purchased logs, which I plan to use to build a public house and boardwalks. He saw your purchase for the school bell and the cross for the church."

"Those are all necessary."

"He believes they can wait. He thinks we need to put more money into expanding the sawmill and enlarging the dam. Lumber is in such demand and he wants to see several saws going."

"If we don't have a school, how will we encourage families to come to town?"

"I agree. A public house is also needed. There are several projects I'd like to see completed to enhance the town's image. Without people, we have no town."

"Does Cheney expect me to stop building the school-house altogether? We have a teacher coming in August."

Hubbard's bald head gleamed from the sunshine streaming through the lone window. "He won't be here until next month, but he's demanded that we stop all extraneous work until he comes and looks for himself. Until then, he wants us to devote our time to the sawmill and gristmill and dam—projects that will actually make us money."

Abram rose and began to pace across his small office. "And if we don't?"

Hubbard sighed. "He said he'll pull his funding."

Cheney's financial support held up over half of their operations—without it, the entire company, and community, would collapse.

Abram paused and gripped the back of his chair. If he had more money, he'd do it himself, but he didn't have a penny to his name. Every last dime was poured back into the company. "It looks like we'll be working on the mills and the dam until further notice." If Cheney came at the end of August, it would put him much too close to Charlotte's September first deadline—but what choice did he have?

Other than Cheney, the only person he knew with money was Charlotte—and she was the last person he would ask.

Charlotte sat inside the church building on the third Sunday in July, reveling in the fresh pine scent of the gleaming new boards. Soft light filtered in through the wavy glass windows, washing over the eager congregants gathered within. The morning was much warmer than usual and the day promised to bring intense heat, but for now, Charlotte sat inside and basked in the presence of the Lord.

Dozens of familiar faces, and some new ones, encircled the church. Robert sat to Charlotte's left, allowing her to interpret the whole service using sign language. Martin sat on her right, between her and Abram, and George sat on Abram's lap. They were offered the front bench on the left and the Hubbards sat on the front bench on the right, their three children surrounding them.

Ben had appeared on Saturday and, finding the new town, had readily volunteered to hold the first church meeting in the new building. Charlotte had shared the news with Mrs. Perry and today over fifty people were in attendance.

Ben read from Psalm 118:24. "'This is the day which the Lord hath made; we will rejoice and be glad in it.'" His dark brown eyes looked out over the congregation and stopped on Abram. "God has planted seeds in the heart soil of His people, and He requires us to water and nurture those seeds with His word and through prayer. If attended to properly, when fully grown, they produce a harvest of fruit, which we can offer to the hungry here on earth.

"This church is the fruit of a seed planted in the heart of Abram Cooper. Through Mr. Cooper's unwavering faith and dedication to God's call, he saw this town spring forth from the wilderness. And, as a dedication to God, he built this building."

Abram squirmed in his seat and adjusted his tie, unable to meet Reverend Lahaye's penetrating gaze.

"What dream has God planted in your heart?" the reverend asked, searching the crowd. "What dream do you need to nurture and water, so it can produce a harvest? I urge you to ask God this question, and seek His answer." He offered a gentle, inviting smile. "I will leave you with this passage from Psalm 37:3–5. 'Trust in the Lord, and do good; so shalt thou dwell in the land, and verily thou shalt be fed. Delight thyself also in the Lord: and He shall give thee the desires of thine heart. Commit thy way unto the Lord; trust also in Him; and He shall bring it to pass.' Let us pray."

It was good to see Ben again. He wore his customary clothing, and his two long braids. Charlotte guessed him to be in his late twenties, but his youthful face and joyful disposition gave him a slightly younger countenance. He was a handsome man and Charlotte had watched several women take notice.

He had bunked with Abram and the boys the night before and had joined them for breakfast, but Charlotte was eager to return home for the noon meal, and spend time with him and Abram. She still recalled the Christmas they'd spent together with fondness.

Ben finished his prayer and the group stood for one final hymn. They sang Charlotte's favorite, "Amazing Grace," and then Ben exited the church and waited on the front steps to greet everyone as they left the building.

It had been a humble service with no piano or organ, no choir or hymnals. But it had been heartfelt and had offered nourishment to parched souls.

Charlotte waited for Abram to leave their pew, but he stood, staring at the cross hanging on the whitewashed wall behind the simple pulpit.

The room filled with the voices of their friends and neighbors, but Abram didn't move to speak with any of them. Instead he took a deep breath. "There are two things I regret in my life," he said quietly, and she had to lean closer to hear.

"Only two?" she inquired with a smile.

He glanced at her and offered a half smile, but lines edged his mouth and eyes. "Two that stand out to me at this moment."

She wasn't sure she wanted to hear his confession but she had nowhere to go.

"I regret not marrying Susanne in a church—and not having a church for her funeral."

Heaviness smothered Charlotte's previous joy and her smile faded. Susanne would have loved this church and loved to see what Abram had accomplished. It still didn't seem fair that her sister had died so young. Charlotte swallowed back a lump in her throat. "There are two things I regret in my life, as well."

Abram met her gaze, his countenance heavy. "What do you regret, Charlotte?"

"Not being at Susanne's wedding and not being at her funeral." In the past she would have reminded him that he had been the cause of these regrets—but not anymore. After their conversation on the night of the dance, she had come to realize she was just as much to blame—if not more so.

"Today is the anniversary of her death," Abram said with a deep sigh. "It's hard to believe she's been gone a year."

How had she forgotten? Guilt and grief choked Charlotte and threatened to cut off her breath. "Today I'll take the boys out and we'll pick some flowers and put them on her grave."

Abram's blue eyes lit with a smile, even though it didn't quite reach his mouth. "May I join you?"

"Of course."

He studied Charlotte for a moment. "I never would have imagined one year ago that I'd be standing in a church, in the middle of this town, with you by my side."

A smile tickled her lips. "Imagine what I would have thought a year ago?"

He readjusted George in his arms and offered Charlotte a tender look. "I think Susanne would be very happy to see us together—reconciled."

Reconciled? Was the word too strong for their tenuous relationship? "I just wish it hadn't taken her death for me to realize so much of this had been my fault."

"Charlotte, don't." He turned and fully faced her. "Don't blame yourself. There's no one to blame. I said those things after the dance because I was hurt."

"No." She shook her head. "You were right. I push too hard."

"Sometimes pushing is a good thing." He used his free hand to indicate the building. "If you hadn't pushed me, none of this would be here."

She glanced around the church and her mood became somber. "If you find a full-time preacher, this building means..." She swallowed and couldn't continue.

"Let's not dwell on that right now," Abram said. "I'd rather try to enjoy this beautiful day and let all my troubles be forgotten for now."

It did feel good to be speaking to him so freely again. "I won't mention it...at least not today."

He smiled and his eyes crinkled at the corners.

"There you are." Ben entered the church and Charlotte realized they were standing in an empty building. Martin had gone to the front of the room and was standing behind the pulpit, murmuring snippets of scripture he had memorized. Robert sat on the bench, holding Charlotte's Bible in his hands, studying the words, and George had fallen asleep on Abram's shoulder.

"Are you ready to join us for dinner?" Charlotte asked.

"I've been looking forward to it all morning." Ben's handsome gaze rested on her face and she felt heat rise to her cheeks.

"Come, Martin," she called and then touched Robert on the shoulder and motioned for him to follow.

They left the church and walked down the wagon road to their home.

Somehow, over the past eight and a half months, it had stopped being Abram's home and had somehow become "theirs," though she knew it could never truly belong to her. Her home was waiting in Iowa, along with her new dress shop. She had tried to daydream about the shop and how she would decorate and operate her business, but it had been hard to concentrate on a place so far removed from her current situation.

But today she wouldn't think of her inevitable departure from Minnesota Territory, or wonder, for the thousandth time, if she was going alone or taking the boys.

They entered the house and were greeted with the scent of roasted chicken. Charlotte shooed the men and children outside to enjoy the day and went into the kitchen to finish dinner preparations. She had put the bird in the oven early that morning, so when she pulled it out of the pot, it fell off the bone. She had also roasted some potatoes, and quickly whipped up some gravy. The biscuits were still fresh from Saturday's baking and there were fresh greens from the garden she and the boys had planted early that spring.

"Do you need any help?" Abram entered the kitchen and, for a moment, it felt like last winter, when it had been just the two of them and the boys, before Hubbard had partnered with Abram.

"I could use your help setting the table."

"It would be my pleasure."

While Abram set the table, Charlotte stole an appreciative glance at him and caught him looking at her. He smiled and she felt her cheeks bloom with heat.

Reconciliation. Maybe it was possible.

Chapter Fourteen

Abram sat at the head of his table, enjoying the easy conversation between him, Charlotte and Ben. It had been many months since he had taken the time to simply sit down and visit with friends. The meal sat with satisfaction in his stomach and Charlotte's coffee warmed his hand through the speckled mug. They had left the dirty dishes on the table, so deep in conversation that no one had noticed.

"And what do you think of Mr. O'Sullivan's idea of Manifest Destiny, Reverend Lahaye?" Charlotte asked.

Ben leaned forward, his eyes flirting with her. "I told you to call me Ben… Charlotte."

Charlotte's cheeks filled with color, just as they did every time Ben teased her or showered her with attention—which had been all afternoon. "All right, Ben."

Ben leaned back in his chair. "I believe in Manifest Destiny as an idea, but not as a government policy," he said. "I believe, as Christians, we are commissioned to go and make disciples of all the nations, and I believe that every knee shall bow and every tongue confess— but do I believe it is the job of the American government to conquer this vast land, with the idea of ultimate control? No, especially if it means the spread of slavery and forcing my mother's people onto reservations." He paused, as if to gather his thoughts. "But I do believe that eventually this land will be full from sea to sea, and there is no way to stop it now."

The boys had been put down for a nap, which allowed the adults the freedom to visit, and Abram sensed Charlotte was in need of this time. He had never seen her so animated—except for the few times he'd watched her dance. She was an intelligent woman and it was fun to hear her thoughts.

She leaned forward. "What do you think of—"

"No more questions." Ben laughed, putting up his hands. "At least not for me. I'd rather learn more about you. It's my turn to ask questions."

She met his gaze with an air of good-natured challenge. "What would you like to know... Ben?"

Ben rested his elbow on the table and put his chin in his hand. "I'd love to know everything there is to know about you, Charlotte."

Abram didn't like the intimate turn in the conversation—or the fact that he felt as if he had been forgotten. He stood quickly. "Ben, I'd like your help with something outside."

Ben and Charlotte both turned to look at him.

"Now?" Ben asked. "It's Sunday. A day of rest—and I was just starting to get to know Charlotte."

"It's nothing hard...just." Just what? What excuse could he make for tearing Ben away from Charlotte's company? "I need to replace a hinge on the privy door."

"Abram," Charlotte chastised, her eyes growing wide.

"Can't Harry do that tomorrow? We were enjoying a nice conversation."

Abram took Ben's coffee mug out of his hand. "I need to talk to Ben—in private."

"At the privy?" Ben asked with a raised brow.

"Abram!" Charlotte said again.

"No." Abram scratched his head, irritation making his pulse jump. "I just need you to come with me." He had to resist the urge to haul Ben out by the nape of his neck. "We'll be back soon, Charlotte."

She stood and started clearing the table, casting a strange look at Abram, but didn't ask any more questions.

Abram strode out the lean-to door and walked around the house. He glanced back only once to make sure Ben was following.

"What's this about, Abram?"

Abram walked to the river, wanting to be as far away from the house as possible. "I need to speak to you about something."

"You couldn't talk to me in front of Charlotte?"

Abram shook his head. "It has something to do with her."

They sat on the bank of the river. Heat penetrated the air and humidity saturated their skin. Abram took off his jacket and rolled up his sleeves. The sun made the heat even more unbearable. Maybe he should have taken Ben to the shade of a willow tree.

Ben leaned his elbows on his upright knees. "What's going on, Abram?"

Abram took a deep breath. "I need a favor."

"Anything."

Abram wished it was that easy. "This one is probably more than a favor. It's a sacrifice, really."

Ben watched him carefully. "Go on."

"I need a full-time preacher in the church…or Charlotte will take my boys back to Iowa with her."

"What?" Ben dropped his arms. "What are you talking about?"

Abram quickly told him about their arrangement. "I have a teacher and a doctor—now I just need a preacher."

"And you need to finish the school."

"That's the least of my worries. I can figure out how to do that—but I can't seem to find a full-time preacher."

Ben shook his head. "You know I'd like to help—but I'm not called to stay in one location. I'm able to reach more people by traveling." He laughed. "I wouldn't even know what to do with myself if I stayed in one place. I haven't lived in a house for more than a week at any given time in the past ten years."

"I can't let her take the boys back to Iowa—it would be like losing Susanne all over again. Those boys mean everything to me. I built this town for them—everything I do is for them. I can't lose them now."

"Then tell Charlotte you've changed your mind."

"I can't do that, either. She's already given up eight months of her life and put her business on hold to help me and fulfill her end of the deal. I don't know what I would have done without her this year. She single-handedly fed over sixty men three square meals a day, every day, for months. If I withdrew now, I couldn't live with the guilt."

"So then let her take the boys to Iowa."

"Didn't you hear me? That's not an option, either. I have to find a preacher."

"If you find one, she'll leave then, won't she?" His dark eyes studied Abram. "Is that something you're willing to accept?"

"It's the only choice I have."

"Abram, what you ask of me is something I cannot decide quickly. I would have to pray and ask the Lord if it's something He would have me do." Ben looked toward the hill and to the church, sitting on the corner of Main Street and the old wagon road. "I confess it was nice to be in a building today and see so many people who could become my flock. And when I rode by the shanty last night, and saw all those men coming and going, I felt a pressure on my spirit to reach out to them." He stopped and squinted, as if in thought. "I will pray about your request."

"You will?" It wasn't yes, but it also wasn't no, either. At this point it felt like progress. "Keep in mind, it doesn't mean you can't travel and minister to people in the area."

Ben nodded.

A sliver of hope wiggled inside Abram's heart. "I will pray, as well. And you can stay here as long as you need to think it over."

Ben was quiet for a few moments and then he lifted his knee and wrapped his arms around it. "Now, I have a question."

"What's that?"

"Do you think there is any chance?" He paused and then hesitantly went on. "Do you think Charlotte might consider staying in Little Falls?"

Abram was silent as he contemplated the question.

"I don't believe there is. She is set on returning to Iowa City and opening a dress shop."

"Do you think she might be persuaded to stay?" Ben asked.

"I really don't know." Abram had known Ben for five years and, in all that time, he'd never been afraid to talk frankly. "Why are you asking?"

Ben offered a sheepish smile. "Isn't it obvious?"

His answer felt like a punch out of nowhere.

"Since she has no other family," Ben continued, "are you the one I need to ask to call on her?"

"Me?" Abram stood quickly. "She is a grown woman. I'm the last person you need to ask."

Ben also stood. "Do you think I have a chance?"

Abram ran his hand over his hair and scratched the back of his neck. "Let's not keep Charlotte waiting."

"My sentiments exactly." Ben started toward the house before Abram could get his feet to work.

In all the scenarios Abram had envisioned, he'd never imagined Charlotte staying in Little Falls to marry one of his best friends.

Could he stand by and watch that happen? At this point, what choice did he have? He had no claim on her heart.

Charlotte usually loved any work that brought her outside, especially in the last part of August, when the weather was close to perfect. But today her heart was too heavy to enjoy the beautiful day. They were only one week away from the first of September, and she would be leaving on the stage…if the schoolteacher arrived, and if the schoolhouse was complete.

Today was Friday, which meant she was cleaning the

house, and she had brought the rugs outside to beat on the clothesline. It afforded her the opportunity to be in the sunshine and to watch the activity at the top of the hill. Now that Main Street had filled in, she could only see the back side of most of the buildings.

Charlotte used all her upper body strength to beat the rugs with the flat metal rug beater. The dust fluffed into the air with each thwack and she had to stop to wipe the sweat from her brow.

George was taking a nap, while Robert and Martin were collecting eggs in the henhouse. Now that Robert could freely communicate, he threw fewer tantrums and had proved to be a gentle boy with an easy smile and a tender heart. Martin, on the other hand, was quick to fight and often disobeyed. But, Charlotte had to remind herself, he had just celebrated his fourth birthday and had a lot to learn.

Harry appeared near the barn door, a shovel in hand. He didn't notice Charlotte, or if he did, he ignored her. He went to the pigpen, where a post had come loose, and proceeded to fix the problem.

Charlotte hit the rag rug one more time and then took all the rugs off the line and set them in her basket. She lifted the basket and rested it on her hip, standing for a moment to watch Harry. Every day, when he came to get his food, Charlotte offered him a smile and tried to start a conversation, but without fail, Harry grunted or scowled, or simply turned away without acknowledging her.

What would he do if she approached him? Would it be more of the same treatment? If she was leaving in a week, she needed to set things right between them.

Charlotte focused her sights ahead and marched

across Wood Street, directly to the pigpen. "Hello, Harry."

Harry turned, his eyes growing round and then narrowing. "What do you want?"

What was the point of small talk? "I want you to forgive my rash behavior last year and start joining the rest of us in the kitchen again."

Harry stopped his work and stood, slowly, mistrust written all over his face. "What did you say?"

She repositioned the basket on her other hip. "I'd like your forgiveness." She swallowed hard, forcing herself to say the next words. "I was wrong about the way I treated you." Though, she wasn't wrong about why she had done it. She should have simply thought of a different way to encourage him to go to church.

"You were wrong?" He leaned on the shovel, his freckled face squinting in the bright sunshine. He looked baffled, as if maybe she was trying to play a trick on him.

"I still hope that one day you'll choose to reform your ways and start going to church, but it's not my place to convict you." She had served many men at her table over the winter, and she had no idea what state their hearts were in, yet she had welcomed them all. Why should it be any different for Harry?

"You're saying I can eat in the kitchen with you, regardless of whether or not I go to church?"

She smiled and nodded. "Yes."

"No." He shoved the spade into the ground with a hard thrust.

Her smile fell. "No?"

"I wouldn't sit at your table if it was the last table in this territory." He stopped and glared at her. "I'm sure you had some religious revelation that made you think you're ready to offer me mercy—but save it for church, lady. Did you ever stop to think I was choosing not to eat at your table? All these months, you thought you were denying me access, but I was the one who was choosing not to eat with you." He went back to work and didn't bother to look at her. "I'm counting down the days until you get out of this town, so I don't have to look at your face anymore."

Charlotte had never been slapped before, but she imagined this was how it would feel. Her cheeks burned and embarrassment sliced through her chest. She swallowed several times but couldn't find the wherewithal to move her feet. "I—I'm sorry you feel that way, Harry."

He snorted. "I'm sure you are."

"Aunt Charlotte, I broke an egg on accident!" Martin called out. "And Robert's crying."

Charlotte turned from Harry and walked slowly across Wood Street and over to the chicken coop. Robert held a broken egg in his little hands, tears streaming down his cheeks.

A thick blanket of melancholy slipped over Charlotte's shoulders as she set down the basket and knelt in front of Robert. "It's okay," she signed.

"Baby chicken," Robert signed.

Charlotte shook her head, her throat tight. "It wasn't a baby chicken yet."

"It could have been." Robert lifted the broken shell, signing as the yellow yolk slid down his arm. "Not anymore. Martin broke it and I can't fix it."

Martin stood by, the realization of his actions sinking in as his eyes grew bigger.

Charlotte hugged Robert and then wiped his hands with her apron.

She caught a glimpse of Harry, working near the pigpen. Was he like the delicate egg, broken and irreparable? Had she cracked him further?

Lord, I thank You that we are not like eggshells that once broken are irreparable. I thank You that You are the God who heals and fixes, and like the fence Harry is repairing, can be useful again. Please forgive me for my part in Harry's brokenness, and help me to be a light in the darkness for him. Amen.

"Let's go inside and have a cookie," Charlotte said to the boys. "And I'll tell you all about how chickens are made."

The boys ran ahead into the kitchen, but a man's approach on Wood Street made Charlotte pause in the doorway—and smile. "Hello, Ben."

He returned the smile and it warmed Charlotte all the way through. Ben had been staying with them for nearly five weeks, and had conducted services in the church on several Sundays. He didn't tell Charlotte why he had chosen to stay in Little Falls for so long, but he spent his days helping Abram, for which Abram had been very grateful.

Ben drew close and his gaze rested gently on her face. "You don't like wearing a bonnet, do you?"

"How could you tell?"

He reached out and touched the tip of her nose. "You have freckles."

She brought her free hand up and covered her nose. "No—do I?"

He laughed. "I think they are very becoming."

Something about Ben drew her to him. Maybe it was

his quiet confidence, or his deep faith. Maybe it was the fact that, though he was a wanderer, unlike her father and Thomas, there was purpose in his wandering. He wasn't chasing the next scheme, but was chasing after the heart of God.

She sensed his attraction to her, but that wasn't what drew her. There were several men in town that paid special attention to her, but she didn't return their affection—not like she did with Ben.

Whatever it was, she had enjoyed his time with them.

He took off his hat and held it to his chest. "Do you have a moment to talk?"

"I will gladly make a moment." She indicated her basket of rugs. "Let me set this down and give the boys some cookies."

He nodded and followed her into the house. She left the basket in the lean-to and then took four sugar cookies out of a cookie jar and handed two to each of the boys.

"That should keep them busy for a few moments." She wiped her hands and found Ben fiddling with his hat. "Shall we go into the other room?"

"I'd like that." He followed her out of the kitchen and closed the door.

"What can I do for you?" she asked. He had mentioned at one point that it might be nice to have curtains on the windows in the church, to close them when the sun was especially bright. "Do you need help picking out fabric for the church?"

He took a step toward her and then hesitated, as if uncertain. "This isn't about the church—well, not really."

It was the first time she had seen him look insecure. She placed her hand on his arm. "What is it, Ben?"

He looked down at her hand and then tentatively placed his over hers. "I'd like to speak plainly to you, Charlotte."

Her heart thudded against her breastbone. She wanted to remove her hand from his but wasn't sure how to do it tactfully. "Of course. Shall we sit?"

He nodded and she moved away from his hold, thankful for the space between them. She indicated Abram's chair and then took a seat in hers.

Ben sat and looked at the ground for a moment. Finally he glanced up. "I have a big decision to make, and it largely depends on what you say in the next several minutes."

Charlotte's hand fluttered to her chest. "What I say?"

He scooted forward on his chair. "Charlotte, ever since the day I met you, I've admired you." He paused and swallowed, as if redirecting his approach. "Abram has asked me to stay here and pastor the church, and I told him I would have to think and pray about the decision."

"You'd give up your travels?"

He moved so far forward, he came off his chair and bent down on his knee in front of her.

She backed up as he reached for her hand. "I would, if you'd agree to marry me," he said. "I never considered marriage, because of my transient lifestyle, but if I stay in one place, I would desire marriage—marriage to you."

Charlotte inhaled.

"I've prayed about this decision," Ben said, his handsome face lighting with a smile. "And I believe this is the right thing for me to do."

"Ben." She wished she could catch her breath. "I don't know what to say."

"Then don't say anything yet." He gently rubbed her

hand. "It took me over a month to come to this decision. I couldn't very well ask you to make yours quickly. I know you'll want to pray and seek the Lord."

She stood, forcing him to stand, too. "I have plans to go back to Iowa City."

"Plans can change." He grinned. "Isn't my revelation proof? I thought I'd live and die on the trail, but sometimes our plans are not God's plans."

"Yes, but sometimes they are."

He nodded, his face growing serious. "You're right, and I would never ask you to go against God's will." He took a step back and lifted his hands. "It's up to you to seek Him and discover for yourself what His will is for your life. I don't want to pressure you."

She couldn't help but tease him. "You said you have a big decision to make, and it largely depends on what I say. You don't think that's pressure?"

He laughed, and it was good to see his confidence return. "You're right. I suppose that was a bit serious of me."

She took a deep breath. "So, you plan to stay on at the church?"

He twisted his hat. "I do."

"Which means Abram has his preacher, his teacher and his doctor."

"Now he need only finish the school."

Charlotte turned from him and looked out the window at the sawmill and new gristmill. "He's meeting with Mr. Cheney and Mr. Hubbard this afternoon, and he's going to request funds to complete the project."

"It looks as if you have a lot of seeking to do, Charlotte." Ben's voice was gentle.

Yes. With the last of her requirements in place, she

was faced with two decisions. Either return to Iowa City, alone, to start her business. Or stay here, with Ben, and become his wife, which would allow her to see her nephews on a regular basis.

It also meant she would see Abram, as well, unless he became restless and moved on to a new adventure. But she would be here for the boys if that happened, and that was the most important thing to consider.

Chapter Fifteen

"Go ahead and finish your school," Cheney said to Abram. "I suppose it's considered a necessary structure for a community."

Abram almost let out a sigh of relief. After several hours of heated debate about how to spend their capital, finally he and Cheney agreed on something.

"I only want the bare essentials," Cheney added, his large mustache twitching. "A chalkboard, benches and a stove. The families can provide their own primers."

"Benches?" Abram asked. "The children will need desks."

Cheney rapped his finger on the ledger sitting on Abram's desk. Hubbard had kept their records with meticulous accuracy. "We spent forty thousand dollars on logs over a month ago," Cheney said, "and they're sitting in the millpond waiting to be milled. Once the logs are milled and sold, you can have your desks, but not a minute sooner." Cheney glanced from Abram to Hubbard. "I'm warning both of you. All of this could fail in the blink of an eye if we're not careful. I know you're eager to make this an appealing community, but we must focus first on the necessary projects that will make us more money. Everything else will come in time."

"I think roads are necessary." Hubbard pointed at the ledger. "This expenditure is for the road running east of town where several people have started farming. We need a road for them to come to town, don't we?"

"If we have no lumber or flour to sell to them, what will it matter?" Cheney asked.

Abram stood, tired of the incessant arguing. "I'll finish the school and get the lumber milled, and then I'll focus my attention on expanding the dam."

"That's another thing," Cheney said, rising from his seat to look Abram in the eyes. "Without the dam, we have no power, and without power, we can't sell river lots to other entrepreneurs. We need that dam expanded across both the east and west channels of the river. Put men on the project right away."

"I can't oversee the project until I finish the sch—"

"The dam has top priority." Cheney closed the ledger and let out a frustrated breath. "I wish I wasn't needed in St. Anthony. I'd stay here and oversee it myself."

Abram reminded himself that he had invited these men to invest in his dream, not the other way around. He owed them a great deal and needed to keep them happy. "I'll get right to work on the dam in the morning, and I'll put some men on the school and the logs."

"Good." Cheney took his hat from the hook near the door. "I need to get going or I won't reach St. Anthony before nightfall. Goodbye, gentlemen. I'll be back next month."

Abram and Hubbard also grabbed their hats and the three men walked out together.

They said their goodbyes and then Abram turned

toward home. His insides felt wound up and his temper was short, but he'd held himself together during the long morning and afternoon.

Right now, all he wanted was to go home and see his children and tell Charlotte about the surprise he had waiting for her.

As Abram neared his house, Harry was by the pigpen, finally fixing the loose post. The mama pig and her piglets grunted inside and rolled around in the mud.

Harry glanced up and then looked back at his work. "I think it's time I take my leave, Abram."

Abram hitched his foot on the pen and leaned his elbows on his knee, not surprised by Harry's announcement. "For good?"

Harry stomped the dirt into place and nodded. "The place is getting too crowded. A man can't breathe with all these people crawling about. I didn't mind when it was just a few of us here. No one was telling me what to do or where to go or what to believe."

"Does this have something to do with Charlotte?"

Harry glanced at the house, but instead of the same look of disgust, Abram recognized fear in Harry's eyes. "I don't like when people go changing on me. It makes me uneasy."

"Changing?" Abram looked over at the house, too— just as Ben and Charlotte exited. Ben put his hat on and dipped his head at Charlotte. She remained near the open door, one hand on the knob. Something about the way she stood and interacted with Ben made Abram's pulse pick up speed.

"I think I'll pull out tomorrow," Harry said.

Abram looked back at Harry. "Tomorrow? Where will you go?"

"Duluth."

"Why Duluth?"

"Several men are getting rich mining copper. I heard there's an abundance of it up there. They're expecting a land rush, and I aim to be one of the first to stake a claim. I figure if someone gets to make money, it might as well be me."

Abram dropped his foot to the ground and put his hand on Harry's shoulder. "If I can't change your mind, I wish you well. I couldn't have done any of this without you."

Harry shrugged away from Abram's hand and started toward the barn without another word.

Ben and Charlotte still stood by the open door, their gazes intent on one another.

Abram strode across Wood Street and cleared his throat.

"Abram." Charlotte looked around Ben, but she didn't offer the smile he'd become accustomed to. "How was your meeting?"

"I got the money to finish the school. I hope to have it enclosed by the end of this week."

"That's good news," Ben said as he turned to Abram. "And I have more good news for you."

Abram looked between Charlotte and Ben, apprehension snaking around his throat. "What's that?"

"I've decided to accept your offer and stay at the church."

Abram grinned and reached for Ben's hand, pumping it up and down. "You will?"

Ben laughed. "I was just telling Charlotte."

Abram glanced at Charlotte, who was quieter than usual.

Of course—this meant he had achieved all his goals and just in time.

Abram dropped Ben's hand and became serious. "That's it, then."

"I suppose it is." Charlotte looked down. The toe of her shoe slipped out from under her skirt and played with the dirt. "You've done something I thought was impossible, and you did it much faster than I imagined." Her voice was filled with a mixture of sadness and respect.

"The teacher hasn't arrived yet," Abram said. "And the school isn't built." He dipped his head to get her to look at him. "It isn't September. There's still time for me to mess up."

She finally looked up at him and tried to offer him a smile, though her lips trembled.

"Charlotte." He itched to reach for her but felt the presence of Ben looming near.

Maybe Abram could cheer her. "I have a surprise for you."

"A surprise?"

"I'd like to take you out for supper."

Charlotte's eyebrows dipped. "Go out to eat?"

Abram chuckled. "Some people do that on occasion— especially in civilized societies like ours."

Charlotte's countenance brightened but then dimmed. "What about the boys?"

"I thought we could ask Mrs. Hubbard to watch them for the evening."

Charlotte glanced at Ben. "Would you like to come?"

Abram's smile fell. He hadn't anticipated a guest— but he should have realized he couldn't extend the invitation to Charlotte with Ben standing there, unless he wanted Ben to join them.

Ben glanced at Abram and then back at Charlotte. "How about I stay with the boys and you two can go enjoy the evening?"

"Are you sure?" Charlotte's voice dropped lower than normal.

Ben nodded. "I think you and Abram have a great deal to discuss."

She smiled at Ben. "Thank you."

"I feel like I'm on the outside, looking in." Abram crossed his arms. "Is there something I need to know?"

Ben looked at Charlotte, his eyes intense. "Is there?"

Charlotte shook her head and swallowed. "Not yet."

"What?" Abram asked, impatience rising up his spine.

Ben put his hand on Abram's shoulder. "Go and enjoy yourself. Take all the time you need. I'll stay with the boys."

Abram didn't like what was going on, even if he didn't know what it was—or especially because he didn't know.

"I'll go and change," Charlotte said. "There's bread, butter and fresh pickles in the pantry for supper, Ben. I hope that's okay."

"We'll be fine."

Charlotte offered Ben one last smile and then left the two men standing in the doorway.

"What was all that about?" Abram asked when she was out of sight.

Ben's face had become serious. He closed the door and stepped away from the house. "If Charlotte isn't ready to talk about it, then neither am I."

Alarm scattered throughout Abram's mind like little

fragments he couldn't pick up and put together. "Did you ask her to marry you?"

Ben glanced at Abram and then paced away, clearly not as confident as he had seemed in front of Charlotte. "If she wants to tell you, she may."

Abram took one giant step toward him and put his hands on Ben's chest to stop his pacing. "Did she say yes?"

Ben paused, clearly surprised by Abram's actions. "No. Not yet."

"So she's thinking about it?"

Ben nodded.

Abram dropped his hands and stared at his friend. "Do you think she'll say yes?"

"I hope she will—but I really don't know." Ben tilted his head toward the house. "Why don't you go inside and get ready? I'll see to the boys. Maybe I'll take them up to the Hubbards' after all, so they can play with the other children."

Abram walked away from Ben and entered the house, but he hardly saw anything in his path. What would he do if Charlotte said yes to Ben? It was hard enough to imagine Charlotte leaving…but even worse to imagine her staying as Ben's wife.

Charlotte put on the dark blue silk dress she wore the night of the barn dance. She didn't have time to curl her hair, but she did restyle it, using the ivory-handled brush Abram had given her for Christmas, securing it with several pins. Her hands shook as she pinched her cheeks and then slipped on her gloves.

Ben's proposal still echoed in her mind, giving her much to think on. She admired him, and found him to be handsome and kind—but that was all she felt. He didn't send her pulse skittering or cause her stomach to fill with butterflies at his appearance. She didn't look for him when he was gone, or try to be near him when he was present. She enjoyed their conversations, but he didn't challenge her—not like Abram did.

Could she marry a man she didn't love? Many people did, and some found happiness—but could she? It would allow her to be near the boys and to be present if they needed her.

A knock sounded at her door. "Are you ready?"

Abram.

She closed her eyes and willed her heart to stop fluttering. It was simply a dinner, like all the other meals they had eaten together.

So why was she so nervous? Why did she anticipate the evening with excitement and dread?

"One minute, please."

She looked at her reflection and took several deep breaths. Abram was all wrong for her. She couldn't allow herself to even contemplate these feelings budding up inside. She must force her guard up once again and resist the twinkling in his eyes, the teasing in his tone. She must not notice the way his hair curled at the nape of his neck or how his voice dipped deeper when he laughed.

She must simply not think of Abram.

Charlotte opened the door, determination making her bold, and stopped short, her breath catching in her throat.

Abram leaned up against the door frame leading into his room, his hands in his pockets, his feet crossed at the ankles. He had shaved, giving his face a youthful look, and combed his hair to the side. When she appeared, he stood straight and the look in his eyes made her knees grow weak.

"Charlotte." He took a step toward her, his eyes roaming her appearance. "You're...beautiful."

Every reasonable thought left her and all she could think about was how wonderful it felt to be noticed by him. For far too long she had tried to resist the feelings his compliments elicited, but at the moment, she wanted to bask in his praise. "Thank you."

His eyes filled with pleasure and he grinned. "You're welcome." He extended his arm toward the stairs. "Shall we?"

She took a tentative step into the hall, hoping her legs would hold her up, and then she descended the steps, as carefully as she could, breathing a sigh of relief when she made it to the bottom without tripping.

He came down after her and together they walked into the kitchen. Charlotte glanced around the empty room. "Where did Ben and the children go?"

"He took them up to the Hubbards' for the evening, so they could play with the other children."

"That was kind of him."

Something darkened Abram's mood and he didn't respond. Instead he opened the door and extended his elbow. She hesitated for only a moment and then slipped her gloved hand around his arm.

They took their time and walked up the old wagon road toward Main Street and then turned left. A new restaurant sat across the street from the Northern Hotel and, from all appearances, it was doing a good business. Dozens of men walked in and out of the restaurant, many of them casting appreciative glances in her direction.

"Do you think there will be room for us?" Charlotte asked.

"It looks pretty crowded in there."

Across the road, the Northern Hotel gleamed under the sun with its white clapboard siding and dozens of windows. It was an impressive building, long and narrow, built in the Greek Revival style.

"Richardson finished the hotel today and Jude Allen at the American Hotel is livid," Abram said. "Richardson won the right to have the first ball, which will be held one week from tonight. August thirty-first."

"August thirty-first." The day before their agreement ended.

He took a deep breath. "I was wondering if I may escort you to the ball."

Charlotte glanced at him and caution prevented her from saying yes. There was still the matter of Ben and his proposal hanging between them—yet she had made no commitment to Ben. She nibbled on her bottom lip and allowed herself to imagine being in Abram's arms as they danced. The thought sent a warm sensation flowing through her midsection. "If you escort me, does it mean you'll finally dance with me?"

The twinkle returned to his beautiful blue eyes. "More than once, if you'll allow me the honor." His free hand came up, rested on the hand she had wrapped around his elbow, and he squeezed it. "I'll be the happiest man in the room."

Instead of walk her to the restaurant, he veered her toward the hotel.

"Aren't we going to eat?" she asked.

"Yes—as the first guests at the Northern Hotel. Richardson asked if I would dine there this evening." He turned and winked at her. "He said to be sure to invite you, too."

They climbed the steps and Abram turned the knob of the large front door. It swung open freely and Charlotte stepped over the threshold into a beautifully decorated room.

"I had no idea," she whispered. White wainscoting circled the large lobby and ran down the long hallway to the back of the hotel. A matching counter filled the corner of the room to her right, while potted ferns sat in the opposite corner near a floral sofa. A magnificent set of steps lifted from the end of the lobby, directly across from the front door. "This was being built, right here?"

"In the middle of the wilderness," Abram added with a chuckle. "Wait until you see the ballroom."

Nathan entered the lobby from the long hallway, and when he saw them, his face lit with a grin. "Welcome to the Northern Hotel."

"Nathan!" Charlotte couldn't hide the surprise from her voice. "You told me you walked all the way from a lumber camp. I assumed it was because you couldn't afford the stagecoach fare—yet you managed to build this magnificent hotel."

"I *couldn't* afford the fare! I had to save every last penny to put into my hotel." He took Charlotte's arm. "Come and see the rest."

Nathan led her down the hall, opened two large doors and then escorted Charlotte into the grand ballroom. Never had she imagined something so extravagant in Minnesota Territory. The high ceiling boasted three enormous chandeliers filled with candles waiting to be lit. Floor-to-ceiling mirrors graced the far wall and made the space feel bigger than it truly was. The walls, painted a creamy yellow, had large wall frames and several windows along Main Street, allowing the evening sunshine to enter.

"I feel as if I'm in a ballroom back East," Charlotte said.

"Now you can see why I wanted to win that silly competition with Jude Allen." Nathan crossed his arms with a satisfied grin. "This is where the balls should be held in this town."

Abram came up from behind Charlotte and spoke quietly. "And this is where I'll dance with you next Friday evening."

Heat filled Charlotte's cheeks.

"It doesn't matter," Nathan said, apparently still talking about Mr. Allen. "The first ball will be here and that's all that matters." He pointed toward the door. "Supper is ready whenever you are."

Abram offered his arm and they followed Nathan across the hall and into the dining room. It was another substantial room with more potted ferns and more windows, these facing Broadway. White-linen tablecloths covered the round tables, with candles set at the center of each. One candle flickered to life on a table near a window.

Nathan led them to the table and pulled out a chair for Charlotte. "The cook has prepared roasted duck and baby red potatoes for supper."

Charlotte offered him an encouraging smile. "It sounds delicious." After she was seated, and Nathan presented her with a linen napkin, she asked, "When will you open to the public?"

"Tomorrow morning at six o'clock," Nathan said. "And from that moment on, the front doors will never be locked again."

His enthusiasm matched that of Abram's and every other man in Little Falls, and Charlotte couldn't help but compare them to her father. She could imagine Father here in the midst of it all, his hopes and dreams pinned to one business venture after another. What would happen to Nathan Richardson? Would he give up on this hotel and move on to bigger and better things in time? When the hotel didn't prove to make him money, or fulfill whatever longing it was in his heart, would he walk away from it, like her father had walked away from the dreams he had followed? How long would Nathan stay in Little Falls before his wandering eye called him farther west, like it had Thomas?

"I'll be back shortly." Nathan left the dining room through a swinging door, leaving Charlotte and Abram alone.

"I imagine this place will be filled with people tomorrow night," Abram said, looking around the room. "Richardson outdid himself." He shook his head. "It's actually a little hard to believe."

"Is this town everything you'd hoped it would be?" Charlotte asked, drawing his attention back to her. "Or is it still lacking something?"

He studied her for several moments before he answered. "It's lacking a great many things, but in time, I imagine it will have all the amenities a town should have."

"So it's not what you had hoped for?"

He leaned back in his chair and crossed his arms. "What are you getting at, Charlotte?"

"Are you satisfied?"

"No."

His simple answer twisted her heart. Her father had never been satisfied—wasn't that why he could never settle down?

"If I was satisfied," Abram said, "I would never reach for more, and I believe God created us to long for more. That way, we never become stale and settle for good enough. Think of the great men and women in history. If our founding fathers had been satisfied, we would still be ruled by the king of England. If the Puritans had been satisfied, we might not be here at all. Right now, there are those who are not satisfied with slavery, and are working hard to abolish it." He leaned forward. "There's nothing wrong with longing for more, Charlotte. The trick is to be content. Satisfaction and contentment are two different things."

"How are they different?"

"Satisfaction comes from a job well done. If it's not done, we are not satisfied. Contentment comes from a heart that is confident in God's provision and plan. It's being patient as we wait for God to move or act on our behalf. It's being happy with where He has placed us, and what He has called us to do." He put his elbows on the table and leaned even closer to her. "So if you're asking if I'm content, the answer is yes. But if you're asking if I'm satisfied with the job I've done here, the answer is no. There's still much more to do."

His words, so heartfelt and confident, offered Charlotte a glimpse into his heart—and what she found made her second-guess everything she'd ever feared about him.

A peal of thunder reverberated through the dining room, startling Abram and Charlotte.

He pushed aside the lace curtain and glanced at the sky. "Where did that come from?"

Charlotte also looked outside and saw a large wall cloud advancing from the west. "It looks menacing."

Nathan entered the dining room with two steaming plates of food. "I almost dropped your duck," he laughed. "That thunder about scared me out of my shoes."

He set their plates before them and Charlotte inhaled the savory scent. "Thank you, Nathan."

"I don't know if it'll compare to your cooking, Miss Lee," Nathan said. "But I hope you enjoy it." He left the room as the cloud began to cover the sun and the room grew dark.

Abram glanced outside again, his eyes filled with concern. "I don't like the look of that cloud."

"Let's eat and hurry home," she said.

Abram bowed his head and offered up a prayer, and then they tasted their food. The duck melted on her tongue and filled her mouth with a gamey flavor. The new potatoes were tender and sweet.

The lone candle wavered, causing shadows to dance on the walls. It offered a warm light for their table alone, but the rest of the room faded away.

"Mmm. This is good," Abram said. "Maybe not as good as your food, but a close second."

"I think it's wonderful."

They sat in companionable silence, each appreciating their meal.

"I don't know the last time I ate something I hadn't prepared," Charlotte mused. "I wish the boys were here to enjoy it with us."

Abram took a sip of water and nodded. "I do miss

having them here. They would be quite impressed, I'm sure."

Charlotte set down her fork, the food suddenly unappetizing.

"What's wrong?"

An ache clogged the back of her throat. "I'm going to miss those boys."

Abram set down his fork, as well. "So then you've decided not to marry Ben?"

Charlotte's gaze shot to Abram's face, heat coursing up her neck. "He told you?"

Abram shook his head. "I guessed."

Now that he knew, there was no point hiding the truth. "I can't marry Ben. I wouldn't do it for the right reasons."

"And what reasons are the right ones?"

Her cheeks warmed at his question. "Love. Attraction. A desire to share one's life with another person."

His blue eyes grew serious. "And you don't feel any of those things toward Ben?"

Charlotte looked down at the napkin in her lap. "No."

"Why didn't you give him your answer right away?"

"Because of the wrong reasons I was contemplating."

He shifted awkwardly in his chair. "I don't think I want to know what those are." He paused. "Or maybe I do."

"I had considered marrying him so I could stay, in case the boys need me..."

His jaw tightened, just enough that she could sense his frustration. "Because you don't trust me."

She studied him for a moment. "Because I *didn't* trust you." Hearing him speak of satisfaction and contentment had offered her hope. Maybe Abram was different than her father and Thomas. "But now..."

He leaned forward. "Now what—"

Another clap of thunder echoed in the dining room and a soft patter of rain hit the windows.

Charlotte spoke gently. "Now I'm beginning to doubt my previous opinions about you."

Abram watched her for a few moments, the slightest smile forming in his eyes. "I'm happy to hear that."

More thunder filled the room and the rain began to pour from the sky.

Abram glanced outside then back at Charlotte, warmth smoldering in his gaze. "We should finish our meal and then get home... We can continue our conversation there."

Charlotte swallowed a flutter of nerves and tried to eat the rest of her duck.

Abram finished quickly and set his napkin on his plate. He looked out the window. "I think the worst is yet to come, but we should have no trouble getting home."

Charlotte dabbed her lips and set her napkin down.

"Ready to leave?" Nathan asked, entering the dining room.

"Yes, thank you. It was a wonderful meal," Abram said. "I wish you great success."

A flash of lightning filled the room, followed by thunder.

"We had better go before the storm gets worse," Abram said.

Nathan nodded and his good-natured smile followed them all the way to the front door.

Rain pounded on the street, turning it to mud. "Here,"

Abram said. He took off his suit coat and held it above Charlotte's head. "Let's make a run for it."

Charlotte lifted her hem and they followed Broadway all the way to Wood Street, and then turned left and raced down the hill to their door. The mud was slippery and Abram's jacket did little to keep the rain off, but they made it home breathless.

Charlotte pushed open the lean-to door and they hurried inside. She shook the water off her silk dress as best as she could, and ran her hands along her hair, pulling out pins that had come loose. Her hair fell down her back in a mass of curls.

She felt Abram's eyes on her and turned to find him standing just inside the door, his gaze riveted to her hair.

"I had no idea how long it is."

Charlotte quickly gathered it in her hands, taking a step toward the door. "I'll go put it up."

"Do you have to?"

It felt far too intimate to keep her hair down in his presence, but something held her in the kitchen.

Abram slowly crossed the dark room and Charlotte stayed rooted to her spot.

He stopped in front of her then reached around her to grab the box of matches on the cupboard. "I'll light a lantern," he said softly, near her ear.

She swallowed and forced herself to take several breaths to steady her pulse as she let go of her hair and allowed it to fall freely over her shoulders.

"Ben must have stayed at the Hubbards'," Charlotte said, her voice a bit shaky.

"I thought something was different about the place," Abram teased as he struck the match and set the flame to the wick. The lantern flared to life. He blew out the match and then set the chimney on top.

His movements were steady and smooth, and when he turned back to Charlotte, she could see something in his eyes that she'd denied for a long time.

Attraction.

The room suddenly felt too small and too warm. "I think I'll go watch the storm over the river." She quickly moved out of the kitchen and entered the main room, which was even darker than the kitchen had been.

Charlotte stood near the window, her arms wrapped about her waist, watching the rain pound across the surface of the river. Sheet after sheet of water poured from the sky, until the river became almost hidden and the world felt as if it was growing smaller—and more intimate—by the minute.

Abram entered the main room and silently went to the fireplace, where he laid a fire. The dry wood crackled to life and offered a pleasant glow.

Thunder rolled outside and lightning filled the dark sky. The rain came harder and soon hail hit the roof and the side of the house, filling the yard with pellets of ice.

But Charlotte wasn't focused on the storm outside. It was the storm inside that frightened her the most. Even as her attraction to Abram grew, her mind offered all the reasons she couldn't have feelings for him—yet the desire to let go and allow herself to explore these wonderful emotions was so strong, she was tempted to throw everything aside and give in—come what may.

"Charlotte." Abram was suddenly behind her and she closed her eyes, reveling in the sound of her name on his lips.

His hands rested on her shoulders and she thought she would collapse from the pleasure of his touch.

Ever so gently, he turned her to face him.

His hands remained on her shoulders and he gazed at her with a longing kindled deep within his beautiful blue eyes—but he hesitated, and she sensed he was seeking her permission.

Oh, but she wanted to grant it! She ached to explore the height and the depth of these feelings swirling inside. She suspected that if he kissed her, it would be but a taste of all that was available to them.

Yet one kiss would send her beyond the abyss and she could never return to common sense and rationality. Was she willing to walk the path her mother and sister had followed? What if Abram did prove to be like her father and Thomas? Was the risk worth the reward? Was she enough for him? She hadn't been for Thomas.

His gaze drifted over her face and he lifted his hand from her shoulder to graze her cheek. "You're so beautiful. It's hard to believe—"

A loud crack split the air, followed by grinding and a deep rumble beneath their feet.

Abram tore his gaze from her and looked out the window. "What was that?"

Charlotte also looked outside, but the rain was coming down so thick, it was impossible to see beyond the front yard.

Abram flung open the door and the horrible sounds increased.

For what seemed like a lifetime, he stood staring.

Suddenly, realization dawned on his face. "No!" Abram raced out of the house and was soon swallowed up in the rain.

Charlotte ran to the open door. The rain blew against her warm face as she searched for a sign of Abram and the cause of his abrupt departure.

A sense of foreboding shivered up her spine as she wrapped her arms around her body and prayed for his safety.

Chapter Sixteen

Abram sat on the soggy riverbank the next morning, his head in his hands, as the sun crested the eastern sky, revealing a world that looked much different today than yesterday. All around him, destruction and defeat taunted. Over forty thousand dollars' worth of logs, washed away by one mighty sweep of fate.

"God?" Abram looked up into the clear sky where twelve hours ago a storm had raged. "Why now? Why when everything was going as I had hoped and planned?" He wanted to rail at God, just as he had when Susanne had died, yet what was the point? God had acted and, like before, He wasn't required to give a reason. It was the hardest part of Abram's faith.

Last night, when Abram had run out of the house during the storm, he had already known what was happening in the river. The dam had given way under the rush of water, and it had broken up the millpond. The logs had let loose and crashed against the brand-new gristmill and the sawmill, causing more damage. By the time he'd reached the riverbank, and seen through the storm, the logs were already floating down the raging Mississippi, with no way to retrieve them, carrying pieces of the mills and the dam along with it.

"Abram." Charlotte's gentle voice broke through his sleepless fog as she appeared next to him and handed him a cup of steaming coffee. "Why don't you come inside?"

He accepted the mug and rested it between his two hands as he continued to stare at the mess. "I can't." He had watched his dreams die in the swirling storm. The least he could do was hold vigil.

"Everyone will be rousing soon," Charlotte said. "I imagine most of the laborers will be here today to help clean and make repairs."

"There's no money to pay them," Abram croaked, his throat dry and his voice hoarse. "There's nothing left. Without the logs to mill and sell, and without the use of the gristmill—the only income we have right now is the company store, but that's not nearly enough." A sob threatened to overtake him, so he paused and looked at the ground, barely gaining control. "We're done."

Charlotte sank down near him, her leg pressed against his. "Abram," her voice pleaded, "there has to be something left."

He shook his head and couldn't look her in the eyes. She had known, all along, that he would fail. Why didn't she just remind him and get it over with? Now there was no doubt in his mind that she would leave and take the boys with her—and he didn't blame her. He had one week left to finish the school, but there was no money.

The boys would be better off with her in Iowa, just as she'd always said. This way of life was too unpredictable and too dangerous. Susanne's death only added more proof.

"The mills are still standing," Charlotte said. "And there are more logs to be cut in the woods." She looked around at the debris floating in the millpond. "There are things you can salvage."

Her words pierced his spirit. She was trying to be optimistic, but there was no point. How would they recoup a forty-thousand-dollar loss? He was done. This dream was over. He had come to the end of it all, and the sooner he accepted it, the sooner he could move on.

"Don't you see?" he asked. "Forty thousand dollars just floated down the river. Forty thousand dollars' worth of logs we bought on credit. And the dam will need to be rebuilt—not to mention the repairs needed on the mills. Where will the Little Falls Company come up with money like that?" He'd sent Caleb with a note late last night to St. Anthony, telling Cheney to come— but he had no idea how he would face him.

"You're just tired and overwhelmed."

"I'm realistic."

She looked around again, this time a bit desperate. "I don't know how you'll come up with the money, Abram, but you have to try. You can't give up. Do you remember when you promised me you would prove me wrong? Well, here's your chance."

The sun rose behind the town site, casting rose-tinted shadows over the land and kissing Charlotte's hair. Her brown eyes, which had once looked at him with mistrust and disappointment, were now begging him to do something, to prove to her that he was not like her father or fiancé. But was he? It would be so much easier to move on to something else that held more promise— yet he couldn't give up on Little Falls. He wanted it for his children, and to honor Susanne's memory.

Was he a quitter—or was he a fighter? "Charlotte, I don't know if I can."

Tears gathered in her eyes and her jaw clenched with anger. "Won't you at least try?"

He had no fight left in him. Four years of work and sacrifice were lost, with nothing but regret to show for it. He was so weary. He could hardly hold his head up.

The thought of trying again was more than he could handle at the moment.

"I don't have anything left in me to try."

Charlotte stood and clutched her coffee mug in her shaking hands. "Don't do this, Abram. Don't be like all the others." She turned away and strode off to the house, her skirts swishing across the wet grass.

Abram let his coffee mug slip out of his hands and he dropped his head to his chest and wept.

Charlotte stood near the window in the main room, willing Abram to get up and fight, but he stayed where she had left him, dejected and defeated on the riverbank.

Maybe Abram wouldn't fight, but she would. She had fought her whole life. It was her only defense. She squared her shoulders and marched away from the window.

She quickly fed the boys and, with George on her hip, and Robert and Martin trailing behind, she went right to Mrs. Perry's home just up the road from the Hubbards' house. The hour was still early, which meant most people were at home eating breakfast. She hoped Mr. Perry was available and Mrs. Perry would be ready to go into action.

Abram had sacrificed everything for this town, and it was time for their neighbors to sacrifice for him. Many of them had invested heavily in Little Falls and they had a lot to lose if Abram failed.

It didn't take long to convince Mr. and Mrs. Perry to help, and Mrs. Perry promised to spread the word.

Charlotte spent the rest of her morning going from home to home, spreading the news about the catastrophe. She invited everyone to help clean up the mess, working the day for free, and was pleased to hear so many agree. Dozens of men and boys picked up their tools to get to work, their community spirit a sight to behold.

Around dinnertime, the women started to appear on the street, laden with food, all of them heading to the mill. Charlotte's stomach growled and Martin yanked on her hand to get her attention as she said goodbye to one final neighbor who lived on the outskirts of town in a covered wagon.

"I'm hungry, Aunt Charlotte," Martin said. "My stomach is making funny noises."

"We'll go home now," Charlotte said, starting down the road toward home. "Why don't you sing for me as we walk?"

They crossed the long ravine bridge on the eastern edge of town and followed Broadway until they came to Wood Street. The downtown was strangely quiet. There were no men working on buildings or walking about conducting business. The schoolhouse sat unfinished and the restaurant was closed.

Charlotte swallowed and couldn't help but feel abandoned. Would this town survive such a terrible disaster, or was everything Abram hoped and dreamed already gone?

The closer they drew to the house and sawmill, the

more noise could be heard. When the site came within view, Charlotte's breath caught in her throat.

Well over a hundred people were working on Abram's property. Dozens of men were in the millpond, gathering debris and putting it on rafts. Some were floating the rafts to the banks and putting them onto piles. Other men were working on the gristmill, which had suffered the most damage, and already the waterwheel was spinning on the sawmill, which meant they were making lumber.

Women swarmed around the yard, placing food on makeshift tables, and children were running about, playing with cast-off supplies.

Abram stood in the midst of it all, directing people and answering questions, though he looked exhausted. His hair stood on end and his face was lined with fatigue.

A movement on the top of the hill caught Charlotte's eye and she glanced up to find Mr. Cheney on his horse. He was too far away for Charlotte to see his reaction, but it couldn't be good.

Cheney spurred his horse down the hill and Charlotte met him near the house.

Terror filled his eyes as he stepped out of the saddle. "We're ruined."

"Everyone is pitching in to help," Charlotte said. "And they're doing it for free."

Cheney didn't appear to hear her. He absently handed her a letter. "The postmaster in St. Anthony asked me to bring this." He didn't look at her, but set off toward the river, where he met up with Abram and Mr. Hubbard.

With George still on her hip, Charlotte glanced down and saw elegant script on the letter. It was addressed to the Superintendent of Schools, Little Falls, Minnesota Territory.

Since there was no superintendent of schools, Charlotte decided to open the letter herself and not bother Abram or Mr. Hubbard.

She set George on his feet, thankful to relieve the burden on her hip, and opened the seal.

Dear Mr. Superintendent,
I regret to inform you that I will be unable to teach for your school. I have become engaged to be married and I plan to stay in Moline. I hope this doesn't inconvenience you.
Sincerely,
Helen Palmer

Charlotte lowered the letter and looked up just as Abram glanced in her direction. The last thing he needed right now was to learn that the teacher was not coming. Charlotte feared it would be the final push for him to give up and walk away.

Her stomach felt queasy and her head began to pound. September first was one week from today. Abram wouldn't have everything in place to fulfill his end of the agreement and keep the boys in Little Falls—but how could she leave him now when he needed her most?

She couldn't.

Chapter Seventeen

Cheney paced in the main room of Abram's home, his face red and his eyes glazed over with anger. "If you would have milled those logs like I asked, we wouldn't be in this mess."

Abram sat on the edge of his rocker, his head in his hands. Exhaustion suffocated him as he tried to keep his eyes open. The sun had already set and everyone had gone after working tirelessly all day. Charlotte had made supper for the Hubbards and Mr. Cheney, and then Pearl had taken the children home, while Charlotte had taken the boys up to bed. Ben had also gone to bed, telling Abram he would give him and his business partners some much-needed privacy.

Now that they were alone, Cheney was letting all his frustrations loose. "What will we do? I've already mortgaged my mill in St. Anthony to help pay for this venture. I have nothing left."

Abram glanced at Hubbard, who looked ten years older in just one day.

"We need to find a way to raise forty thousand dollars," Hubbard said.

"The banks won't loan us any more money." Cheney continued to pace. "And I have nothing left to mortgage." He looked at Abram. "What about you? Do you have anything left to sell or mortgage?"

Abram shook his head, too tired to speak.

"And you?" Cheney asked Hubbard.

"I have a few lots in Moline I could sell, but that would only buy us a little time before the creditors come knocking."

Cheney ran his hand through his hair and dropped into Charlotte's rocking chair.

Abram's mind began to wander and he couldn't focus on Cheney's voice. All he could think about was his bed and the sleep he needed. It would feel good to forget about everything that had happened in the past twenty-four hours.

Almost everything. He didn't want to forget about how close he had come to kissing Charlotte, or how wonderful it had felt when he'd seen longing in her eyes—yet he needed to forget about that, too. It would do no good to dwell on the memories. He didn't deserve a woman like Charlotte, and even if he did, she wouldn't have him. He had nothing to offer and no prospects left.

"What we need is another income source, not related to the river and the mill," Hubbard said. "Some other investment that could pay for this venture."

Abram's mind returned to the conversation he'd had with Harry yesterday. If what Harry said was true, and men were making money mining for copper, maybe that could be the answer to the Little Falls Company's problems.

"I think I might know of another income source," Abram said, suddenly feeling energized. "Harry is planning to go to Duluth and start mining copper. If he strikes the right vein, he could have more than enough money within a few short months."

Cheney and Hubbard were quiet for a moment.

"That might be a viable option," Hubbard said. "We need a man to go up there immediately and do some research."

As the idea grew, the darkness in Abram's mind seemed to lighten. He still believed in Little Falls, and what it could be, but they needed money to rebuild what they had lost. Once that was done, they could continue on the course they had set for themselves.

Abram's conversation with Charlotte from the Northern Hotel returned. He wasn't satisfied yet, because Little Falls hadn't reached its full potential—and until it did, Abram would do whatever he needed to do. If it meant mining copper in Duluth, then that was what he would do.

"I don't like it," Cheney said. "There's too much risk and we'd be spreading ourselves too thin. We need money, and we need it fast. I think the only thing we can do to remain solvent is create a joint stock corporation and sell public shares."

"A stock corporation?" Abram swiveled his head to stare at Cheney. "We're having enough trouble managing with three opinions. How will we manage with hundreds of shareholders' opinions, not to mention a board of directors? It's a terrible idea."

"It's the only way to generate the cash we need to regain what we've lost." Cheney leaned toward Abram, his posture intense. "We can retain fifty percent of the shares and hand-select the board. Other than an annual board meeting, you won't even know anything has changed."

"Everything would change," Abram said. "I'd have to answer to a board of directors." And he'd only own five-twelfths' share of fifty percent of the company. One year ago he had owned one hundred percent. "I can't do it."

Cheney turned away from Abram and looked toward Hubbard. "What do you think?"

Hubbard shrugged. "It's also a reasonable idea."

"What are you thinking, Hubbard?" Abram leaned forward. "You've hated to get permission to spend money the way you want. What happens when you have a board to answer to? This will no longer be our company. It will belong to hundreds of people."

Hubbard looked between Abram and Cheney, his eyes clouded with indecision. "Both ideas have their merits and their risks."

"I'm the majority partner." Abram crossed his arms. "I vote we go with my plan."

"Together, Hubbard and I are the majority," Cheney said. "If the two of us decide a joint stock corporation is the way to go, we outvote you."

Abram rose from his seat and looked between them. "I have four years invested here." He couldn't hide the incredulity from his voice. "You'd go against my wishes?"

Cheney also rose. "You might have time invested, but the money I've invested came from years of hard work. If this venture folds, not only will I lose what I've invested here, I'll lose my other businesses."

"We're all tired," Hubbard said. "Maybe we should wait until tomorrow to finish this discussion."

"I plan to leave first thing in the morning," Abram said, his voice tight. "I'm going to Duluth to do research."

"And I'm going to speak to a lawyer about forming a joint stock corporation," Cheney said, his voice equally tight. "I won't wait to see what comes of your research."

"If Hubbard and I decide selling shares isn't the way to go," Abram said, "then your talk with the lawyer will be a waste of time."

Again, Cheney looked at Hubbard. "What will it be?"

Hubbard swallowed and shook his head. "I can't make a decision without knowing all the facts." He looked at Abram. "How quickly can you be back from Duluth?"

Abram paced to the window, where the moonless night hid the wreckage from view. Duluth was a hundred and fifty miles northeast. If he pushed hard, he could make the trip in a day, and would need a few days to look around and talk to people who had already started mining, and then a day to come back. He turned and looked at his business partners. "I think I could be back by Friday."

Cheney's eyes narrowed. "Fine. But I expect you back here on Friday with answers, and in the meantime I'm talking to a lawyer." He went to the hook by the door and grabbed his hat. "I'm going to the Northern Hotel. If you change your mind, that's where I'll be until you return."

"Wait." Abram glanced up the stairs where Charlotte was sleeping. He lowered his voice. "Keep my trip to yourselves. I don't want anyone speculating about why I left. We need people to keep coming to town, thinking the company is thriving. If they hear we're facing trouble, they'll move on by."

Cheney nodded once and then walked out, slamming the door behind him.

Hubbard slowly stood and put his hand on Abram's shoulder. "I hope you find what we need. I'll see you on Friday during the ball at the Northern Hotel."

The ball.

Abram planned to escort Charlotte.

"Good night, Abram." Hubbard left the house and gently closed the front door behind him.

Abram stood for a few moments, the fog of exhaustion returning.

Footsteps fell on the stairs and the hem of Charlotte's dress slipped into view. Soon her entire body was visible and she looked around the room. "Are they gone?"

Abram nodded, but couldn't move. What had she heard?

"You should go to bed, Abram. It isn't healthy for you to be awake for so long, especially when you've been working so hard."

He pulled his feet over to the stairs and stopped in front of her. He didn't want to ask her what she had heard, in case it made her suspicious. But she needed to know something. "I'm leaving first thing in the morning, and I won't be home until Friday night."

She blinked up at him, her face half hidden by the shadows. "Where are you going?"

He wanted to tell her, but if he did, she wouldn't understand. "I'm going with Harry for a few days, but I'll be back."

"Harry?" She put her hands on his forearms, her eyes pleading. "Abram, I know you're upset, but you can't follow in Harry's footsteps."

He shook his head. "It's not like that. I'm going with him to look into business for the Little Falls Company. I'll be back on Friday."

She studied his face, as if ascertaining if he was telling the truth. "The ball is on Friday."

"I hope to be back by then."

"I hope so, too. Won't you tell me where you're going?"

What would it hurt to tell her? "I'm going to Duluth."

"Duluth? But why? Especially now?"

"I'll tell you more when I return, but this is urgent, so I need to go immediately." If he was successful, he could put the money back into the Little Falls Company and he could stay here and raise the boys.

"Will you be safe?" Her eyes were so tender in the lantern light, he wished he could stare into them forever.

He wanted to reassure her, and somehow capture the essence of last evening, before everything had gone wrong, so he lifted his hand and placed his palm against her soft cheek. His fingertips nestled into her hair and he lowered his head to look her in the eyes. "I promise I will be safe, and I'll return home on Friday evening to dance with you at the ball. You have my word."

She looked intently into his eyes. "Can I trust your word?"

Charlotte had never had a man she could trust, and the weight of the responsibility almost buckled his legs. Not only did he have the Little Falls Company to save, but he also needed to prove to Charlotte he was a man of his word. "You can trust me."

Quiet strength flickered in her eyes and she put her hand up to rest on his. "Then I'll be here waiting for that dance on Friday."

He wanted to kiss her—but there were still so many unanswered questions, and he didn't want any regrets between them, especially when they had come so far.

He lowered his hand and took a step back. "I'll ask Ben to find somewhere else to stay while I'm gone. It wouldn't be right for him to be here alone with you." He took another step away from her, afraid what he might say or do with his emotions so frayed. "Why don't you go to bed? It's been a long day."

She nodded and started to turn back to the stairs, but she paused and looked a bit uncertain. "A letter came. I wish I didn't have to show it to you, but you'd find out sooner or later." She extracted a letter from her apron pocket. "It's from the teacher, Helen Palmer." She offered it to him. "Sh-she's not coming."

Abram stared at her. "She's not coming?"

"She decided to get married instead."

Abram closed his eyes and turned away from Charlotte, not wanting her to see his disappointment. Defeat lay heavy upon his shoulders and he feared he'd lie down and never stand under the weight of it again. "While I'm gone, you should start packing for your move back to Iowa. It will take you some time to get the boys' things ready to go."

Charlotte took a step toward him and laid her hand on his shoulder. "Abram, I can't hold you to that deal now—not after—"

"Yes, you can, and you will." He shook his head. "You were right all along. This is no place for the boys. They'll be better off with you in Iowa."

"You need to get some sleep, Abram. Things will look better in the morning." Charlotte let go and waited for a moment, but when he didn't answer, she walked up the stairs and disappeared.

Abram finally gave way to the defeat and fell to his knees.

"Are you sure you don't want to go to the ball?" Charlotte asked Rachel the following Friday night as they stood in Abram's kitchen.

Rachel shook her head slowly as she admired Charlotte's silk gown and curled hair. "No. I'm happy to stay with the children. You should go and have fun, though."

Charlotte glanced out the kitchen window, toward the road. The sun had already set and dusk had fallen on the last day of August, and still there was no sign of Abram. His absence had been more difficult than Charlotte realized it would be, and the only thing that had seen her through the week was the knowledge that she would dance with him one more time.

But the ball had started an hour ago.

"It's not right for you to be alone here tonight, Charlotte—especially all dressed up like that." Rachel handed Charlotte her long gloves. "It's still light enough for you to walk to the hotel."

Charlotte took the gloves but shook her head. "I spent the last six years alone." She tried not to let her voice catch. "I can stay home from a ball." Charlotte had grown close to Rachel, and appreciated their ease in conversation. Rachel, like Ben, was the daughter of a fur trader and an Indian mother, and she spoke flawless English.

"You've had many invitations to the ball," Rachel said. "Surely, if you go, someone will escort you home."

Charlotte let out a disappointed sigh. "I wanted to go with Abram. I just hope he's all right."

Work had resumed in the community as it had been before, with buildings going up and new citizens arriving every day. If anyone noticed Abram's sudden absence, they didn't comment. At least, not to Charlotte.

Basic repairs had been made to the dam and gristmill, with Mr. Cheney's supervision. The sawmill had continued to run, but the schoolhouse remained unfinished.

Despite Abram's orders to move back to Iowa, Charlotte had not packed. She couldn't leave him now. None of this had been his fault.

Charlotte looked outside once again and this time there was a man walking toward the house on Wood Street—but it wasn't Abram.

She tried not to look crestfallen when she opened the door and smiled. "Hello, Ben."

He stopped midstride, his face filled with pure delight. "You look lovely."

"Thank you. Will you come in?"

He approached the house but glanced over his shoulder toward the barn. "Is Abram back yet?"

Charlotte shook her head.

Ben stopped just outside the door and offered her a sad smile. "I'm sorry he didn't come. You're too pretty to be sitting home in that gown."

She couldn't help but smile.

He wore an evening coat and his customary braids, but tonight he had taken out the hoops in his ears. He looked dashing.

"Why aren't you at the ball?" she asked.

"I was. But when you didn't show up, I thought it was a shame that the prettiest lady in town wasn't there, and decided to come get you myself."

"Thank you, but I don't think—"

"Charlotte." He took a step forward and lifted her hand. "I know you had promised to go with Abram, but I also know how much you had looked forward to dancing tonight." He bowed over her hand. "Would you do me the honor of accompanying me to the ball?"

She still hadn't given him an answer in regard to his proposal. He had kept his distance while Abram was gone, and she hadn't had a chance to seek him out. Tonight was the first time she would have a chance to speak to him. She owed him an answer. The least she could do was put aside her unhappiness and go with him to the ball.

"Yes."

He looked up, a light in his brown eyes. "Yes?"

She nodded.

He kissed her hand. "You've made me the happiest man in town."

"Let me get my shawl and say goodbye to Rachel."

He let her go and she went back into the house.

Rachel was still standing in the kitchen, where Charlotte had left her, and she had a smile on her face. "I see you have an escort."

Charlotte lifted her long white shawl from the back of the chair and quickly slipped on her gloves. "Reverend Lahaye will bring me."

"Have fun, and don't worry about the children."

"Good night." Charlotte waved as she passed through the lean-to and met Ben outside.

He offered his elbow and she took it.

They walked up Wood Street and then down Broadway toward the Northern Hotel.

Neither one spoke for a while, but then Ben took a

deep breath. "I know I said I didn't want to press you for an answer, and that's why I gave you time to think and pray this week—"

"Thank you for that."

He stopped and his face was barely discernible in the dying light. "I thought I could be patient, but I need to know what you're thinking." He tilted his head toward the hotel. "Before we go in there, and I have to share you with all those other men, I'd like to know where we stand."

Dread knotted Charlotte's stomach and her throat became dry. She had grown to care for Ben like a brother, and she hated to break his heart—but it wasn't fair for him to wonder any longer. Not when she knew the answer. "I'm sorry, Ben."

His shoulders dropped. "I had hoped—but I think I already knew."

"I am sorry."

He held up his hand. "You don't owe me an apology, Charlotte. Really, you don't." He lowered his hand and studied her for a moment. "Are you in love with Abram?"

Her heart leaped at his name but she shook her head, unable to answer him.

He tucked her hand inside his elbow once again and held her close to his side. "I'll pretend like I believe you."

"Come." Charlotte tugged on his arm. "Let's go try to have some fun and leave all our troubles out here on the street."

They entered the Northern Hotel and Charlotte was even more impressed than the first time. The lobby was filled with laughter and conversation. The majority of the occupants were men, and when she entered, she was swarmed with attention.

They made their way through the crowd and passed into the ballroom.

The candles were lit and a three-string orchestra played on a raised platform to their left. Here, three or four dozen women spun about the room in the arms of their partners, while other men waited on the outskirts for their chance to dance.

Charlotte was handed a dance card, and quickly surmised how many dances she had missed and how many were left. She penciled Ben's name in for the first and the last dances. The other spaces were quickly filled by men she had come to know sitting around her kitchen table earlier that winter.

When the next song began, Ben offered his hand and he walked Charlotte onto the dance floor. "I warn you," he said. "I'm not very good."

She grinned and felt the joy from the other dancers bubble up within her. "Neither am I."

They joined the dancers as they swirled about the room and, within seconds, Ben was laughing.

"What?" she asked.

"You lied to me. You're a magnificent dancer."

She added her laughter to his. "Will you forgive me?"

"Always."

The evening continued much the same, with one dance partner after another. Charlotte enjoyed herself immensely, but worry began to visit her when she wondered why Abram had not returned.

As each dance was checked off her dance card, Charlotte's disappointment mounted. She found herself looking toward the door every chance she could—and each time her melancholy grew a bit deeper.

The last song was finally announced and Ben found her in the crowded ballroom. "You must be exhausted," he said. "Have you had a break since we danced last?"

She shook her head and glanced at the door one more time, but still Abram had not appeared. Tears threatened but she looked back at Ben, determined to enjoy this last dance.

He took her into his arms as the first note struck against the violin. "Shall we?"

She followed his lead and he spun her around the room in a lively waltz.

"Have I improved since our last dance?" he asked with a laugh.

She offered a halfhearted smile, wishing she could enjoy herself. "Have you heard word about Abram?"

Ben shook his head. "I asked Hubbard and Cheney, but neither one have heard from him since he left."

A sinking feeling overcame Charlotte as a thought took root. What if Abram had left...for good, just like Thomas had? What if the lure of something better, or easier, had been too great and he had simply walked away from all of them?

The song ended and the couples stopped dancing. Everyone cheered loudly for the orchestra and each member stood and took a bow.

"Shall I take you home?" Ben asked.

Charlotte offered a quick nod, hoping to hold in her emotions until she was home, alone, and in her own room.

"Just a moment," one of the orchestra members called out. "We've just had a special request from our town's founder, Mr. Abram Cooper. At his request, we will have an encore performance of 'Wings of the Phoenix.'"

"Abram?" Charlotte looked about the room, desperate to see him healthy and whole. "Where is he?"

She turned, her heart beating rapidly, searching—and then she saw him, coming toward her, his eyes focused solely on her. She wanted to soak up the sight of him. Memorize every plane of his handsome face and every nuance of his blue eyes. He wore his evening coat, but he hadn't taken the time to shave—though he looked more attractive than ever.

"Abram."

She didn't realize she had reached for him until he took hold of her hands. The music played and she found herself in his confident hold, twirling her around the dance floor. All else faded as she lost herself in the longing in his eyes.

"Charlotte—" He broke off his words and pulled her closer. She rested her head on his chest and they danced.

She was so secure in his arms, she closed her eyes and allowed him to lead her. She remembered their first dance and how well they had moved together. But she also remembered why she had put him at a distance that evening. Because he was a wanderer—or so she thought.

Please, Lord, let me be wrong about Abram Cooper.

Neither one said another word as the music played and they waltzed on.

Abram rested his cheek against Charlotte's head and she inhaled his scent, reveling in the feel of his arms around her.

She wanted the song to last forever, but all too soon it ended and they came to a stop. The other dancers clapped for the musicians, but Abram only stared at Charlotte.

"I'm so sorry, Charlotte. I tried to get here——"

"It's all right."

"It's not. I made a promise——"

"And you fulfilled it."

She realized he was still holding her hand when he squeezed it. "May I walk you home?" he asked.

She opened her mouth to say yes but then remembered how she had arrived at the ball. "I came with Ben."

The disappointment on his face was strong and swift.

Ben must have been watching, because he approached them now. "Welcome back, Abram."

"Ben." Abram nodded at him. "Thank you for bringing Charlotte to the dance for me."

"It was my pleasure." Ben glanced between Charlotte and Abram, understanding in his eyes. "I imagine you'd like to take her home."

Abram grinned at his friend. "I would."

Ben bowed. "By all means." He took Charlotte's hand and placed a chaste kiss on her knuckles. "Thank you for a lovely evening."

"Thank you for coming to get me."

Ben bowed one more time and then walked away.

The room filled with conversation and Abram stepped closer to Charlotte. Her pulse beat hard at the thought of walking home with him and finally telling him what she had come to realize.

"Are you ready to go?" he asked.

"Abram." Mr. Hubbard appeared behind Abram. "I'm happy you're here. We're eager to hear what you learned about the venture in Duluth. Is there really copper up there?"

"Copper?" Charlotte frowned. "What does he mean 'the venture in Duluth'?" She paused as dread filled her soul. "Are you leaving Little Falls, Abram?"

Abram glanced around and leaned closer. "This is not the time nor the place to talk about my plans, Charlotte. I've just returned and there are many things to discuss with Cheney and Hubbard."

She looked at Hubbard and then back at Abram, disillusionment creeping into her heart. "Is that why you went, because you heard there's copper in Duluth? Are you planning to chase another scheme?"

"It's not like that. We need money for the Little Falls Company, and if we strike now, we'll get more than we need in Duluth. The talk up there—"

"The talk. That's exactly right. It's only talk." She wrapped her arms around her waist, feeling sick to her stomach. All her father had ever done was talk. "It's gold fever is all it is—" She paused, incredulity in her voice. Thomas had left her for gold fever. "I knew you couldn't stay, Abram. I tried to tell myself I was wrong—but I wasn't." She shook her head, anger and disappointment blurring her vision.

"Charlotte, Cheney wants to turn the Little Falls Company into a joint stockholders' corporation." Abram's voice was desperate—pleading. "I can't let him. I've fought too long and too hard to give my company over to a board of directors."

"So you're going to go mining for copper?" She fisted her hands at her sides. "That makes no sense, Abram. It's just another scheme. And it will fail. If something sounds too good to be true, it usually is. Real success comes from hard work and dedication. You have to stay with something for it to flourish." She could hardly look at him. "It's called commitment." She bit her bottom lip to stop its trembling then pushed past him and Hubbard.

She maneuvered through the crowd and several people tried to stop her, but the only thing she wanted was to go home.

To Iowa.

Chapter Eighteen

"Charlotte." Abram moved to follow her but Hubbard took his arm.

"Cheney's madder than a tickled rattlesnake," Hubbard said. "We've been waiting for you all evening."

"I have to talk to Charlotte." He had to convince her that he wasn't following another scheme but had Little Falls' best interest at heart.

"Miss Lee can wait." Hubbard nodded toward a side door in the ballroom. "Cheney can't."

"She can't walk home alone. It's not safe."

"Look. She found Reverend Lahaye. I'm sure he'll walk her home."

Abram let out a frustrated sigh then followed Hubbard through the ballroom. He turned his head several times to make sure Charlotte was safe with Ben and then entered a small parlor adjoining the ballroom.

Cheney stood near a window overlooking Broadway but swiveled toward them. "Well? What did you discover?" He crossed his arms, clearly indignant to Abram's report even before he gave it.

What Abram had learned had both excited and frustrated him. "I met a man named Reuben Carlton, who is a blacksmith for the Chippewa Indians. He has already created a company and they're actively locating copper deposits. He told me he expects a land rush in the next year, and if we're going to get the Little Falls Company involved, we need to act immediately."

"How much will it cost to get started?" Hubbard asked.

This was the part that frustrated Abram. "Several thousand dollars—but Carlton expects a return on the investment within the year."

"No." Cheney slashed the air with his hand. "We need to stick with my plan and form the corporation. I already had my lawyer draw up the papers."

Abram shook his head. "I can't do it." He couldn't hand over all he had worked for.

"It's already done," Cheney said. "Hubbard and I agree."

Abram looked toward Hubbard, feeling as if the wind had been knocked from him. "You did this, without my approval?"

"Abram." Hubbard took a step toward him. "We don't have much choice. We need the money or everything disappears."

Abram ran his hands through his hair and walked over to the cold fireplace. He couldn't give over that much control.

"If you don't like it, Abram, I'd be happy to buy your shares." Cheney spoke with little emotion. "Then you can leave Little Falls and do whatever you want in Duluth."

"Leave Little Falls?"

"We've made our decision." Cheney strode to the

door. "Let me know in the morning what you decide." He exited the room, leaving Hubbard with Abram.

"I'm sorry, Abram. This isn't personal—I need to do what is best for me and my family. You understand, don't you?"

Abram couldn't talk. He couldn't even look at Hubbard.

Hubbard sighed. "I hope you decide to stay. It would be a shame to work so hard for all of this and then leave it behind because you weren't satisfied with how things turned out."

"I didn't have a choice about how things turned out."

Hubbard clapped Abram's shoulder. "We rarely ever do. We simply have to make the best of it and let go of our disappointment. It's the only way to move forward. You can choose what you want your legacy to be. You can either be known as a man who stayed the course or one who never found his way. It's up to you." Hubbard dropped his hand and walked to the door. "Good night, Abram."

Hubbard left the room and Abram stood for a long time staring into the lifeless fireplace.

He had allowed himself to get caught up in an easy fix, but Hubbard was right. Abram must choose his course and then be persistent to stay on track. He would never move ahead if he spent his life wandering from one path to another.

He strode from the room, determined to convince Charlotte he wasn't a wanderer—even if for a brief moment he was drawn to that course.

Abram would stay in Little Falls, regardless of the obstacles in front of him.

* * *

Charlotte's bedroom was cloaked in darkness when she heard Abram's footsteps on the stairs. Quiet sobs shuddered through her body as she buried her face in the pillow. She had sent Rachel home with Ben and had extinguished all the lights. She had quickly gone to her room, undressed, slipped into her nightgown and climbed between the sheets before Abram came home.

The last thing she wanted was to talk to him. How many times had Father begged Mama into forgiving him? And then how many times had he squandered away what little money they had on a scheme, only for him to beg her to work harder until he could pick himself back up? It was a vicious cycle; one Charlotte had no desire to embrace.

A light knock sounded at her door and she held her breath, hoping Abram would think she was sleeping and go to his own room.

She waited, hearing her pulse in her ears—but then he knocked again. "Charlotte, I know you can't possibly be asleep already."

Time moved slowly as she lay there.

"Please. Let me explain."

Her heart tugged at her to open the door but her mind demanded she stay where she was. He was charming and convincing, and would tell her everything she wanted to hear.

"Charlotte. Please. I want to talk to you. I'm not going anywhere until you open this door."

She sat up and ran her long sleeve over her cheeks. "Go away, Abram. There's nothing you can say to convince me you've changed. Just go to bed."

There was silence and then a light thud. Was that his head against the door?

"I haven't changed, Charlotte. That's the point. I'm the same man who married Susanne and the same man who was working in the sawmill that day last fall when you marched in. I'm the same man—but I'm not the man you've always assumed I was."

Charlotte pulled her legs up and put her forehead on her knees. Tears of anger and frustration wet her nightgown. "You are the man I thought, and you proved it by chasing a rumor up to Duluth."

"Will you please open this door so we can talk face-to-face?"

"I'm in my nightgown."

"Put on a wrapper."

She wanted to see him, but that was the problem. She shouldn't want to see him, or talk to him, or believe in him.

"Charlotte. Please."

She let out a sigh and pushed back the covers. The moon shone bright and offered a scant light as she grabbed her wrapper from the foot of her bed. She wiped at her cheeks again but knew it was pointless. Her tears would not quit easily, because she had allowed herself to trust—and her trust had been betrayed.

Charlotte cracked the door open a fraction but didn't look out at him. Instead she stared at the back of the door. "I'm only opening this door to tell you that tomorrow is September first, and you failed to provide what I required. The boys and I are leaving on the stagecoach when it comes through on Monday."

"Charlotte, let me explain—"

"I wanted to believe in you, Abram—I was even

willing to stay as long as it took—" She choked on a sob. "But then you lied to me—"

"How did I lie?"

She flung open the door and found him standing there, his elbows pushed against either side of the door frame and his fists clasped over his head.

"You said you were different than my father and Thomas. Yet you did exactly what both of them would have done."

"I had to go."

"Why? You had other options. But you chose to follow the rumors."

He dropped his hands. "It doesn't matter now. I realized you're right. I was looking for the easy way out, but I've discovered there's only one way and that's forward on the path I've already chosen."

She turned away. "Stop. I don't want to hear any more."

"Charlotte, you have to believe me."

It was like hearing her father all over again. She wanted to cover her ears and hide under the blankets like she did when her parents fought. Tears fell down her cheeks once again. "It's no use. There's nothing you could say to change my mind. I'm taking the boys back to Iowa City."

"Charlotte, I'm going to join Cheney and Hubbard as they start the corporation. I'll finish the school this week and I'll find a teacher. I'm not leaving Little Falls."

Promises upon more promises.

"Until something else goes wrong and you want to run again."

Abram's shoulders sagged and he let out a long breath. "I can't convince you, can I?"

Charlotte's legs felt heavy and she lowered herself

into the rocker near the bureau. Even if Abram was telling the truth, and he would stay in Little Falls, she was afraid she could never fully trust him. Her father and Thomas had ruined her from ever trusting a man's promise.

"I'm sorry, Charlotte." Abram slouched against the door frame, emotion shaking his voice. "I didn't hold up my end of the agreement. I give you permission to take them back to Iowa."

She had thought she would be satisfied with his permission—but it only made her more heartsore. She didn't want to take the boys away from him, but she couldn't leave them in good conscience, either. "We'll leave on Monday."

He stood tall and reached into her room to grab the doorknob. "Good night, Charlotte."

The door closed and she was left in the quiet darkness. "Goodbye, Abram."

There was no way forward for either of them. She had chosen her path when she had first come to Little Falls and had almost veered off, but was now back on course.

Chapter Nineteen

A light rain dripped off the edge of Abram's brim as he held the umbrella over Robert and Martin. Up ahead on the old wagon road, Charlotte held George in her arms, a black umbrella protecting them from the predawn rainstorm. The streets were dark and empty, and the only sound to accompany them was the pitter-patter of raindrops splashing in puddles and landing on buildings.

Now that Little Falls had a real downtown, Andrew stopped the stagecoach in front of the Northern Hotel. He still came from St. Paul on Fridays, and headed back to St. Paul on Mondays.

Abram had already hauled the trunks and valises to the hotel earlier that morning when he couldn't sleep and then he had helped get the children ready while Charlotte finished her last-minute preparations. He had buttoned up the boys' jackets and answered all their questions about riding a stagecoach and what it would be like to live in Iowa. Robert asked when Abram was coming to see them, and he had signed that he would come as soon as he could—but he didn't know when that would be.

Charlotte wore the same dark green traveling gown she'd worn the first day she arrived, and a matching green bonnet. George looked at Abram over Charlotte's shoulder as he waved his chubby little hand around in excitement. His dark brown eyes sparkled with happiness and Abram couldn't help but think of all he would miss in the coming years. How old would his sons be when he saw them next? Would they remember him?

Charlotte turned left onto Main Street and glanced back at Abram and the boys. He wanted to feel animosity toward her but he couldn't find the strength or the inclination. They had made a deal and he had not met the conditions. He couldn't expect her to stay in Little Falls forever, even though everything in him wanted to call out and ask her to do just that. Even if he did ask her, she would never say yes. She had a life to go back to.

"Will the horses go fast, Papa?" Martin asked.

"Yes. The horses will go fast."

"Will we sleep in a hotel?"

"Yes." He'd already answered this question several times. "Tonight you'll sleep in a hotel in St. Paul and then tomorrow you'll get on another stagecoach that will take you to another hotel. You'll travel for six days and sleep in five hotels."

When they arrived at the Northern Hotel, Charlotte opened the door and stepped inside. Abram followed with the boys.

The lobby was virtually empty, except for a clerk who sat behind the counter, a book in hand.

"You two wait on the sofa," Abram said to his two older sons. "Be on your best behavior."

Their trunks were still near the door, so there was nothing left to do but wait.

Charlotte stood with her gaze directed out the window looking onto Main Street.

Abram stepped close to her, having no interest in the hotel clerk knowing his business. "I'll be sure to send you a regular stipend." Abram played with the rim of his wet hat. "Please write if you need more or if something comes up and you can't afford—"

"I will."

Abram glanced at his sons, who suddenly looked very young. Robert glanced around the hotel lobby with his quiet reserve, while Martin sat close to his big brother, inspecting the room from around Robert's shoulder.

"Charlotte, are you sure this is what you want?"

She closed her eyes for a moment and then looked at Abram. "You and I both know it's for the best."

Was it? He had full confidence in her, and knew she would raise them well. There would be schools for them, and a church. They would have friends their age and all the conveniences they needed for a happy life.

The stagecoach pulled up to the hotel and Abram's chest tightened. Everything within him wanted to keep his family together—yet Charlotte would never agree to stay and he couldn't go back to Iowa and give up on Little Falls. No matter how hard it would be, he would succeed for his boys. One day, when they were older, hopefully there would be a legacy waiting for them when they returned.

"Come, boys." Charlotte signed for Robert and Martin to follow her. She opened the door, but Abram put his hand on her wrist.

She looked up at him, her brown eyes filled with tears.

"Charlotte, I'm sorry everything came to this. I'm sorry I couldn't do what I said I would do." He swallowed. "But most of all, I'm sorry I couldn't prove you wrong."

She studied him for a moment. "I am, too." She moved away, wiping her cheeks, and spoke to the boys. "Say goodbye to your father."

Martin leaped into Abram's arms and squeezed him tight. "Goodbye, Papa. Come and see us soon."

Abram squeezed him back, burying his face in his son's shoulder. "I love you, Martin."

Martin wiggled to get out of his father's arms.

Abram reached for Robert, who also came to him with a big hug, and spoke a silent prayer. *Lord, I pray for this boy and all the obstacles in his path. I pray You would ease his burden and pave a straight and narrow way for him.*

Robert pulled back and signed goodbye.

Abram took George from Charlotte's arms, which allowed Charlotte to go out into the rain with her umbrella to speak to Andrew. He climbed down from the top of his stagecoach and entered the hotel with Charlotte to help with the luggage.

Abram gave his youngest son a hug and a kiss then handed him back to Charlotte.

He helped Andrew load the luggage and strap it down on top, and then Andrew resumed his place on the driver's seat and Abram reentered the hotel.

"It looks like you're ready to go." Abram looked at Charlotte and his three sons, sorrow clogging his throat.

Charlotte's eyes filled with sadness as she put her free hand on Robert's back to guide him out of the hotel.

When she passed by, Abram said, "Goodbye, Charlotte. And thank you."

Charlotte paused and turned to him. "For what?"

"For everything. Maybe I didn't fulfill all the requirements, but this town wouldn't be here right now if it wasn't for you and all the hard work you did." He wanted to take her into his arms, as well, but refrained. "And thank you for taking such good care of the boys. There isn't anyone I'd trust more."

She looked like she might say something but then she closed her mouth and nodded. "Goodbye, Abram."

Charlotte led his boys out to the stagecoach and they all loaded inside. She pulled the door closed and the boys looked out the open window and waved at him.

Andrew clicked the reins and the horses went into motion, pulling the stagecoach away from the Northern Hotel.

Abram waved at his sons, trying to smile for them, and watched Charlotte, waiting for her to offer him one last glance.

She never did.

The stagecoach disappeared down Main Street but Abram remained in the rain for several minutes. All around him, buildings stood where only trees and grass had been before, and over two hundred people now lived in a town that had been virtually empty one year ago. But, despite the two hundred new friends and neighbors, Abram felt lonelier now than he had when it was just him and his four employees.

"Abram." Hubbard appeared from around the corner of the Northern Hotel, an umbrella in hand. "You're just the man I want to see today. Let's go inside and get out of this rain."

With one last glance down Main Street, Abram followed Hubbard into the hotel.

Hubbard closed his umbrella and set it in the stand next to the front door. "Why don't we get something warm to drink in the dining room?"

Abram didn't say anything but followed his business partner through the lobby and into the dining room. His feet felt heavy and his heart was sore. He was afraid he wouldn't be good company and almost told Hubbard he'd rather go home. But the thought of being in the house without Charlotte and the boys made his melancholy almost too much to bear.

Several patrons had arrived for their breakfast and a low murmur filled the room.

They found a table in a quiet corner and ordered coffee.

"I'm happy I found you." Hubbard leaned his elbows on the table and his long beard almost touched the top. "I've been thinking more about what you said concerning Duluth."

"It doesn't matter anymore." Abram's shoulders sagged as he sat there. "I've decided to go along with Cheney's plans to form a corporation."

"But that's the thing I've been thinking about." Hubbard's eyes became animated. "Why can't we do both? I can stay here with my family and manage our company's affairs in Little Falls, and you can go up to Duluth and stake a claim and work the copper mines. That way, we'll have several income generators."

Abram had already come to terms with the idea of staying. The sudden invitation to leave didn't set well—

until he started to think about all the possibilities a new adventure could bring.

"It might be a good time for you to leave, with Charlotte taking the boys to Iowa," Hubbard said. "A change in scenery might make the adjustment easier."

Abram couldn't deny the thought was tempting.

The waiter arrived and set their steaming cups of coffee on the table.

"So what do you think?" Hubbard asked. "Are you ready to try something new?"

Thoughts of Charlotte filled Abram's mind and he knew the answer. For the rest of his life, there would be many opportunities that would come his way, but he had made a commitment to stay in Little Falls.

"No." He shook his head. "Little Falls is my legacy, and I intend to stay here for as long as God allows. This is my home."

The only thing his home lacked was his family.

The stagecoach rolled through the darkening streets of St. Paul, jostling Charlotte and the boys. George was asleep in Charlotte's arms and the older two boys had curled up on either side of her, with their heads in her lap. The stagecoach had been uncomfortable and hard for the boys, but Charlotte had kept them entertained—which had distracted her from thinking of Abram. But now, with them asleep, she allowed the memories to engulf her in both joy and sorrow.

She was in awe of how Little Falls had grown up around her. How often did a dream materialize in such a short time? Yes, it had taken Abram years of hard work and sacrifice before she had arrived—but then it had come together like a well-timed dance, swirling out of the dust.

The memories with Abram spun about in her mind, twisting and turning, until they created a bittersweet taste in her soul. When she closed her eyes, she could see his twinkling blue gaze and hear his deep laughter—and she recalled the way he had looked at her the night of the storm. What would have happened if the dam hadn't broken? Would she have allowed him to kiss her? The question left an aching hole in her heart, begging to be answered.

The coach came to a stop and Charlotte opened her eyes to see a two-story clapboard hotel in the dying light.

Andrew climbed down and opened the door. "I'll help you get the little ones into the hotel, and then I'll have a boy come out and give me a hand with your luggage."

Charlotte indicated for him to take Martin and then she roused Robert. It took her several attempts to get him to climb out of the stagecoach. His head hung low and his feet dragged as they walked into the hotel.

The establishment wasn't fancy, but it would do for the night. The lobby was clean and simple, with a fireplace and several wooden chairs spread throughout. One chair by the smoldering fire was occupied with a young woman who rose upon their entry and quickly approached.

"Are you Andrew, the stagecoach driver?" she asked.

Andrew held Martin in an awkward position, with the boy's head flopping to the side. "Yep."

The lady let out a relieved, somewhat dramatic sigh. She had blond curls and the biggest blue eyes Charlotte had ever seen. Her clothes were well crafted and looked new.

"The hotel proprietor said you run the stage north on Fridays," the lady said. "I'm wondering if there's a way I could persuade you to go tomorrow instead."

"On a Tuesday?" Andrew lifted a gray eyebrow, clearly perplexed by the question. "I never heard of such a thing."

Charlotte went to the counter and smiled at the diminutive man behind the desk. "I'd like to check in, please."

"I need to get to Little Falls as soon as possible," the young lady said.

"Little Falls?" Charlotte turned to look at her more closely.

"I just came from that direction today," Andrew said. "I don't aim to head back until early Friday morning."

"That means I have to stay here for four days?" The lady glanced around the lobby. "What will I do here? I should be in Little Falls, getting the school ready for my pupils."

"School?" Charlotte stepped away from the counter, George heavy in her arms and Robert lagging near her side. "Are you Miss Helen Palmer?"

The lady blinked her pretty eyes several times. "Why, yes, I am! How do you know?"

"But I thought you were getting married. Abram— Mr. Cooper isn't expecting you."

"He's not? Oh, dear. I called off my engagement almost immediately after writing to the superintendent of the school, but I decided to come anyway. I thought maybe I'd get here before my letter. Do you think they'll send me back?"

"Mr. Cooper will be relieved to have a teacher for his school." The thought of Abram's joy brought a smile to Charlotte's lips.

"Are you from Little Falls?" Miss Palmer asked.

Was she from Little Falls? "No. I'm from Iowa City."

"But you've been in Little Falls?"

"Yes, for several months."

"Oh, I'd love to hear all about Little Falls. Do you have the time?"

Andrew cleared his throat and Robert swayed with exhaustion.

"I'm leaving first thing in the morning. I'm afraid I won't have time."

"Oh, please." Miss Palmer twisted a handkerchief in her hands. "I must sit here for four days and fret. I'd appreciate any information you may have to relieve my anxiety."

Charlotte adjusted George. How could she refuse to visit with the new teacher? "I need to check in and put the boys to bed. Would you like to come to my room?"

"Yes." Miss Palmer nodded emphatically. She glanced at Robert and offered a sympathetic look. "Would you like me to pick up your son? He looks so tired."

Her son? "He's not my—" She paused, realizing that, for all intents and purposes, these were her sons now and she was their mother. Though she knew she would never replace Susanne, she would do her best to make her sister proud. "If he'll allow you."

Miss Palmer took a step toward Robert and smiled. "May I hold you?"

Robert simply blinked his tired eyes.

"He's deaf," Charlotte explained.

"Oh." Miss Palmer squatted to Robert's level and her

smile grew softer, though there was no pity. "Would you ask him if I may hold him?"

Charlotte signed the request, telling Robert this was a teacher and she was very kind.

To her surprise, Robert acquiesced and Miss Palmer lifted him.

Her bright smile and infectious personality drew Charlotte to her immediately. She would make a good teacher, and would be a welcome addition for the male population in Little Falls.

Charlotte checked into a clean room overlooking the crude downtown streets of St. Paul. Andrew brought up her trunks and placed them in her room. She thanked him and wished him well.

Miss Palmer helped Charlotte prepare the boys for bed. Afterward, she sat quietly in one of the chairs near a window and waited for Charlotte to finish changing George's diaper.

All three boys fell back to sleep on the only bed in the room, and Charlotte joined Miss Palmer near the window, sighing as she collapsed in the chair.

"You must be exhausted," Miss Palmer said. "Are you traveling back to Iowa City?"

Charlotte nodded. "I *am* exhausted, and, yes, I'm traveling back to Iowa City."

"Is your husband in Little Falls or Iowa?"

"No." Charlotte shook her weary head. "I'm not married."

Miss Palmer's blond eyebrows rose to her hairline. "You're not married—but I assumed…"

"The boys are my nephews. I went to Little Falls to take them from their father and bring them back with me."

She bent forward to whisper, "Was their father... *unfit* to raise them?"

"Unfit?" Charlotte shook her head. "No, nothing like that." She paused, thinking of Abram and all his qualities. "He is a wonderful father." Her voice betrayed the depth of her feelings and she felt her cheeks grow warm. It was true. Abram was a helpful, loving and compassionate man. Now that she had some distance from him, she realized he was the most fit father—and man—Charlotte had ever met.

"Oh." Miss Palmer nodded, a depth of understanding in the one word. "He couldn't raise them on his own, so he asked you for help?"

She was asking personal questions, but Charlotte didn't mind. It felt good to talk to another woman.

"He didn't actually ask me for help, but he needed it."

"It's nice that you're able to help him."

Charlotte didn't want to talk about herself any longer. "What would you like to know about Little Falls?"

Miss Palmer nearly bounced in her seat. "Anything you'd like to tell me."

Charlotte told the new teacher everything she could about the town and the people, preparing her for all the single men.

"And may I ask why you changed your mind about coming to Little Falls after you wrote the letter?" Charlotte asked.

Miss Palmer sighed. "I decided I didn't want to settle down and marry Ned. He was just so...so stable. He never wanted to take any risks. If I married him, my life would be the same, day in and day out, forever." She wrinkled her nose and laughed. "And where's the fun in that?"

"There's a great deal of reassurance with a life like that."

"Reassurance?" She shook her head. "Nothing is sure in life. We're not guaranteed tomorrow, so why not be adventurous and take some risks today?"

Charlotte looked at the boys, asleep on the bed. She couldn't afford to take risks. She had responsibilities. So many things could go wrong. "Aren't you afraid?"

Miss Palmer tilted her head. "Of what?"

"Of never being content. When do you stop taking risks? When is enough good enough?"

"I don't know." She laughed. "I suppose it's never 'good enough' until we're home with God. I think maybe God enables us to long for more, so we keep seeking, and pursuing, and going after Him and all He has planned for us. That might mean being a mama to three little boys, or being a teacher, or a wife—but whatever He has planned for us, we should never let fear stop us from going after it." She leaned back and became serious. "I don't want to get to the end of my life and realize I missed a chance to walk in God's will, just because I was afraid."

"You sound much bolder than me."

Miss Palmer studied Charlotte with a penetrating gaze. "What are you most afraid of, Miss Lee? It's obvious you're in love with Mr. Cooper, so why didn't you stay in Little Falls?"

"In love?" Charlotte clasped her hands and tried to laugh. "I'm not in love." But was she?

Her chair suddenly felt uncomfortable, so she stood and walked over to the bed to check on her sleeping nephews.

Why was she so afraid of falling in love with Abram? Was she afraid of death? Meeting the same fate as her mother and sister? No. Death wasn't the end. It was only the beginning for those who believe in Jesus.

Was she afraid of marriage? She thought about her parents' marriage and visions of her father clouded her thoughts. She could almost hear him talking about a new plan—one that Charlotte knew would fail to satisfy him like all the others. It always left her wondering why his family wasn't enough—why she wasn't enough— to satisfy him.

She also thought of Thomas and how the lure of gold had been greater than the prospect of spending a life with her. She wasn't enough to satisfy him, either.

And in that moment Charlotte finally understood what she was afraid of.

It wasn't death, or marriage, or even following a husband who had grand dreams—it was the fear that she would never be enough for him.

Her father had chased countless dreams and schemes, when all along his greatest treasure, his family, was right in front of him. Thomas had run after riches when all along his greatest possession, her heart, had been in the palm of his hand.

Charlotte looked down at the boys again and with blinding clarity realized Abram's greatest treasure was lying in the bed, cuddled up together, with her—not because they couldn't satisfy him, but because he thought they would be better off with her. He had entrusted them to her care and he believed she was enough—more than enough—for them.

But was she enough for Abram?

"Miss Lee?" Miss Palmer stood and put her hand on Charlotte's shoulder. "Are you all right?"

"Yes. I'm sorry." Charlotte turned back to the young lady. "I was just thinking."

"I'm sorry. I tend to overstep my boundaries. I won't keep you longer. You have a full day ahead of you, and you'll need your rest. Good night—and God bless."

"Good night." Charlotte opened the door and allowed Miss Palmer to exit. She closed it and leaned against the hard surface. The last time she stood this close to a door, Abram had been on the other side, begging her to listen and understand…and forgive. Fear had prevented her from hearing the truth—but the truth was that he deserved to stand on his own and to not be judged by other people's mistakes.

She had been unfair to Abram and she owed him forgiveness and trust.

But was it too late?

What would Abram do if she went back to Little Falls? Would he tell her to return to Iowa City? Or would he tell her she was enough for him?

There was only one way to find out—but it would require taking the greatest risk of her life.

Chapter Twenty

Abram stood back and surveyed the outside of the schoolhouse in the dying light, but found no joy or sense of accomplishment in his work. He wished Charlotte could see the building completed—but as soon as the thought struck him, he forced himself to think of something else.

His mind had dwelled in a vicious cycle for the past five days. He promised himself he wouldn't think about Charlotte, or mourn for his sons, but everywhere he looked he was reminded of each of them in little ways. As soon as he began to think about them, he wondered how far they had traveled and if they had met with any problems along the way.

If he didn't think about where they were, or how they were doing, he replayed each moment of his time with Charlotte, revisiting their dance and the evening of the storm, before the dam had washed out. He thought of her standing in front of the stove, flipping flapjacks and tapping her toes to a lively tune. He thought of her sitting in the rocker, near the fireplace, knitting needles in hand. He thought of the joy on her face when she'd received the book of sign language, and then her patience in teaching Robert how to communicate.

He thought about a hundred precious moments, and each time he did, it was as if he was adding one more delicate snowflake to a branch laden with snow, about to break under the heavy weight of its burdens.

And then he would stop himself and try to forget all over again.

"I think it's a right fine school," Caleb said as he gathered together their supplies. "I should have the floors installed on Monday, and Milt and Josiah are working on those benches."

Abram sighed and picked up a scrap board. "I don't know if we'll have a teacher yet this fall—"

Caleb stood straight, his gaze riveted across the street. Abram glanced in that direction and found a charming young woman with blond hair walking their way.

She crossed the street, holding up the hem of her pink gown. "Is this the schoolhouse?"

Caleb took off his cap and grinned like an idiot.

"It is. How may I help you?" Abram asked.

"Are you Mr. Cooper?"

He nodded.

"You're just the man I wanted to find."

Abram glanced at Caleb, surprised by her admission. "What can I do for you?"

"I'm Miss Helen Palmer." She paused, as if her name alone should be introduction enough, but Abram couldn't place her.

"The new teacher," she said with a giggle in her voice.

Abram's mouth slipped open. "But I thought you refused the job."

She laughed and it sounded like tinkling bells. "All of that has changed. Do you still need me?"

"I'd say we do." Caleb grinned.

Her cheeks turned a becoming shade of pink.

"Yes, of course," Abram said. "Welcome to Little Falls."

"Since it's getting late," she said, "I thought I had better find a place to sleep, so I left my trunk at the Northern Hotel."

"That's not necessary." Abram wiped his hands on his trousers and offered to take her carpetbag. "You'll be rooming with the Hubbards. I'll show you there myself."

She tilted her head back toward the south. "The stage driver delivered several packages to your home. I imagine you'd like to go and see what they are." She offered Caleb a smile. "Maybe this young man can show me the way to the Hubbards' home."

Caleb's ears turned red and he dropped all his tools in a pile by the schoolhouse door. "I'd be honored, Miss Palmer."

Packages from the stage? Since Little Falls was now an established village, Hubbard served as the postmaster, so all packages were delivered to him. Why would Andrew deliver packages to Abram's house?

"Packages, you say?" Abram crossed his arms and leaned back on his heels. "Do you know what they might be?"

Miss Palmer batted her eyes and shook her finger. "I do know what they are—but I promised not to tell." She lifted her bag toward Caleb. "Are you ready?"

Caleb took her bag in one hand and put out his other

elbow for her to hold. He nodded like a schoolboy trying to impress his teacher. "Yes, Miss Palmer."

"Good day, Mr. Cooper. I plan to start school one week from Monday, so spread the word." Miss Palmer practically pulled Caleb in the direction she wanted to go and sashayed down the street on his arm. Several men stopped their work and many called out to her from the tops of buildings and the inside of passing wagons.

Abram stood for a moment, trying to think of what could be waiting at his home. Caleb's tools were lying on a pile, where anyone could trip over them, so Abram took them inside the building and picked up the remaining boards and stray nails.

He had several reports waiting for his attention back in his office at the company store, and some papers to sign for the new corporation—but all of those things could wait until he went home and discovered what Andrew had brought him.

Abram walked down Main Street, past the church next to Susanne's grave, and then turned right on the old wagon road. His home sat at the bottom of the gentle slope, with the sawmill and gristmill just beyond on the banks of the Mississippi. The wing dam had been fixed, and as soon as the corporation was finalized, and the shares were sold, they would begin work on the expanded dam, stretching it all the way across the east channel and connecting it to the island dividing the river.

The house stood quiet, just as it had since Charlotte and the boys had left. There were no sheets fluttering on the line or children running about the yard collecting eggs, and bugs, and mosquito bites.

Where would Charlotte and the boys be today? He

calculated the trip and figured they should be arriving in Iowa City tomorrow. Would Charlotte write to tell him they arrived safely? Would she update him on the boys' achievements and milestones? He had instructed her to find out when Robert could start attending the school for the deaf and how much it would cost.

He looked forward to her letters more than anything.

Abram stopped walking and closed his eyes, taking a deep breath.

He must stop thinking about Charlotte and the boys so much. It only made their departure more difficult to bear.

A bald eagle dipped from a tree near the river and flew low over the water, looking for its supper. Evening had arrived and Abram would have to decide if he would stay home and face the deafening silence or go to the store and work until he couldn't keep his eyes open any longer.

He continued down the road and looked around his yard to see if Andrew had left his packages outside.

Nothing looked amiss.

With a glance toward the barn, he opened the lean-to door and stopped short at the sound of voices inside the kitchen.

Martin and Robert sat at the table, the wooden toys Abram had given them for Christmas in their hands, while George sat in his high chair, banging a spoon.

Abram blinked several times—and then he heard the sound of Charlotte humming while the scent of fried bacon and coffee filled the lean-to.

He took two wide steps and then he was in the kitchen—and there she was, her left hand on her hip, her right toe tapping. She still wore her green traveling gown, but her bonnet had been discarded and he had a view of her beautiful brown curls.

"Papa!" Martin jumped off his chair and rounded the corner of the table—and then all at once everyone noticed him.

George threw his spoon to the floor in his excitement and Robert began signing about the coach ride and sleeping in a hotel all week.

But it was Charlotte who arrested his undivided attention. She had turned from the stove, with a fork in hand and an apron tied about her slender waist, uncertainty and joy mingling in her gaze.

Martin continued to talk, and Robert signed, but Abram could only focus on Charlotte. "What are you doing here?"

She nibbled on her bottom lip. "That's exactly what you asked me the last time I showed up unexpectedly."

"Last time you came, it was to take the boys away from here." He took a step toward her, wanting nothing more than to take her into his arms and assure himself that she was real. "That can't be why you've come this time."

She blinked and a stray tear slipped down her soft cheek. "This time I came to bring the boys back."

"Charlotte—" His voice caught with emotion. Did she plan to return to Iowa City or had she come to stay, too? "Why?"

She studied him for a moment, as if trying to gauge how he would react to her admission. "I realized I never gave you a fair chance."

"A fair chance to do what?" Hadn't she given him ten months to prove he could build a town?

"A chance to show me who you really are—and not who I perceived you to be."

Her words felt like a balm to his aching heart. He moved toward her, until he was so close she had to look up into his face. "Charlotte."

"I assumed you were just like my father and Thomas," she said. "And because of that assumption, I never fully discovered the real Abram Cooper."

"What if you don't like what you find?"

Another tear slipped from her eye. "I'm certain I'll love what I find."

"Love?" he said softly.

She nodded and this time a beautiful smile spread across her lips. "I knew I was risking everything to come back, but I had to tell you… I love you, Abram."

He needed no other invitation. He slipped his arms around Charlotte and pulled her into his embrace, loving the feel of her in his arms. "I'm so happy you did, because I love you, too." He lowered his lips to hers and kissed Charlotte Lee for the first time.

The Hubbard home was filled with dozens of people. All of them were busy downstairs moving furniture, preparing food and filling vases with wildflowers. Charlotte stood upstairs in the room she had shared with Helen Palmer since their arrival in Little Falls just over a week ago. Helen helped slip Charlotte's wedding dress over her corset covers and then stood back as Charlotte secured the etched-brass buttons up the bodice.

"It's lovely, Charlotte." Helen glanced over Charlotte's shoulder and looked at Charlotte's reflection. "I can't believe you had time to sew it."

"You and Pearl and Rachel have been so helpful, I hardly had anything else to do this week."

It was true. Charlotte had moved into the Hubbard home, sleeping there at night, but she had spent her days at Abram's taking care of the boys. Her three friends, and many other neighbors, had helped with chores so she could complete her dress on time.

"It's the prettiest gown I've ever seen," Helen said. "Now I know who to ask when I need a dress for my wedding."

"Oh? Is there someone you have in mind?"

Helen laughed. "Several, actually." She took another step back from Charlotte and her eyes glowed with approval. "You'll be the most beautiful bride this town has ever seen."

"I'm the only bride this town has ever seen!" Charlotte looked at her reflection and had to agree the dress was stunning. There hadn't been much fabric to choose from at the company store, so she had gone with a chocolate-brown silk with small, gold-floral brocade and buttons down the front. The dress hugged and accentuated her in all the right places and belled out in a wide skirt.

Helen had helped style her hair with ringlets coming down the sides of her temples, drawing out the deep brown of her eyes. Her cheeks glowed pink from excitement and she couldn't stop smiling.

"It's almost time to go to the church." Helen gathered up Charlotte's shawl and handed her a pair of long white gloves. "Are you ready?"

Charlotte took a steadying breath and nodded. She was more than ready to embark on marriage with Abram. She could hardly believe how happy and content she felt knowing he would be standing at the front of the church when she arrived.

In the week since her return they'd had several moments together, and she marveled at the depth of character and commitment she'd found once she started looking for it. As Abram shared his heart and his dreams, Charlotte had come to realize that dreaming wasn't wrong. On the contrary, dreams gave hope and meaning to so many aspects of life.

And for the first time since she was a child, she had dreams of her own. A home, a family, a husband and maybe more children to add to their already busy household. She planned to sell her building in Iowa City and purchase a lot on Main Street. One day, when the children were a bit older, she could open a dress shop if she liked. But for now, she would be content to sew for her family and friends.

Helen opened the bedroom door and Charlotte moved past her into the long hall. The smell of spice cake filled the air and Charlotte's stomach growled, though she was too nervous to eat.

They descended the stairs just as Rachel passed with a stack of plates, on the way to the dining room. She paused and smiled. "You look lovely, Charlotte."

"Thank you for all your hard work." Charlotte glanced into the dining room and found the table ready to receive their guests. The Hubbards were hosting a meal after the ceremony and everyone had pitched in to help.

"We're so happy for you and Mr. Cooper."

"Time to stop work," Pearl said, coming into the front hall as she removed her apron. "We'd better hurry over to the church or we'll be late."

Butterflies filled Charlotte's stomach and she swallowed down the rush of nerves.

Someone opened the front door and Charlotte was guided out by Mr. Hubbard, who would walk her down the aisle. She nestled her hand inside his elbow and allowed him to lead her through town.

They rounded the corner onto Main Street and Charlotte's mouth slipped open in amazement. Standing outside the church, people—mostly men—had lined up on the steps and down the sidewalk, two or three deep.

When she appeared, a great shout filled the air and dozens of men threw their hats above their heads.

"Oh, my."

Mr. Hubbard squeezed her hand. "They're all very excited for you and Abram."

"Congratulations, Miss Charlotte," several of them called out.

"Thank you," Charlotte said as she smiled at familiar faces.

"Are you ready, my dear?" Mr. Hubbard asked.

Charlotte nodded, though everything was happening so fast, how would she recall all these little details in the days to come?

The doors were pushed open and the inside of the church was just as full as the outside.

A violinist played the "Wedding March" and all the people inside stood and turned for a glimpse of her.

Charlotte recognized more dear faces. Mr. and Mrs. Perry, along with Maude. Mr. and Mrs. Ayers from the mission. Mr. Cheney and his wife. Nathan Richardson and Pierre LaForce. Josiah, Milt and Caleb—and one person she didn't expect to see: Harry. He stood with the others, his face turned toward her. When she caught his eye, he offered her a simple nod.

She nodded back and then her attention was captured by the man standing at the front of the church, his two older sons on either side of him and his youngest in his arms.

Tears gathered in Charlotte's eyes and joy flooded her soul. Abram, Robert, Martin and even George all smiled at her as if she was the most important person in the room—and for the first time in her life, she believed she was enough.

Ben stood at the front, next to Abram, his long braids lying on his chest. He smiled at Charlotte and nodded his approval. "Who gives this woman away in marriage?"

"The citizens of Little Falls," Mr. Hubbard said with great pride.

Cheers rose all around the church and Charlotte's cheeks hurt from smiling.

Abram grinned and Martin clapped.

Charlotte looked at Robert and realized he didn't know what had been said. She quickly signed the words for him and he clapped his hands and smiled.

Rachel came up from behind Charlotte, took George from Abram's arms and then ushered the boys to a bench.

Abram extended his left hand to Charlotte, his brilliant blue eyes looking at nothing and no one else but her.

She took his offered hand and he entwined his fingers through hers, squeezing her hand ever so gently in his strong grip.

Ben began the ceremony but Charlotte hardly noticed

what he said. All she was conscious of was Abram's steady presence beside her. It wasn't until it was time for the vows that she finally focused.

"Abram." Ben spoke in a grave voice. "Do you take Charlotte to be your wedded wife, to live together in marriage? Do you promise to love her, comfort her, honor and keep her, for better or worse, for richer or poorer, in sickness and health, and, forsaking all others, be faithful only to her, for as long as you both shall live?"

Abram grasped Charlotte's hands and faced her with no hesitation or doubt. "I do."

His simple vow filled Charlotte with a sense of awe. She didn't know where life might take them, or if they would stay in one place for the rest of their days—but she did know that Abram would always love and honor her.

"And do you, Charlotte, take Abram to be your wedded husband, to live together in marriage? Do you promise to love him, comfort him, honor and keep him, for better or worse, for richer or poorer, in sickness and health, and, forsaking all others, be faithful only to him, for as long as you both shall live?"

Every word—every promise—was filled with risk, but it was a risk she would gladly take for Abram. "I do."

"Do either of you have a token of your commitment?"

Abram produced a simple gold band, which he placed in Ben's hand.

"May this ring be blessed as the symbol of this affectionate union." Ben smiled. "These two lives are now joined in one unbroken circle. May these two find in each other the love for which all men and women yearn. May they grow in understanding and in compassion.

May the home which they establish together be such a place that many will find there a friend, and may this ring on Charlotte's finger symbolize the touch of the Holy Spirit in their hearts."

Ben handed the ring back to Abram and said, "Put this ring on your bride's finger and repeat after me, 'Charlotte, with this ring you are now consecrated to me as my wife from this day forward.'"

Abram slipped the cool ring on her left ring finger and looked her in the eyes. "Charlotte, with this ring you are now consecrated to me as my wife from this day forward."

Ben continued. "'I give you this ring as the pledge of my love and as the symbol of our unity, and with this ring, I thee wed.'"

"I give you this ring as the pledge of my love and as the symbol of our unity." Abram lifted her hand to his lips and placed a kiss over the ring. His eyes filled with tenderness. "And with this ring, Charlotte Lee, I thee wed."

"Now, by the power vested in me by the Territory of Minnesota, and by Almighty God," Ben said, closing his Bible, "I now pronounce you man and wife. You may kiss the bride."

Abram gently put his hand on her cheek and lowered his lips to hers. The kiss was sweet, yet passionate, and made Charlotte wish they were alone and not in a room with hundreds of well-wishers.

A great cheer arose from the congregation, followed by much back-slapping and congratulations all around.

Robert and Martin ran up to Charlotte and wrapped their arms around her legs, while Rachel handed George to Abram.

"Now you belong with us forever." Abram put his free arm around her waist and pulled her close to his side. He looked down into her face, devotion shining from his beautiful eyes. "I'm never letting you go again, my love."

Her heart was full of all that lay ahead. Evenings by the fireplace, early mornings with mugs of steaming coffee, late nights in each other's arms, birthdays and holidays and Sundays. The good and the bad, the easy and the hard—life, in all its glory.

She looked up into his dear face, amazed at the depth and breadth of her love for him, and was reminded of Ruth's promise to Naomi in the Book of Ruth. She stood on tiptoe and whispered for his ear alone. "'Entreat me not to leave thee, or to return from following after thee: for wither thou goest, I will go; and where thou lodgest, I will lodge; thy people shall be my people, and thy God my God.'"

She rested back on her feet and watched his eyes fill with affection just before he placed another kiss on her lips. "Those words are the greatest gift you could ever give me, Charlotte Cooper."

She took his hand in hers and they were led away to celebrate their new union in the presence of their community.

Now Charlotte understood why her sister had risked everything to follow Abram to the wilds of Minnesota Territory. Wherever Abram went, Charlotte would follow all the days of her life.

* * * * *

If you liked this story,
pick up this other heartwarming book
from Gabrielle Meyer

A MOTHER IN THE MAKING

Available now from Love Inspired Historical!

Dear Reader,

Sixteen years ago, when I was a college intern at the Charles A. Weyerhaeuser Memorial Museum in Little Falls, MN, I discovered the incredible history of my hometown. I began to dream of writing stories that would follow the rise and fall of a unique American community on the banks of the Upper Mississippi River.

This story was born from that dream. It is a work of fiction, but it's strongly influenced by true events. The cast of characters is closely related to the original founders, but these men and women are the work of my imagination. It is my hope that through this story you will be intrigued to learn more about the real people who sacrificed everything to build Little Falls. Please visit www.gabriellemeyer.com to discover more.

God Bless!
Gabrielle Meyer

REQUEST YOUR FREE BOOKS!

2 FREE INSPIRATIONAL NOVELS
PLUS 2 FREE MYSTERY GIFTS

Love Inspired HISTORICAL

YES! Please send me 2 FREE Love Inspired® Historical novels and my 2 FREE mystery gifts (gifts are worth about $10). After receiving them, if I don't wish to receive any more books, I can return the shipping statement marked "cancel." If I don't cancel, I will receive 4 brand-new novels every month and be billed just $4.99 per book in the U.S. or $5.49 per book in Canada. That's a saving of at least 17% off the cover price. It's quite a bargain! Shipping and handling is just 50¢ per book in the U.S. and 75¢ per book in Canada.* I understand that accepting the 2 free books and gifts places me under no obligation to buy anything. I can always return a shipment and cancel at any time. Even if I never buy another book, the two free books and gifts are mine to keep forever.

102/302 IDN GH6Z

Name	(PLEASE PRINT)	
Address		Apt. #
City	State/Prov.	Zip/Postal Code

Signature (if under 18, a parent or guardian must sign)

Mail to the **Reader Service**:
IN U.S.A.: P.O. Box 1867, Buffalo, NY 14240-1867
IN CANADA: P.O. Box 609, Fort Erie, Ontario L2A 5X3

Want to try two free books from another series?
Call 1-800-873-8635 or visit www.ReaderService.com.

---

* Terms and prices subject to change without notice. Prices do not include applicable taxes. Sales tax applicable in N.Y. Canadian residents will be charged applicable taxes. Offer not valid in Quebec. This offer is limited to one order per household. Not valid for current subscribers to Love Inspired Historical books. All orders subject to credit approval. Credit or debit balances in a customer's account(s) may be offset by any other outstanding balance owed by or to the customer. Please allow 4 to 6 weeks for delivery. Offer available while quantities last.

Your Privacy—The Reader Service is committed to protecting your privacy. Our Privacy Policy is available online at www.ReaderService.com or upon request from the Reader Service.

We make a portion of our mailing list available to reputable third parties that offer products we believe may interest you. If you prefer that we not exchange your name with third parties, or if you wish to clarify or modify your communication preferences, please visit us at www.ReaderService.com/consumerschoice or write to us at Reader Service Preference Service, P.O. Box 9062, Buffalo, NY 14240-9062. Include your complete name and address.

UHI1

SPECIAL EXCERPT FROM

Love Inspired HISTORICAL

*When cowboy Logan Marshall and schoolteacher
Sadie Young discover three abandoned children, they
are determined to help them. But working together to
care for the children while searching for their parents
might just leave Logan and Sadie yearning to make
their temporary family permanent.*

*Read on for a sneak preview of
MONTANA COWBOY FAMILY by Linda Ford,
available January 2017 from Love Inspired Historical!*

"Are you going to be okay with the children?" Logan
asked.

Sadie bristled. "Of course I am."

"I expect the first night will be the worst."

"To be honest, I'm more concerned about tomorrow
when I have to leave the girls to teach." She looked back
at her living quarters. "They are all so afraid."

"I'll be back before you have to leave so the girls
won't be alone and defenseless." He didn't know why
he'd added the final word and wished he hadn't when
Sadie spun about to face him. He'd only been thinking of
Sammy's concerns—be they real or the fears of children
who had experienced too many losses.

"You think they might have need of protection?"

"Don't all children?"

Her lips trembled and then she pressed them together
and wrapped her arms across her chest in a move so self-
protective that he instinctively reached for her, but at the
look on her face, he lowered his arms instead.

She shuddered.

From the thought of him touching her or because of something she remembered? He couldn't say but neither could he leave her without knowing she was okay. Ignoring the idea that she might object to his forwardness, wanting only to make sure she knew he was concerned about her and the children, he cupped one hand to her shoulder. He knew he'd done the right thing when she leaned into his palm. "Sadie, I'll stay if you need me to. I can sleep in the schoolroom, or over at Uncle George's. Or even under the stars."

She glanced past him to the pile of lumber at the back of the yard. For the space of a heartbeat, he thought she'd ask him to stay, then she drew in a long breath.

"We'll be fine, though I would feel better leaving them in the morning if I knew you were here."

He squeezed her shoulder. "I'll be here." He hesitated, still not wanting to leave.

She stepped away from him, forcing him to lower his arm to his side. "Goodbye, then. And thank you for your help."

"Don't forget we're partners in this." He waited for her to acknowledge his statement.

"Very well."

"Goodbye for now. I'll see you in the morning." He forced himself to climb into the wagon and flick the reins. He turned for one last look before he was out of sight.